Accident

Joanne Simon Tailele

To Mary & Jim
Enjoy

Joanne Simon Tailele

Joanne Simon Tailele

Chapter One

She was fifteen years old and alone. The first gulp of the dark liquid scorched her throat and burned all the way down. Her eyes stung and she fought the urge to vomit. The second gulp went down a little easier. By the third, the warmth inside began to surface toward her skin. As it settled like a warm blanket around her, she knew she had found a way to keep her secret, for at least one day at a time. By the time she finished the bottle, she was no longer ripping long strands of red hair from her head.

***

Susan Jennings awoke from the dream, shaking off the old memory that had haunted her for twenty years. As her eyes adjusted to the harsh fluorescent lights, she noticed the sterile green walls and the metal rails on either side of the bed. When her vision cleared she saw her husband, Thomas, slumped in a straight-backed chair, his dark head cradled in his hands. "What happened?" she whispered.

Thomas jerked up when he heard her voice. Shadowy circles surrounded his deep brown eyes. His rumpled shirt suggested he had slept in the chair. Tears brimmed in his eyes. His words were jagged and raw as he recapped the accident in halting phrases. He was still in a state of shock as he toggled back and forth between his wife's and his daughter's rooms on different floors.

"You missed the sign, the stop sign, Susan. The other car couldn't stop. Your car . . . the whole passenger side crushed . . . the other car rolled."

He sucked in his breath and wrung his hands, a nervous habit. Absentmindedly, he reached for the tube which pushed oxygen through the cannula in her nose. He squeezed the tube, blocking off the air. A lock of his jet-black hair fell over his forehead.

His words brought back flickers of recollection to her, the children laughing in the back seat, a white sedan approaching from the right . . . crawling from the ditch . . . her late model station wagon crushed almost beyond recognition . . . the sedan rocking on its hood.

Susan gazed down at her body. A few bandages covered superficial cuts on her arms. She reached for the mirror on the bed tray and noticed long strands of red hair twisted in the palm of her hand. She shook her hand and the hair fell to the tile floor. Her left eye was turning a muddy purplish-brown. Dried blood caked at her hairline. She fingered the few stitches above her right eyebrow.

Thomas continued, "Deanna and your mother were pinned inside. The EMT's talked about taking Deanna's leg off to get her out, but they didn't . . . at least . . . not yet. The doctors say she has internal bleeding and several broken ribs. Her leg is a mess. They still don't know if they can save it. Shit Susan, she's in a coma." Without thinking, he squeezed and released the tube, causing the air to come in spurts through her nose.

"No," Susan whispered. "That can't be right. We were on our way to the mall. Maybe the rain . . . ." Her words trailed off as Thomas shook his head. "And . . . what else?" A sense of dread caused a shiver down her spine.

"The car folded like an accordion. They found your mom wedged between the windshield and the dashboard in the front seat. Her arm is pretty fucked up. Your dad said she might have had a stroke too."

It's all so hazy. Why can't I remember? Panic began to set in. "What about Daniel?"

Thomas let go of the tube and cradled his face in the palms of his hands. His shoulder-length jet-black hair hung loose and obscured his face. Racking sobs shook his body and a near-primal growl escaped his lips. Finally, angry eyes looked up at her. "He's dead, Susan!" He spat the words at her. "He got thrown from the car. They found him in a field. He hit his head on a rock and he broke his neck."

His words bit into her, sucking the breath from her lungs. She couldn't speak. She couldn't scream. Her heart pumped wildly. It felt as if a boulder had landed on her chest. The heart monitor went off, sending screeching alerts to the nurses' station.

A nurse rushed into the room. "You'll have to leave, Mr. Jennings. She's too upset. Her blood pressure and heart rate are going through the roof."

"I'm sorry, I should have waited." His anger was quickly spent. Thomas moved out of the way, allowing the nurse to administer a sedative. Shaking his head, he turned and walked out the door, heading to the intensive care unit to sit with his daughter, Deanna.

The room started to get dark and blurry. Susan was glad. She wanted to slip into that dark void of nothingness. Just before the blissful darkness descended, she thought, how can this be? They were fine, having fun, laughing and playing. Daniel is dead? Mom and Deanna hurt? Did I really do this?

***

The attending physician wanted to treat her for shock, but Susan refused. They released her the next day with a prescription for Valium. She threw it in the trash on the way to Deanna's room.

Susan's hand flew to her mouth when she saw her daughter. Multitudes of wires, drips and hoses protruded from Deanna's body. The sounds of machines created a rhythmic percussion of beeps and gurgling water. She staggered to the bed and caressed Deanna's red swollen cheek. Most of the girl's thick blond hair had been shaved on the right side of her head and a gauze bandage did little to cover the twenty-eight stitches that drew a ragged C from her right eyebrow to behind her ear. Susan lifted the sheet to look at her daughter's right leg, wrapped from her ankle to her thigh. In the course of a few days her athletic five-foot frame appeared to have shriveled. She looked much younger than her fifteen years.

Susan sank quietly into a chair beside her daughter's bed. A constant beep of a heart monitor indicated a steady heartbeat. She watched for the slightest movement— a twitch of her hand, a blink of her eye, but. Deanna lay motionless, still in a coma.

Susan didn't think she believed in God. She hadn't for a long time now. But just in case she was wrong, she folded her hands to her chest. "Please dear Lord. Don't let her die. Please, please. She needs to live. Don't take her from us too. Isn't Daniel enough? Please don't take Deanna too." She hadn't prayed since she was fifteen, Deanna's age. She didn't know if He would listen to her pleas or if He even existed.

She pleaded, "Oh, Deanna, I am so sorry. Can you ever forgive me? Please baby, please wake up. Mommy is right here. Wake up baby, please wake up. Please baby, open your eyes." Susan stroked Deanna's arm and kissed her fingertips. She didn't notice Thomas had stepped into the room and was sitting quietly in the corner until she heard him cough. She looked up and met his eyes. They didn't speak.

"You'll have to step out for a bit." A young nurse with soft gentle eyes prodded Susan to get up from the chair. "We need to change her dressings. It won't take too long." She looked at Susan and Thomas and gave them a feeble smile.

Susan didn't want to leave, but reluctantly, they both left the room. Thomas stayed by the door, waiting for a signal from the nurse he could go back in.

Four floors below, Daniel lay in the morgue. She found her way there through a maze of corridors. She asked to see her son. One lone man seemed to be working in this cold sterile room. He asked if she didn't want someone to be with her. She shook her head. The man in the white lab coat led her to a wall of drawers. After double checking identification, he pulled a drawer that had Jennings,D written on a tab on the front. An unbelievably small shape lay under a white sheet. He looked at her for confirmation before he gently folded away the sheet to reveal Daniel's head and shoulders. Susan sucked in her breath and her knees began to give out under her. Somehow a chair appeared that she sank into. Besides being chalky white and blue lips, he looked like he could be asleep. She could see that there was some type of bandage on the back of his head and a portion of his hair had been shaved away. He looked so tiny. Susan wanted to shake him to wake up but when she touched his bare shoulder and felt the coldness of his body, she jerked her hand away. She was appalled at herself that touching his cold skin frightened her and steeled herself to try again. Gently, she touched his tiny little face. His skin was so soft, but it felt slack, as if all the muscle had instantly vanished. Oh my God! My baby! She had no idea how long she sat there, staring at his lifeless form. The tears on her face had dried and her body ached from somewhere deep inside she could not reach. The gentle man in the white lab coat helped her to her feet and led her to the door. Her legs moved in response but she did not feel them.

Susan found herself in the lobby. She asked at the information desk for the number to Esther Lundgren's room. With instructions from a disinterested and grumpy volunteer, she located her mother on a wing two floors above Deanna.

Susan stood in the doorway, fresh tears streaming down her cheeks as she looked at her mother. Esther tried to give her daughter a reassuring smile but only one corner of her mouth turned up. She patted the left side of the bed with her good hand, inviting Susan to come closer.

Her knees barely held her upright as she made her way to the cushioned armchair beside the bed.

Esther looked at Susan through mummy-like bandages around her head that squeezed her bruised cheeks and pinched her drug-induced eyes into slits. Her right arm, bandaged from her hand to her shoulder hung from a sling supported by a pulley system above the bed. She tried to speak, but the words were jumbled. She reached for her husband Nils' hand, knowing he would understand her every need, even if she couldn't say the words out loud.

Nils stroked her face and kissed her swollen lips. Without even realizing it, he slipped back into their native Swedish tongue. "Oroa dig inte min kärlek. Jag är här. Don't worry my love. I am here. Just rest my love. Everything is alright. The Lord will see us through this."

Esther tried to comprehend what he was saying. She saw his lips moving, but his words sounded far off, as if coming from a distance. She strained to hear him and rolled a finger on her left hand in a circle. He understood; he raised his voice and spoke more slowly. He explained the accident to her, telling her Deanna was in a coma and Daniel had died in the crash.

A tear rolled down Esther's cheek. She rolled her bandaged head back and forth on the pillow.

Susan choked up on hearing him speak about her children. "What do the doctors say, Dad, about Mom?" She looked to her father, who was trying to put up a good front.

"She's fine, she'll be fine," he almost whispered. But the worried look in his eyes gave him away.

Susan laid her head on the left side of the bed. Her tears spilled onto the white sheets. "Oh Mama, I am so sorry." The words sounded empty, even to her. Look what I have done. She doesn't deserve this. She's always been so good to me.

Esther patted Susan's head and gently stroked the strawberry curls with her slender, age-spotted hand.

Time slowed to a crawl as everyone sat in silence. A nurse in green scrubs came in and told Susan she needed to leave.

Why is everyone always asking me to leave?

Susan kissed her mother gently on the forehead and went around to the other side of the bed toward her father. She hesitated, not knowing if he blamed her for the accident.

He stood, opened his arms, and wrapped them tightly around his daughter.

Esther smiled looking at her husband and daughter. It gave her comfort to know Nils held no hard feelings toward his daughter. Susan was going through enough. She needed her father by her side.

Nils held Susan tight and whispered in her ear. "We trust in the Lord, Susan. He'll get us through this. *Bara lita på Herren*. Just trust in the Lord."

Susan clung to her dad, wishing she could just curl up in his lap like she did when she was a little girl. He was a calming force, in spite of the worry lines that crossed his brow. She was grateful for the respite she felt in his arms and buried her face in his soft argyle sweater. It smelled of Tide laundry detergent.

"Hello Susan. I'm sorry we have to see each other again under such awful circumstances."

Susan spun out of her father's embrace to face the man standing in the doorway. The hairs on the back of her neck stood up. "Brother Jim" she stammered. "What are you doing here?"

The man smiled at her, his words soft and buttery. "Well, I'm Reverend Olson now. I'm here for your mother, of course. I heard about the accident. Please accept my condolences on the loss of your son. Would you like me to pray for you and your family?"

Nils nodded at the man in the conservative black suit and spoke for everyone. "Thank you, Reverend Olson. That is very kind of you. We appreciate your prayers." Nils looked at his daughter. "I guess you would remember him as Brother Jim, when he was your youth pastor. They transferred him to another church many years ago, but he's back now, as our senior pastor this time. Isn't that nice?"

The nurse cleared her throat to let them know she still needed everyone to leave. Susan was glad she did not have to answer her father. Nils and Reverend Olson followed Susan out into the hall, the first time her father had left the room since the he arrived at the hospital.

Susan avoided the minister's intense gaze. She pleaded with her father for more information. "The truth, Dad —, how is she really?"

Nils took a deep breath. It was hard to believe what the doctors were saying. "They say she is in stable condition, but she suffered a stroke during the accident. It's going to be a long road. But we'll get through it. The Lord will help us." He gave a weak smile to the clergyman.

Susan kept her eyes focused on her father. "What are they saying about her arm? It looks bad."

Nils shrugged. "They just don't know yet. She may not have any use of it at all. It's just too early to tell."

The nurse passed by them as she left Esther's room.

Nils gave his daughter a kiss on the cheek. "I've got to get back to her, Susan. You know how Mama is —, she'll be afraid without me there.

"I know Dad. Go to her. I've got to get back to Deanna."

The minister and Susan were alone in the hall. He stared at her then his smile broadened and a dimple popped from his cheek. His hair was thinner and gray strands blended with the blonde; he looked like a washed out version of who she remembered. But he still had those Robert Redford looks, the kind that made grown women and young girls go weak at the knees. "Would you like me to come with you to pray for Deanna?"

Susan backed away, not wanting to get too close. "No," she answered a little too briskly. "Thank you. I'm sure you're a busy man. It's not necessary, and I am not much of church-goer these days."

Reverend Olson shook his head. "There is always time to come back, Susan. But we will still pray for her in church. We will start a vigil."

"Fine, okay, whatever you say. I've got to get back to her now." She turned on her heel and headed to the elevators, hoping he wouldn't follow. When the elevator doors opened and then closed around her, she leaned against the railing for support. Her face burned from the memory of the last time she had seen him. Brother Jim. He's back.

Chapter Two

Thomas sat motionless, save his wringing hands, back on his watch beside Deanna's bed. He looked up when Susan stopped in the doorway. Red-rimmed eyes stared at Deanna as they listened to the pulse and beeps of the machinery keeping her alive.

Susan was about to tell him about her encounter with Reverend Olson when Thomas began to speak, so softly she had to ask him to repeat what he just said.

"You killed Daniel and Deanna may die too."

"No, no, it wasn't my fault." Susan whispered. "The other car hit us. I tried to stop. I couldn't stop."

Thomas shook his head. He looked at her with so much pain and anger in his eyes Susan winced.

His words came quickly, escalating in volume as each word pierced Susan's heart. "Your blood alcohol level was two times the legal limit Susan . . . . You were drunk! You ran the stop sign! That man had the right of way and you killed him too. You killed both him and Daniel!" His voice cracked with emotion. "You did this, damn it, Susan, you and your drinking!" He pounded his fist on the nightstand. The pink plastic water pitcher tipped over and spilled water onto the floor.

Susan's mind contested. Am I really responsible for all this? Was I drinking? Why can't I remember?

Susan looked toward the door when two policemen arrived.

"Susan Jennings?" A tall thin officer with grayed temples stepped toward her.

She nodded affirmatively.

He tipped the rim of his hat, almost as if greeting her instead of arresting her.

A much younger but stockier Hispanic officer read her rights. "You are under arrest for the deaths of Daniel Jennings and William O'Donnell. You have the right to remain silent. You have the right to an attorney. If you cannot afford an attorney, one will be appointed for you . . ."

The words echoed in her ears but she no longer paid attention to what he said. Numb, Susan didn't resist when they fastened tie-straps to her wrists behind her back. She knew the drill. It was not her first arrest. She looked longingly at Thomas for help.

Thomas avoided meeting her eyes but he offered a weak attempt at help. "I'll see what I can do for an attorney. We don't have much money."

They escorted her by the elbow out the door. A sense of dread washed over her. It will be different this time. This time someone got hurt. Susan looked at the faces of the nurses and visitors in the hallway as the officers flanked her sides, one with his arm on her elbow directing the way. Their faces registered distain, openly accusing her even before knowing all the facts. Susan's shame made her look away. She wanted to shout out to them, "It was an accident, an accident! I didn't mean to do it." But she kept silent, privately condemning herself.

Charged with vehicular homicide and driving under the influence, they took Susan directly to the Mahoning County jail. Blood and urine tests taken at the time of her admittance to the hospital confirmed their suspicions. Thomas was right. She had been drunk.

"Do you have council to make your bail, Ms. Jennings?" said the matronly clerk. She looked like she had seen and heard it all.

"My husband said he was going to call someone." Surely Thomas is sending someone. I can't stay here. I don't belong here.

Susan waited for her arraignment. The holding cell was a maze of bars. She had never spent more than an hour in jail before. It looked different this time . . . not knowing if anyone was coming for her. Most of the prisoners sat in a large holding area in the center on benches and waited for their attorneys or to be called into court. The perimeter of the large cell held other smaller cells, with more prisoners, perhaps more dangerous criminals that needed to be kept away from the lessor offenders. Even more bars separated the hallways and the exits. The Sheriff's deputies had a miniscule office, smaller than her master bathroom, off to one corner. Everything was steel gray. Seedy looking characters, mostly young, with jeans falling off their hips and huge gold chains around their necks crowded the smoky lobby. Vagrants, unshaven and dirty, looked happy to have a place to sleep off their drunk. Prostitutes paraded by, brazen and confident their pimps would bail them out. Some of the prisoners argued and got into fist fights. The guards broke up one scuffle, then another one started by two other detainees. The noise was deafening.

Susan never felt so out of place. *How did my life come to this? I had it all. The American dream . . . a soccer mom in a nice house in the suburbs, two beautiful children, and a man that loved me.* For the second time in her life, she questioned why God had not protected her and her family. *Surely there can't be a God if He could let this happen.* The first time laid buried deep in her past . . . until now. *Mom and Dad have always believed in me, even when I had no faith in myself. I've disappointed them all. I've let down my husband and my daughter. Oh my God, Deanna! How will she ever* forgive me? I want my life back... and Daniel. Can he really be gone? He is just a baby. This has to be a nightmare. I have to wake up. I have to wake up.

Finally, a rumbled little man with a bad comb-over called her name. "Excuse me, Ms. Jennings?"

"Yes, I am Susan Jennings." Susan looked him up and down. Nothing about him eluded confidence or even competence. Where did Thomas find this guy? "Are you making my bail? Do I get to go home now?"

"Not now. I am Herbert Miller, your attorney. Mr. Jennings put up your house as collateral for your bail. After the arraignment, you should be free on bond. It is scheduled for two days from today."

Susan pleaded "not guilty" under the advice of the defense attorney. They released her with a $50,000 bond and an ankle bracelet putting her on house arrest. The police officer accompanied her to the house and explained that if she went farther than 100 yards from her front door, the alarm would go off on her ankle and she would be brought back to the county jail. Susan mumbled she understood and waited for the officers to leave before she sank into the blue nylon sofa under the window. Thomas was nowhere around. She wondered if or when he would be coming home.

After 10 P.M., Thomas pulled his 1980 Chevy truck into the driveway. Susan waited for the cab door to slam. Five minutes passed . . . nothing. Then ten minutes passed and still . . . nothing. She began to wonder if he was ever coming in when she finally heard the thud of the heavy door.

Susan watched him come through the side garage door into the house and set his black metal lunchbox on the counter.

He hesitated in the kitchen before making his way into the dimly lit living room. "I see you are home."

"Yes, thanks for making my bail, Thomas. I was afraid you weren't going to." She hung her head in shame. "I'm . . . I'm sorry, Thomas. I'm sorry for everything."

Thomas stood in the doorway, wringing his hands. "I found this guy in the phone book. I didn't know any lawyers. And the first three I called, well, we didn't have enough money for them."

"I'm sure he'll be fine, Thomas." I hope. "He said something about the house."

Thomas shoved his hands in his pants pockets to keep them still as he rocked back and forth on the heels of his work boots. "Yea, it was all I could do. We don't have money, not that kind anyway. Hmm, I'm tired Susan. I've been at the hospital with Deanna all day. I'm going to take the guest room. You can have our . . . um . . . the master bedroom." He turned and walked away, never once looking her in the eye.

"What about Deanna, Thomas? Any change?" She looked hopefully for some word her daughter had suddenly woken up.

Thomas never turned as he shook his head and continued into the guest bedroom and quietly shut the door behind him.

She wandered around the house, opening closet doors, staring into one child's bedroom, then the other. A drink would calm my nerves. Maybe just one little sip.

Thomas had removed every bottle from the house. He must have spent half a day checking in all her normal hiding places. Every spot was empty.

The gnawing in her stomach would not go away. She filled it with food. Still there. She drank a whole liter of Diet Coke. It still gnawed at her.

By the end of the week, she was in full blown withdrawal. Her hands shook constantly and her she felt the nerve ending in her body had surfaced above her skin. Her skin felt on fire where it touched her clothing. She broke out in cold sweats, but could not stand the feel of the blanket on her skin.

Two weeks later, the official at the preliminary hearing determined there was probable cause to try her. She would wait another one hundred and twenty days before the trial.

Time had no meaning, days and nights blended together into one. The knot in her stomach would not go away. Food wouldn't stay down. Thomas was practically non-existent and came and went with groceries before he quickly left again with little or no conversation. She had to plead with him to get any updates on Deanna. The news was always the same, stable but still unconscious.

She wandered about the house, pausing at Daniel's room. Her hand trembled as she turned the knob. The light cascaded through the window with the blue curtains producing a muted blue glow to the room. Daniel's favorite stuffed animal, Curious George, lay on the floor, one floppy leg tossed over the other, his stitched-on smile mocking her. Susan picked up the doll and laid it gently on the low single bed that took up most of the small room. She sank to the floor beside the bed. Above her head, a border of marching Disney characters circled the room, eye level for a little seven year old boy.

Hours later, she made her way slowly out of the room to find Thomas sitting at the kitchen table wringing his hands, his hair pulled back in a ponytail, his shoulders slumped in defeat. Susan met his glazed expression.

He spoke quietly, his voice ragged. The anger had been replaced with a deep sorrow. "I made all the arrangements. I picked out a mahogany casket. I gave them his Ohio State football jersey to bury him in. He would like that, don't you think?" It had taken two weeks for Daniel's autopsy and the police to release the body from the morgue.

Has it only been two weeks? It feels like two months.

Thomas brushed a tear away from his cheek, trying not to break down in front of his wife. His dark hair looked greasy, as though taking the time to bathe was too much of an effort for him. Susan didn't know what to say. She nodded her head, unable to speak.

What about his coat? Will he need his OSU jacket? Of course not, what am I thinking? He doesn't need anything anymore.

Susan thought there couldn't possibly be any more tears left, but the vision of her baby lying in a casket in his football jersey was more than she could take. She saw his face as he lay in the morgue, white and chalky with blue lips. Her body began to shake. She sank into a kitchen chair across from Thomas and laid her head on the table. She dissolved into tears.

"And Deanna? How is she? Talk to me Thomas! They won't let me leave this house to even go see her! " She pleaded with her eyes for him to give some good news.

Thomas shook his head. "Still in a coma- no change there." Susan stared at him in disbelief, no words sufficient to express her grief. They sat in silence and stared down at the scarred table between them. I remember this scar. I threw an empty bottle of vodka at him when I discovered he had poured the contents of my hidden stash down the drain. The bottle broke and cut this scar into the wood. In the distance a phone rang at the neighbor's house across the street. No one answered it. Thomas finally rose and walked toward the guest room. He never looked back or spoke as he quietly closed the door.

Chapter Three

The unseasonably cool April air and steady drizzle only intensified the solemn mood as the small entourage gathered around the gravesite with a small mahogany casket as the centerpiece. The sheriff's car arrived last. They had picked Susan up at the house, granted special privilege to leave the house for the funeral. She stepped out of the back of the police car, her hands cuffed in front of her.

Susan tried to pull the navy blue jacket tighter around her, but the sleeves were caught in the handcuffs. She wore nothing on her head and no one offered her an umbrella. The light rain quickly soaked her head and droplets streaked down her cheeks, blending in with her silent tears.

No one spoke to her at the funeral. The clouds broke loose and a steady rain pummeled the small canvas gazebo over the casket and few folding chairs. She shivered as Reverend Olson performed the service. He talked about little Daniel being in

God's hands now and safe from harm or pain. The words gave Susan no comfort. His presence made her unconsciously reach for her hair, one hand pulling the other along by the handcuffs as she tugged at the wet tendrils that came off in her hand.

Esther and Nils tried to approach Susan, offering their support, but the police officers blocked their way. She looked into her parents' eyes and saw love and forgiveness. Esther still looked weak, wrapped in gauze over much of her face and right arm, yet managed a knowing smile. It was the first she had seen either one of her parents since she left the hospital.

Thomas clutched his sister's arm throughout the entire service and stared at the little casket until they lowered it into the cold ground. When he finally looked up to meet Susan eyes, hollow eyes pierced through her, showing neither love nor hatred.

As the service ended, Nils helped Esther maneuver between the headstones back to their car with an umbrella tightly clutched in one hand and his other firmly supporting his wife's elbow. They stopped momentarily at a stone two plots over. It read MSG. Raymond Lundgren, June 22, 1943 – November 6, 1963. Vietnam War Veteran.

Esther placed her bruised lips on the top of her son's stone. Nils turned, his tan trench coat flapping open in the wind and met Susan's stare. He gave a nod and a slight smile, trying to reassure her everything was going to be okay.

Susan watched them leave and wondered if she would ever see them again. She thought about her broken family. Ray . . . gone. Daniel . . . gone. Deanna, now laying in a coma, unable to attend her baby brother's funeral.

Chapter Four

On July 3rd, Deanna woke up. It was three months from the exact hour of the accident. She heard voices in a long tunnel, far away at first, then slowly drawing closer. She recognized her grandmother's voice, then her dad's. Everything came back in slow motion, hazy, like when she first woke up from a dream and didn't know if she was awake or still dreaming.

Esther and Thomas were whispering to each other from either side of her bed, not knowing she was awake. They were discussing how they should tell her something.

Deanna heard her father's deep voice. "She deserves to know. As soon as she wakes up, I need to tell her."

Tell me what? Deanna fought to come out of the deep fog.

Esther said she wanted to wait until Deanna was stronger. Thomas shook his head, saying he couldn't keep pretending Daniel was still alive.

With a start Deanna's eyes came into focus and she tried to sit up. They stared at her in disbelief. Both jumped up from their chairs and reached to touch her.

"Det är ett mirakel. It's a miracle." Esther cried.

"Baby, you're awake. Thank God." Thomas whooped with exhilaration.

What are you talking about? Did you say funeral? What do you mean, pretending Daniel was alive? Deanna struggled to talk, but a tube down her throat choked off her voice. She grabbed at the sleeve of her father's shirt.

Alarms went off from the machines attached to her body. A nurse rushed in, surprised to see her awake and shooed them out of the way. She checked Deanna's vitals. She shouted at Thomas . . . something about heart rates, blood pressure, keeping her calm. He mumbled an apology. She administered a sedative and Deanna watched everything begin to fade and the voices withdrew deep into the tunnel.

It was several more days before the doctors felt Deanna was strong enough for them to tell her all the details. Her grandfather, Nils told her that she had been in a coma for three months.

Esther and Nils sat on either side of their granddaughter's bed, each holding her hand, Esther with her bandaged one. Thomas watched silently from the end of the bed. Nils explained what had happened. Daniel had been thrown from the car and died instantly. He'd hit his head on a rock. Deanna looked at her father, and then to Esther, waiting for her grandmother to say he must be confused; he didn't have it right, Daniel was still alive.

She just patted Deanna's hand.

Tears trickled down the wrinkled furrows of Nils' face. "I doubt he felt any pain, sweetheart, it happened so fast."

Deanna's wanted to scream but no words would come out. What? NO...NO, this can't be true. They have to be wrong. I can see Daniel's face, the look in his eyes. He was laughing because he just beat me. But then his expression changed from laughter to surprise as his little mouth formed a perfect O. He must have seen the car coming over my shoulder, just before it hit us.

Deanna shook her head. "Where's Mom? She'll tell me . . . truth. Why?" The words came out garbled. "Gramps . . . you're lying . . . why . . . say that?"

Nils stared at Deanna, and then looked toward his wife and Thomas for support. He squeezed her hand tighter. No words could give her the comfort she wanted.

It hurt to talk. Deanna clutched at her throat. "Is she . . . dead too? Why . . . Mom . . . not here?"

Nils shook his head. "She's not dead, darling. She's okay. She's at home, under house arrest. She is awaiting trial. They won't let her come darling."

Deanna jerked her hand from his. Esther bowed her head and whispered a prayer. Then Nils told Deanna the rest of the details, how both Esther and Deanna had been pinned inside, that they had arrested her mother for drunk driving. Two people were dead, Daniel and the driver of the other car.

Deanna felt her anger erupting like a volcano. Her chest constricted and her heart thumped loudly in her chest. She cried out the best she could in a twisted voice. "I'm glad she's not here! I don't want her! I don't ever want to see her again!" They were her first clear sentences. "I wish she was dead instead of Daniel! I hate her! I hate her!"

Both grandparents hung their heads.

Thomas didn't say anything. He stood there, wringing his hands, his eyes downcast to the floor. He didn't reach for his daughter to comfort her.

Deanna glared at him, filled with unresolved anger, an emotion that felt all too familiar. One she felt for everyone. Why didn't you say something? Why didn't you stop her from drinking? You knew, you all knew! She pounded her fists on the bed. Looking down, she detected the sheets lying flat below her knee. Unthinkable visions formed in her mind. She grabbed at the sheets and tried to pull them away.

Esther used all her strength, her good arm and much of her body, trying to stop Deanna from pulling away the sheets. They struggled, but Deanna managed to yank the sheet and blanket away. She gasped in horror. For a moment, no one spoke. Everyone froze in place. All eyes were on the white bed sheet where Deanna's shin and foot should have been. A big bandage covered the stump just below her right knee. Deanna heard something wild, animal-like screaming. "NO, NO, NO!" Then she realized it was her own voice.

Her stomach convulsed and she vomited all over her grandmother's floral dress. She couldn't hold back the tears. They came in torrents, washing over her again and again until she collapsed in exhaustion.

Esther and Nils never left her bedside, stroking her cheeks or patting her arm. Thomas came and went. He fidgeted around, wringing his hands or flipping his lighter open and shut over and over again. Deanna sensed he was fighting the urge to run.

Maybe I'm too ugly for him to look at now. Go ahead Dad, run. I'm a freak. I know it. I think I'm ugly too. Hours later, emotionally as well as physically spent, Deanna calmed down enough to think about the day of the accident.

Did I see Mom drink that morning? I hardly paid any attention anymore. It had become such a normal thing, maybe I just didn't notice. I blame all of them, but I knew too. Maybe I could have stopped her. It's just as much my fault that Daniel is dead and my leg is gone.

As the days passed, physically, Deanna was recovering. The nurse removed the feeding tube and began her on soft foods, puréed vegetables and baby food that she hated. She tossed them across the room. Forming words were difficult. The doctor clarified her concerns by explaining it was most likely only temporary brain damage. She may have to learn to talk and walk all over again, but she was young and strong. Eventually it would all come back to her.

The period after the amputation was crucial to Deanna's healing process. Before the doctors could fit her with an artificial limb, they wrapped the wound to reduce the swelling. The therapists told her exercise helped to heal the stump and forced her to do the exercises. After a few weeks and the healing had progressed, they wrapped the stump in an elastic bandage made of cotton. They told her it must be worn at all times.

Thomas quit coming to the hospital shortly after they moved her out of the ICU. Esther explained to Deanna that he was having his own problems dealing with Daniel's death. "Give him time, he needs to grieve in his own way."

"He can go to hell too." Deanna scribbled on a note pad by her bed. It still hurt to talk and forming the words took a lot of effort. I don't need either of them.

"Young ladies don't talk like that, Deanna." Esther frowned. She didn't tolerate bad language or disrespect. "Perhaps we should have Reverend Olson come by. He could pray with you."

Deanna turned her head away from her grandparents. She was angry and didn't care who knew it. And she didn't need any old preacher hovering over her and telling her to forgive her mother.

Chapter Five

Susan went through the trial in a haze. The Prosecuting Attorney for the State of Ohio spoke first. The tall, distinguished man, striking in his impeccable pin-striped suit, made an eloquent opening statement, reading Susan's prior arrests.

Dec. 23, 1966: Driving while intoxicated.

Feb. 14, 1968: Domestic violence, defendant intoxicated

May 28, 1973: Running a stop sign, driving while intoxicated

Nov 21, 1979: Public nuisance, defendant intoxicated

Susan waited for her attorney, Herbert Miller, to object, to say those incidents were not relevant to this case. He sat silently, fumbling with his notes.

The Prosecutor directed his speech to the jurors. "Ladies and gentleman, I thank you for your service by being here today. The sacrifice of your personal time toward the pursuit of justice is greatly appreciated. My name is Alexander Bronson. We are here to seek justice for those whose lives have been cut short due to the actions of Susan Jennings sitting before you. My job is an easy one. Susan Jennings is a drunk. I will prove to you, beyond a reasonable doubt that she is a habitual offender. She has twice been convicted of driving while under the influence of alcohol, twice been arrested for being intoxicated and demonstrating violent behavior. This time her drinking has caused the death of two people, William O'Donnell, a respected member of society, sixty nine years old, an innocent man traveling across town to spend the day with his grandchildren, and Daniel Thomas Jennings, Susan's own seven-year-old son. According to Ohio Revised Code 2903.06, after all the evidence is presented, you will have no choice but to convict Ms. Jennings of first degree vehicular homicide on both counts.

Bronson called an eye witness and the accident reconstruction expert. He addressed the court.

Prosecuting Attorney: "If it pleases Your Honor, at this time I would like to submit into evidence this rendering of the accident scene."

The Court: "Any objections?"

Attorney Miller rose and gave a slight bow to the judge. "No, your Honor."

Prosecuting Attorney: "This clearly illustrates how the Defendant failed to yield for the stop sign, entered the intersection, and thus caused the collision that took the life of Mr. O'Donnell as well as the life of her own son."

Defense Attorney: "Argumentative, your Honor. This isn't Closing Argument."

The Court: "Sustained"

Prosecuting Attorney: "The State calls Sergeant James Nelson to the stand."

Bailiff Jenson: "Raise your right hand please. Do you swear to tell the truth, the whole truth, and nothing but the truth so help you God?"

Witness Nelson: "I do."

Bailiff Jenson: "Please be seated and spell your last name."

Witness Nelson: (spelling) "N E L S O N".

Prosecuting Attorney: "Are you employed?"

Witness Nelson: "Yes, I am."

Prosecuting Attorney: "Where are you employed?"

Witness Nelson: "I am employed by the Mahoning County Sheriff's Department assigned to the Forensics Division."

Prosecuting Attorney: "How long have you been so employed?"

Witness Nelson: "I have been with the Sheriff's Department twenty five years, the last ten with the Forensics Division."

Prosecuting Attorney: "In your job with the Sheriff's Department, Sergeant Nelson, did you investigate an accident at the corner of South Range

Rd. and South Ave. during the afternoon of April 2, 1982.

Witness Nelson: "I did."

Prosecuting Attorney: "Tell the jury what you saw that afternoon."

Witness Nelson: "I arrived on the scene at 3:11 P.M. I observed a late model Buick sedan upside down on the north side of the intersection. Another car, a Ford station wagon was almost in the ditch with smoke coming from the hood of the car. Ambulance personnel were already on the scene assisting the victims and placing two people on the gurneys. I used my department-issued camera and took several pictures of the road, the cars, the stop sign, the bodies, and the survivors. I also measured the skid marks on the road and the blood stains on the victims' clothing and in the vehicles."

Prosecuting Attorney: "I show what has been marked as Peoples Exhibit 35-45. Can you identify these photographs?"

Witness Nelson: "Yes sir, these are the ones I took. They have my mark in the lower right hand corner."

Prosecuting Attorney: "Do these photographs accurately depict the scene as you observed that afternoon?"

Witness Nelson: "Yes sir, they do."

Prosecuting Attorney: "Has anyone tampered with these photographs since you took these pictures?"

Witness Nelson: "No sir, they have not. I have kept these photographs in a file in a locked cabinet and no one has access to the cabinet except me."

Bronson paused briefly and waited as one of the jurors broke into a coughing fit.

The older gentleman pulled a white handkerchief from his breast pocket and covered his mouth. The bailiff handed him a bottle of water.

Prosecuting Attorney Bronson gave the man a reassuring smile and directed his attention back to the witness. "Based on your twenty five years' experience as an officer with the Mahoning County Sheriff's Department, and observing the scene on the date of the accident, and later reviewing your pictures and your measurements, Sergeant Nelson, did you form an opinion as to the cause of that accident?"

Witness Nelson: "I did."

Prosecuting Attorney: "And what is that opinion?"

Witness Nelson: "It is my professional opinion, the Defendant, Susan Jennings, entered the intersection, failed to stop at the stop sign, and thus caused the collision that took the life of Mr. O'Donnell and young Daniel Jennings."

Prosecuting Attorney: "Do these photographs taken by you on the afternoon of the accident clearly illustrate and support your position that the Defendant's failure to stop caused the collision?"

Witness Nelson: "Yes sir, they do."

Prosecuting Attorney: "Your Honor, I offer Exhibits 35-45 into evidence."

The Court: "Any objections?"

Defense Attorney: "No Your Honor".

Attorney Bronson mounted the Exhibits to the right of the jurors' box on a large easel, alongside the previously admitted drawings of the intersection. The jurors grimaced at the graphic photos of the mangled station wagon with the front hood folded into the front seat. An elderly lady turned her head away and covered her mouth with a white handkerchief. A second photograph showed the sedan was upside down on its hood with the driver's door ripped off and the seat tattered and blood stained. Still another photo clearly showed a stop sign on the road Susan was driving, while the other street had the right of way.

A slight man in his mid-thirties was sworn in and he took his seat in the witness box. He looked self-conscious and his cheeks flamed red.

Prosecuting Attorney: "Mr. Adams, can you tell me where you were on the day of April 2, 1982, at approximately two p.m. in the afternoon?"

The eye witness nodded his head. "Yea . . . I mean, Yes sir. I was traveling north on South Ave., approaching South Range Rd. There was a white sedan approaching me from the opposite direction."

"And what occurred next, Mr. Adams?"

"Well, it happened so fast. A car, a station wagon sped right through the stop sign and hit the sedan in the left side. It pushed the car right up onto two wheels. Then the car rolled onto its roof. I had to swerve out of the way to keep from running into the overturned car."

Prosecuting Attorney: "Can you show us on this drawing where each of the cars were and the direction they were traveling?"

"Like this." Mr. Adams moved the magnetic cars on the map indicating the direction of the cars.

Bronson walked away from the exhibit, and rested his hand on the witness stand. "What did you do next Mr. Adams?"

Witness Adams: "I pulled my car to a stop and got out to see if I could help. But there was a lot of smoke coming out of the station wagon. I thought it was going to blow up. The front end was clear in the front seat. I couldn't get close. And . . . um . . . the white sedan . . . well that guy looked dead. I got sick . . . you know. I threw up. Then I saw her climbing out of the ditch." He looked toward Susan.

Prosecuting Attorney: "Please indicate who you saw climbing out of the ditch."

Witness Adams: "Her." He pointed at Susan.

Prosecuting Attorney: "Let the report indicate Mr. Adams identified Ms. Jennings."

Attorney Bronson stroked his cleft chin as he slowly reviewed the drawing and the photographs. "Thank you Mr. Adams. That will be all."

The Court: "Cross examine, Counselor Miller?" The judge glanced toward the defense attorney, who startled at the mention of his name, and dropped a stack of papers he was shuffling.

He stood awkwardly, straightening his crooked polka-dot bowtie, offering a slight bow toward the judge. "Not at this time, your Honor."

Attorney Bronson ran a perfectly manicured hand through his wavy blonde hair. He called the toxicology expert next. Round-faced with thick coke-bottle glasses, he took the stand and swore to tell the truth and nothing but the truth.

Prosecuting Attorney: "Mr. Fleming, did you examine the blood sample taken from the defendant when she was admitted to the hospital on the afternoon of the accident?"

Witness Fleming: "I did."

Prosecuting Attorney: "And what did you find?"

He lifted his thick glasses from the bridge of his nose and stared at Susan, a look of obvious disgust on his face. "I found, to a reasonable degree of certainty, the defendant's blood alcohol concentration was 0.18479% — twice the legal limit. She was drunk."

The jurors sucked in their breath. The men glared at Susan. Women shook their heads in disapproval. The prosecutor paused, letting the information percolate with the jurors before he continued. "Did you prepare a report for this trial?"

Witness Fleming: "I did."

Prosecuting Attorney: "Is this a copy of the BAC (Blood Alcohol Concentration report)?" He handed the witness the report to examine.

The witness glanced over it and concluded, "It is."

Prosecuting Attorney: "Your Honor, I submit Exhibit 43-27." Bronson handed the bailiff the document, who in turn offered it to the judge. Walking over and leaning on the rail before the jury box, the prosecuting attorney opened a law book. He smiled, moving his eyes slowly from juror to juror, making deliberate eye contact with each one. "If I may, ladies and gentlemen, let me read to you from the Ohio Revised Code, statute 4511.19, operating a vehicle under the influence of alcohol or drugs. A-1 No person shall operate any vehicle, streetcar, or trackless trolley within this state, if, at the time of the operation, any of the following apply:"

He looked up in a friendly, compassionate way. "I am only going to read the applicable passages so as not to bore you." He smiled and nodded affirmatively. Their heads bobbed back.

"If the following apply; (a)The person is under the influence of alcohol, a drug of abuse or a combination of them; and (f) The person has a concentration of seventeen-hundredths of one percent or more by weight per unit volume of alcohol in the person's whole blood." He snapped the book shut causing the jurors and Susan to jump in their chairs. "I would say it did indeed apply."

Judge Bishoff raised an eyebrow and looked at Attorney Miller. "Any objections, Counselor?"

Miller rose, straightening his rumpled jacket, dropping even more papers onto the floor, which floated over and settled at the feet of the bailiff. A strand of his comb-over hung over his left ear. "No objections, your Honor."

Sitting quietly, Susan kept her hands folded on the table. Perspiration beaded on her forehead and dripped under her arms. She looked down at the scratch marks embedded into the dark wooden table. Scars, more scars. We all have them, don't we? Her finger traced the grooves that some other defendant had etched while awaiting the verdict that would forever change his or her life. Two ceiling fans whirled above her head. She shivered.

A sketch artist caught the beads of perspiration around her red hairline. The rendering portrayed a broken spirit, eyes downcast, shoulders sloped in resignation.

Susan's defense attorney, Herbert Miller called a lone witness on her behalf. He didn't glance at his client. The witness, a mild timid woman of about seventy, raised her hand and took the stand.

Defense Attorney: "Mrs. Wiltmeyer, isn't it true that the intersection in question has a low hanging branch covering a portion of the stop sign on South Range Road?"

She spoke so quietly, the Judge looked at her kindly, smiled and asked her to speak up so the jurors could hear her.

Witness Wiltmeyer: "Well, I thought so. I complained to the Department of Transportation and they sent someone to look at it. But they didn't trim the branches. They told me the obstruction was not sufficient to send out a truck and two workers. I think they are just lazy, if you ask me."

The audience and the jury chuckled. The judge stifled a smile behind a well-manicured hand.

The Court: "Just answer the question, Mrs. Wiltmeyer. That will be sufficient. Please strike the last sentence from her testimony. Cross examination, Mr. Prosecutor?"

Prosecuting Attorney: "No your Honor. The State rests."

The Court: "You may step down, Mrs. Wiltmeyer."

Susan's council had advised her not to testify on her own behalf. He explained to her that anything she said would only be damaging. She didn't know how her testimony could possibly make things any worse.

The judge instructed the jury regarding deliberations and admonished the jury not to discuss the case except in the courtroom. The court recessed for the day. The jurors did not deliberate for long. The next day, as the jury filed back into the courtroom, Susan perused their faces, trying to read their minds. They all looked somber. One stately older man with a silver cane, briefly caught her eye, and then, quickly turned away. All the others averted their eyes from her. She knew it was not good news.

The Court: "Will the defendant please rise?"

Susan rose to her feet on shaky legs. Beset with fear and sleep deprivation from endless nights of worry, she grasped onto the edge of the table for support.

The judge unfolded the paper the bailiff had handed him from the head juror, read the verdict, nodded, and handed it back to the bailiff before addressing the jury.

The Court: "In the case of the State of Ohio versus Susan Jennings, on the count of vehicular homicide in the first degree in the death of Mr. William O'Donnell, how does the jury find?"

Lead Juror: "We find the defendant GUILTY Your Honor."

Susan felt her knees going weak, but she gripped tighter to the table for support and stayed upright.

The Court: "In the case of the State of Ohio versus Susan Jennings, on the count of vehicular homicide in the first degree in the death of Daniel Jennings, how does the jury find?"

Lead Juror: "We find the defendant GUILTY Your Honor."

Susan's knees gave out and she sunk to the floor. Flashbulbs went off. Voices rose from whispers in the spectator galley.

Judge Bishoff pounded his gavel on the bench and spoke firmly. "We thank the jury for your service. Sentencing shall take place one week from today at 10:00 a.m. This court is adjourned."

Only her parents, Esther and Nils Lundgren, wept silently at the back of the almost empty courtroom. The wife and two sons of Mr. O'Donnell exchanged empty smiles. The verdict would not bring back their loved one. Thomas was not in attendance.

***

At the sentencing the judge addressed Susan. "Ms. Jennings, seeing that you have two other arrests relating to intoxication, and two prior convictions for DUI, and this time your drinking caused the death of two individuals, it is my duty to protect the public from drivers like yourself who can't refrain from drinking and driving. I sincerely offer my condolences for the loss of your son and I advise you to seek help for your illness and dry yourself out while in prison."

Susan nodded in silence, her body sagging as she tried to remain upright, her wrists in tie straps in front of her. She stared straight ahead but saw nothing but a white void.

"Pursuant to Ohio Revised Penal Code 2929.14, on the felony count of first degree vehicular homicide in the death of William O'Donnell, I hereby sentence you to the maximum ten years in the Women's Correctional Facility in Marysville.

On the felony count of first degree vehicular homicide in the death of Daniel Thomas Jennings, I hereby sentence you to the maximum ten years in the Women's Correctional Facility to be served concurrently with the previous sentence. You will be eligible for parole after two years."

Susan slumped to the floor as flashbulbs exploded from eager newspaper reporter's cameras. She fainted. Two deputies lifted her up and escorted her out of the courtroom.

Chapter Six

Susan wiped her brow with the sleeve on her uniform. It was a hot August day when the van transporting the prisoners from the Mahoning County jail to the Women's Correctional Facility of Marysville made its way out of Youngstown and into the countryside. Susan watched her life slowly slip away from her.

The busy downtown city streets melted into tree-lined suburban neighborhoods. Susan stared through the mesh wire and tinted windows of the van as they continued south, past her own small hometown of North Lima, passed the soccer field Deanna played on every Saturday. She could see the roof of the house she grew up in from the highway. She closed her eyes and tried to picture it. How long will it be before I see it again? Opening her eyes, she saw the landscape had given way to rural farms. A three hour drive to Marysville, the penitentiary sat on two hundred and fifty acres, far enough away from the neighboring farms not to make anyone nervous.

Marysville was the oldest women's correction facility in Ohio. It opened in 1916 as a functioning farm, complete with dairy cattle, hogs and grain which the inmates ran. Among the prison population, it was still commonly referred to as 'The Farm' even though it was no longer working as such.

Susan glanced at the four other women who shared the back of the van, all cuffed at the ankles to the base of their seats with their wrists bound in front of them. They looked resigned, almost bored, while Susan quivered with fear in spite of the heat. If there was air conditioning in the van, she did not feel it. Perspiration dripped off the tip of her nose and she had to bend down to reach her shackled hands to wipe it away. She was the oldest and the only white woman among them. In contrast, the four black women were in their early twenties, appeared very street smart and familiar with the routine.

They don't look frightened. I wonder if they have been here before. Susan wanted to ask them so many questions, but she was apprehensive. This new life was far removed from the soccer mom world in her three bedroom ranch and tree lined streets.

No one spoke as the van pulled up the long driveway, and approached the large complex of gray buildings surrounded by high concrete walls.

Electric barbed wire twisted and looped atop the wall. Four tall guard towers loomed like sentries at their post at each corner of the complex.

The van pulled to a stop in front of the secured gates. The driver and the guard exchanged a few words before it proceeded up the drive turning left to an unmarked door in the largest building for new arrivals. Through double steel doors, the women entered single file, chained to each other at the ankles. The only sound came from the links as they dragged the ground, scrapping against the concrete floor.

Inside a door marked 'Intake', the Warden stood, hands clasped behind his back, as he glared at them behind thick tortoise frame glasses. His age showed on him; his hair spun into a ring around the crown of his head and a paunch where once-firm abs settled into a puddle and hung over his belt. His dreams of a political career had long vanished like the many different dreams of his detainees.

"Ladies, welcome to The Farm. I am Warden Fisher. There are only two rules here. Rule number one! My word is law. Keep your nose clean and you might make it out of here alive. Rule number two! Follow rule number one. This has been my house for thirty years. I plan on retiring with a perfect record in twelve months and you are not going to do anything to jeopardize that. If you think you have any rights, let me tell you right now, in here, you have none."

With a nod to the guards, he turned and sauntered back through a faded wood door with his name, "Roland Fisher, Warden" etched on the opaque glass.

The correction officer ushered them to another building which housed the infirmary and instructed them to strip. Their chains were released allowing them to undress, while two huge women in khaki uniforms with black belts and billy-clubs hanging at their side stood in the doorway and faced them with bored, expressionless faces.

The other inmates stripped quickly and stood naked beside the examination tables. Susan nervously followed their lead, slowly removing all of her clothes. She didn't know what to do with her clothes and couldn't just stand there and do nothing. She folded them and set them on the examination table in a neat pile. The vent from the air conditioner blew cold air onto her body and caused goose bumps to rise over her naked skin. She looked around for some paper wraps like in the doctor's office to hide her nakedness. There were none.

A female doctor in her mid-forties, dressed in green scrubs entered and tossed her neatly folded clothes into a wicker basket in the corner. She checked Susan's head for lice, looked in her mouth and ears. She then told her to lie back and put her feet in the stirrups. She performed a female exam and cavity search. Susan kept her eyes closed but could feel the eyes of the guards staring between her legs. After sitting up, the nurse offered a patronizing smile and a small stack of clothing before she continued on to the next intake without saying another word.

Humiliated beyond belief, Susan donned the pull-over sleep bra, scratchy stiff underwear and new orange jumpsuit with WCF stenciled on the back that would be her only wardrobe.

The inmates were divided according to their offenses. The WCF (Women's Correctional Facility) housed inmates from four classifications: minimal security, medium security, maximum security and one specifically for death row inmates. Each building housed a different classification dissected again into quads or wings in each sector. A corrections officer escorted three of the other intakes to a different building.

Along with one other woman from the van, Susan followed an officer down the damp hallway of the quad to which she was assigned. The inmates screamed out graphic promises of what they planned to do to the new inmates. Susan tried to block out the sounds as she fought off the tears that pooled in her eyes. She knew if she gave in to the tears, it would be a big mistake.

"Hoowee, white meat! Look at that one. I get first bids on the redhead!"

"Not on your life, Bitch. That one's mine. She'll be dancing to my jam before the end of the week."

"I think that white meat needs some tenderizing. You kin have'er, after I git'r broke in."

The hoots and cat calls continued down the hall until she reached her own corner of hell.

Susan didn't look up at the source of the voices as they led her to an 8 x 9 cell. On one wall, a metal bunk bed with two thin, stained mattresses took up most of the room. A single sink and steel commode in the corner offered no privacy. High on the wall, one small dirty window, about twelve inches square, cast a small patch of light onto the wall.

Her cellmate didn't look up from the old issue of Ebony magazine that covered her face as she lay on the bottom bunk. On the opposite wall, two small shelves bolted to the wall hovered over matching foot lockers. One shelf held a few photos of three young children with dozens of little braids protruding out from their dark heads. Susan could not discern if they were boys or girls.

The clang of the metal door as it slammed shut caused her to jump. For a minute, Susan stood there, not believing this was going to be her home for the next ten years. This is the same size as my walk-in closet at home. It was hard to breathe. She fought back the panic rising in her throat. She swallowed hard, trying to gain some control while the air around her closed in, suffocating her. She grasped the cold wall to steady herself. She swallowed hard, trying to gain some control over her mind and body.

Once she felt safe to move without her knees collapsing, she unrolled the bedroll at the foot of the top bunk. The stained sheets that were once white and the threadbare grey wool blanket did little to brighten the room. Looking around for a pillowcase and not finding one, she placed the single wash cloth and towel over the flat, thin pillow and poked the protruding feathers back through the seams. She deposited her meager belonging of three identical sets of her wardrobe, a small Bible her father had given her and a standard issued toiletry bag into the foot locker under the empty shelf.

Down the hall, static rap music blared on someone's radio and muffled the sounds of deep voices of inmates arguing and laughing among themselves.

The laughter made Susan think of Deanna and Daniel. She remembered them playing a game in the back seat just before the impact. Daniel was laughing. It registered that was the last time she would ever hear her baby boy's voice. Maybe Deanna's too. Unable to hold them back any longer, she succumbed to the strangulating sobs and buried her face in her hands. She sank down onto the hard foot locker. Life had been like a bad dream, culminating with the accident. A hollow feeling in the pit of her stomach reminded her of a baby being ripped from her womb, a baby like Daniel. She needed a drink.

Eventually she gained enough control of her emotions to speak. "Hello." Her voice was shaky and soft. She stood up with her back to the wall, looking down at the magazine masking the girl's face. Her nose ran. She looked for a tissue. Not finding any, she took the three steps to the stainless steel commode and wiped her nose on the scratchy, thin toilet paper.

She cleared her throat, thinking perhaps her cellmate didn't hear her. "I'm Susan."

"Gladys." The voice behind the magazine sounded deep, almost manly, flat and not too friendly.

Susan swallowed hard. "It's a pleasure to meet you."

Gladys dropped her magazine on the bunk, turned her head to face Susan and erupted in a bellowing laugh, exposing a large gap where front upper teeth should have been. Her hair matched the children in the picture, albeit a bit shorter. A deep scar ran down her dark left cheek from her ear to her chin. Susan guessed her to be in her mid-twenties.

"Well, lookie here. A real lady. If you wanna survive 'round here, just keep yo mouth shut. Dey gonna eat yo 'live. One word of advice. Stay tough and NEVER let 'em know you be 'fraid." With that, Gladys disappeared behind the magazine again.

Susan survived her endless first night on the quad. The ceiling crushed in on her as she lay in the top bunk, trying not to move and wake her cellmate. She needn't worry. Gladys slept soundly, a rhythmic snore counting the hours.

It had been one hundred and fifty two days since her arrest and her last drink. But she still craved the alcohol. Pains still ripped through her body. She alternated between ice cold shivers and raging sweats. She suffered through the dry heaves, grateful she didn't have any food in her stomach

The quad never quieted down the entire night. Cries of loneliness and angst mingled with the sounds of movement on squeaky springs, projected images in Susan's mind which she tried to shut out. Exhausted from fear, she merely drifted in and out of sleep. Finally dozing off about five a.m., she dreamed of Daniel and Deanna. They called for her. She tried to reach them, but the faster she ran toward their voices in her dream, the farther away they sounded.

Morning brought no relief; only her worst fears were brought to fruition when they announced shower call. Trooping to the community shower, she had no idea how to protect herself. Susan moved to the opposite corner of the room to be as far away from the others as possible. Her heart raced and bile rose in her throat when four over-sized naked women started to surround her. It was too late. She realized she had picked the worst possible spot. She was cornered. Susan remembered what Gladys had said and conjured up as much bravery as possible, and met their stares head on. Cold heartless eyes laughed at her futile attempt at bravery. She looked toward the corrections officers for help, but they had turned their backs leaving her vulnerable to the attack.

"It's your birthday, Red." The largest of the four black women approached her. She rubbed her body up against Susan, her heavy breasts almost at Susan's eye level. Susan turned her head away and tried to cover herself with her hands.

"Welcome to the first day of the rest of your life!" laughed the large inmate as she stepped back, skimming her eyes over Susan's whole body.

The other women laughed too, cold-blooded echoes that bounced off the walls.

"I ain't never seen a red bush before." She groped between Susan's legs and tugged on the triangle of hair.

Susan flinched from her touch, and opened her eyes in shock, but had nowhere to go.

"How 'bout we give you a little shower?" The shortest of the four, still several inches taller than Susan, seized her by the arm and pinned her against the cold concrete wall.

Another one, weighing nearly three hundred pounds, with rolls of fat supporting her huge breasts, turned on the faucet. Cold water pummeled Susan's body from the industrial strength sprayer. The huge attacker licked her lips in triumph. Freezing water teemed onto Susan's face, running into her eyes and mouth, and caused her to choke. Through watery eyes, Susan could scarcely make out something in the ringleader's hand. She braced herself for certain death.

With a crushing force, a hard, metal object hammered down on Susan's collarbone. She cried out and fell to the floor. Two women kicked her in the stomach. The heaviest-set one flipped her face down on the cold tile floor, pressing her foot into the small of Susan's back, forcing her legs apart with the pipe. She knew they were going to sodomize her.

"Help", she tried to cry out. "Someone, help me." The pain in her shoulder ripped through her body. A scream escaped her lips just before they shoved a cloth into her mouth, causing her to gag.

When Georgia stepped into the shower room, fully clothed, the other women moved aside, assuming she would want to have the honor. Close to six foot tall, built like a linebacker and no stranger to the gym, she towered over even the largest of them. Her massive white arms were tattooed from her wrists to her exposed biceps in geometric designs and zodiac signs. Short cropped dark hair did little to soften the chiseled chin. If Susan had looked at her face, she would have been surprised to see light blue penetrating eyes. But Susan didn't look up from the tiles. She only saw large worn sneakers under orange pant legs.

"Get out," Georgia commanded the gang in a flat monotone as she turned off the faucet. Georgia had been the queen of the quad for ten years. There was an unspoken hierarchy which was rarely contested. They didn't argue with her and abandoned the pipe, dropping it by Susan's head in a deafening ring on the tile floor. They retreated to the locker room, leaving Georgia and Susan alone.

Georgia didn't assault her. To the contrary, she sat down on the floor beside Susan. Fully clothed, the orange jumpsuit darkened as the water from the floor seeped into it. Susan pulled the rag from her mouth and curled into a ball on the icy tile floor, naked and trembling with fear and cold.

"So you killed your kid huh?"

Shocked by the accusation, Susan didn't know what to say. Through chattering teeth she said, "It was . . . was . . . an ac . . . accident, a c . . . c . . . car accident." Susan wondered if admitting killing a child would be the trigger to set Georgia off.

To Susan dismay, Georgia sympathetically nodded her head as though she understood. The sounds of the others making their way out of the locker room echoed in the background. Suddenly it was eerily quiet, just a few drops of water dripping onto the tile, rhythmically in sync with Georgia's tapping foot.

"Was never s'pose to happen", Georgia began. "Damien was s'pose to stay in the car. It went down all wrong. Then he was lying in the street with blood all over his tummy. He tried to say Mama, but only red bubbles of blood came out of his mouth. Then he died, right there in my arms."

Susan let her talk. Georgia's little boy had been caught in the middle of a shoot-out between her boyfriend and a drug dealer to whom he owed money. Grabbing the gun from her boyfriend, she took the dealer out, but it didn't save her son's life. And her price was life imprisonment.

There they were. Two grieving mothers mourning the death of their little boys. A connection was sealed, a bond solidified. Susan sat up, futilely attempting to cover her nakedness, but grateful to Georgia for saving her from the assault. It was then Susan noticed her eyes, like calm pools of respite. How did I acquire this unusual friend and ally? The officer entered the shower and barked at them to move along.

Chapter Seven

Esther and Nils arrived at the hospital with a small cake with sixteen candles on it. The nurses and aides joined them in Deanna's room to sing Happy Birthday.

Deanna sat motionless as they sang, almost as still as when she was in the coma, she neither looked at the cake nor into their eyes. She stared blankly ahead. Go away, just go away. I will choke on that stupid little cake and you are all off-key

Nils leaned in close to his grand-daughter. "Can't we even get a little smile from my flicka? Your Gram baked your favorite cake, chocolate with mint chocolate chip frosting. How about I sing to you in Swedish?"

Deanna's lips finally curled upward at the corner. "Don't sing in Swedish, Gramps. I'm sorry. Thank you for the cake." She reached over and grasped her grandmother's hand.

As the revelries settled down and the hospital staff went back to their chores, Esther and Nils spent the rest of the afternoon reminiscing with Deanna about past birthdays, theirs and hers. Nils told her about his birthdays by the lake in Sweden. Thomas arrived just at the end of visiting hours with a bouquet of flowers and a small teddy bear he had picked up hastily in the hospital gift shop.

***

It was a week later when Susan stared at the calendar on the library wall. It was late October. She had missed Deanna's sixteenth birthday. Was she was still in a coma? Will she even be alive by the time I get out?

Susan knew not to expect many visitors so when Thomas arrived she was anxious for news about Deanna. Susan sat across from him, through the bullet-proof glass divider. He needed a shave and his face looked drawn and aged for a man of thirty-five.

"They tried everything. It was just too damaged. Gangrene had set in. They asked me to sign the papers. She was still unconscious. We weren't sure if she would ever wake up."

Susan knew what he meant, but she needed to hear the words to make it real. "Sign for what, Thomas? What did you do?"

His eyes flashed in anger. "What did I do? Are you fucking serious, Susan? I didn't cause her to lose her leg, YOU did. I HAD to agree to the amputation. I was saving her LIFE. Shit Susan, YOU caused this, not me." The outburst sucked all the energy out of him. He slumped into his chair, staring blankly over her shoulder.

"She's awake now? Is she okay?" Susan words were barely audible through the phone she held close to her mouth.

Thomas looked blankly through the glass. The anger was gone from his voice, replaced with deep sorrow. He began to nod his head, and then shook it instead. "She's awake, but not good Susan. She's scared and angry and misses her brother. Your parents and I had to tell her about Daniel. How did you think she'd be?"

Susan had to know. "Does she ask for me?"

He shook his head. "I don't see much of her. They're talking about moving her to a rehabilitation center soon."

"But Thomas, you must know how she is? Why aren't you going to see her? Isn't it bad enough she lost Daniel, and me? She needs you!"

Susan watched him squirm in his seat, alternating the phone from one ear to the other.

"I . . . I don't know Susan. It's just so hard to see her like that. My whole body starts to shake with just the thought of seeing her leg, or missing leg, I guess I'm not good at this Susan. I can't stand to look at her leg, er' stump, but I also can't look away. I look at her and see Daniel lying in that casket . . . maybe later. I'm sorry — I just can't."

Susan shook her head in disbelief. How can he just walk out on her now, when she needs him the most? She's only sixteen. Susan got up from the booth and motioned for the officer to let her go. She didn't have anything else to say to him. She looked over her shoulder as she passed through the door. He still sat there, fumbling with his hands.

Susan stumbled back to her cell. Gladys looked at her but kept silent. Susan's mind exploded with visions of her daughter, alone and afraid. How did things go so wrong? Deanna must be so afraid. Is she in pain? I need to put my arms around her, wrap her up and make her feel safe. I guess I was never very good at that. I've failed her miserably as a mother. I HAVE to get out of here. She needs me. Susan had sent a letter every week to Deanna, even before she knew if she was awake. She wanted them to be there for her when she did. Now she wondered if they had ever been opened. There was never a response.

Nils and Esther made the three hour drive to Marysville as often as they could. Esther's physical therapy and Nil's numerous doctor visits to monitor his worsening heart condition occupied a lot of their time. Their visits to Susan were not enough to satisfy either daughter or parent.

"What can we do sweetheart?" Nils touched the glass separating him. "We miss you so much. Deanna is doing much better. Rev. Olson has been by to see her a few times. I think his prayers are helping her recovery."

"Why?" Susan almost shouted. A guard stood up to see what the noise was about. "I mean," she lowered her voice. "Isn't there a youth pastor? One closer to her age?"

Esther's furrowed brows looked at her husband. Nils tried to explain. "We don't have a youth pastor right now. Attendance is so low; hardly any young people come anymore. He is only trying to help, sweetheart. I know you don't go to church anymore, but how can you object to his prayers? Do you blame Him for Daniel's death? You must not question the Lord's will, Susan. Even though, it may be hard to understand. You still believe in the good Lord, don't you Susan?"

Susan didn't have the heart to tell her father no, in fact she did not. She let out a sigh. "Maybe, Dad, I don't know. But you believe, and your prayers are enough."

Chapter Eight

The pretty little candy striper with her hair pulled high into a chestnut ponytail greeted Deanna with a big smile and placed a letter on Deanna's nightstand. "You have another letter." Her words slurred slightly by the mass of metal in her mouth. "I always love getting letters, don't you?"

Deanna looked down at the envelope and recognized the return address of the Marysville Correctional Facility. Her face darkened with anger and she grabbed the letter, "Get Out!" She screamed at the startled young girl. She tore the letter in half and flung the pieces at her. The two halves floated to the floor and slipped under the bed.

The young girl jumped back from the bed, "Oh, I'm sorry . . . I thought . . . it's just that . . ." She turned on her heels and sped out the door in tears, her face flushed with embarrassment. Deanna sunk back onto her pillow, fighting back her own tears of anger. I don't want anything from my mother, not now, not ever!

Deanna's life had centered on her rehabilitation. Learning to accept the word "amputee" as part of her life was an immeasurable feat. The orthopedic doctor explained that the prosthesis would be fitted once the wound was closed and the stitches removed. Sometimes Deanna thought she could still feel her leg. The pain was so real, coursing through her missing foot and traveling all the way up to her thigh. The doctor explained it as "phantom leg syndrome." He said eventually it would go away and the wound on her stump was healing nicely. Deanna still didn't want to look at it, even when they insisted she learn to change the cotton dressing by herself. They said she would be fitted first with a metal prosthesis, and eventually with a natural, flesh looking leg as her swelling reduced and her leg was back to its regular size.

They took her to physical therapy every day. The room was full of exercise equipment, bars and benches. Bare wooden tables had stacks of children's toys, blocks and tubes, plastic cups and plates. Most days, Deanna was in tremendous pain. The goal was to build up her arm strength so she could first use a walker, then crutches, and later be fitted for the prosthesis.

She hated the parallel bars the most. The weight of her body caused her shoulders to protest in pain. She'd fall and hang by her armpits until the therapist helped lift her back up onto her arms. "I can't. It . . . hurts. Please stop."

But they didn't stop. If she refused, two brawny male aides lifted her out of the wheelchair and placed her between the bars. She had no choice but to do it or just hang there. Afternoons, the speech therapist came to her hospital room. Props such as balls or a stuffed pig or a hat were brought in to encourage her to use her words.

I know what a damn ball, a pig and hat are, you idiot. Deanna fumed behind words that would not form. The therapist patiently dodged the items Deanna whirled at the wall in frustration. She picked up a plastic cup and threw it against the wall. It didn't have the same satisfying effect as smashing a glass into a million pieces. It just cracked as it hit the wall with a light ping and rolled under the empty bed next to hers.

The late October air still clung to an Indian summer. It was ten weeks since Deanna had woken up when the doctors came into her room. They said they had good news. "You are being discharged from the hospital. You've made remarkable progress and are out of danger. Now we just have to get you walking again."

"Walk?" She looked down at her stump in disgust. "Aren't you forgetting something?"

"That's why we need to get you out of here. You'll get fitted with a wonderful new leg and you'll be walking again before you know it."

Deanna thought they were sending her home. She was wrong. They were transferring her to a rehabilitation center where she would continue with her therapy.

Chapter Nine

Susan's withdrawal from alcohol addiction was brutal. Even though it had been five months since she had a drink, every day she wanted one. When she had a bad day, she craved a drink to get to sleep. On better days, like when she received a letter from her parents, she needed one to celebrate. The nights were the worst.

Susan worried Gladys could feel the entire frame of the bunks shake as she trembled in a cold sweat, coiled in a ball as pain racked through her body. Those horrible nights were coming less and less frequent, but she was a far cry from clean.

In a different lifetime, Gladys and Susan never would have been friends. But they both missed their families and shared their mutual alcohol addictions. Gladys shared her pre-prison life, as did Susan. Susan confessed about her drinking problem and reminisced about her life as a soccer mom. Some things she couldn't say. Some things were buried too deep.

Gladys understood her caution, and her addiction. She was going through the twelve steps of AA. She suggested to Susan she should attend the meetings with her. "I get it," she responded to Susan's refusal to attend a meeting. "Been there, done that. I had my first drink at twelve years old."

Susan thought about Deanna and wondered if her daughter ever experimented with the many bottles around their house. She certainly had access to it all. She stared at the ceiling from the top bunk.

"Never knew my old man," Gladys spoke from the bottom bunk, staring at the springs of Susan's bed. "But my Ma was around, and my 'uncles'. She gave a short cynical laugh. She turned and stared at the pictures on the small shelf opposite the bunk.

"My sisters each got dif'ent 'uncles' as their baby-daddy. When dey leave, like dey always did, it be me that had to make sure them lit'uns got fed and all. Seems I was der Mama most da time. Dey all be in dif'ent foster homes now.

Susan nodded her head, slid down from the bunk and sat on the metal foot-locker, leaning her back on the cold concrete wall. "That's rough. What happened to them?"

"The county took 'em away from Mama. When she finally pass out on da couch an' da kids be asleep, I'd dig through her favorite hiding places and help myself to whatever was left in the bottle. It be my only 'scape. Sometime dem uncles come after me, but I kep a butcher knife under my bed. I tol 'em I cut it off if dey wave dat thing near me. So dey lef me lone. "

Gladys jumped up from the bunk so fast she startled Susan, shaking off the feeling like discarding an old coat. "Come wit me to a meet'in". She pleaded again. "You don't have to say nuttin'. Just sit there. You need help, and I'm tired of my whole bunk shaking me ta sleep." She winked at Susan, letting her know it was said good-naturedly.

"Maybe someday," was all Susan could muster.

There was AA meetings every day for those that wanted to attend. Susan dragged herself grudgingly behind Gladys two weeks after she arrived. Ten women sat in a circle in the middle of the cafeteria. Gladys and Susan pulled over two more chairs and joined the group.

"Hello, my name is Gladys and I am an alcoholic."

The group responded, "Hello Gladys".

Susan knew she was supposed to repeat the same line. An admission of what she was. She couldn't do it. "Susan," she mumbled to the group, averting her eyes from their sympathetic stares.

Step One of the twelve steps required admitting she was an alcoholic and powerless over alcohol. She listened to them talk. She knew in her mind the alcohol had been the cause of Daniel's death, and why she sat in prison, but she couldn't admit it out loud, to herself or anyone else. Not yet.

Chapter Ten

Esther and Nils were there to help Deanna with the move.

"Why can't I go home?" Deanna looked toward her grandfather. Nils shook his head. "You need more therapy, darling. You'll go home someday, just not yet."

The orderly helped her into the wheelchair and maneuvered it into the elevator. Deanna gave one last plea to Esther. "Please Gram, why can't I go with you? Or Dad? I don't want to go . . ." Esther bent down and kissed her head. "I'm sorry. Be a good flicka and listen to your Gramps. You'll go home in the Lord's good time." Nils settled a pink stocking cap Esther had knitted for her on Deanna's head. The right side of her head had about two inches of blonde hair growing back around the stitches that stretched across her head. Her left side had been trimmed to a close Pixie cut. A few thick curls nestled against her ear.

The transport van lowered the ramp and they strapped her wheelchair to it. Deanna never took her eyes off of her grandparents until the chair was in the van and she could no longer see their faces. The young driver tried to make small talk. Had it been a different circumstance and a different time, Deanna would have noticed that he was cute, with freckles across his nose and dimples in both cheeks. But she only saw the blur of light posts through her tears as they whizzed by her window.

The rehabilitation center was red brick, spread out across several city blocks. Brighter colored brick showed where the new wings had extended the facility over the years. A well-manicured lawn with huge pots of burnt-orange chrysanthemums surrounded the wide concrete paths wound around the building and reached to the large parking lot and circular driveway at the entrance.

A short, stocky nurse's aide in a bright yellow happy-face smock smiled at Deanna as they lowered the ramp from the van to the entrance. "Welcome Miss Deanna. We're so happy to have you here with us. Another young face is just what this place needs."

Deanna shook her head. She wasn't going to dignify the statement with a response. She hated the facility already. Shriveled old patients with blank stares watched from their wheelchairs scattered about the lobby and hallways. One skeletal man babbled on about something unintelligible and tried to grab her wheelchair as they moved her down the hallway. Another ancient woman waved her arms at her, calling out, "Penelope". Agitated, Deanna gave her a scowl and glared back at her. Most of the patients were in their seventies and eighties. Many had fallen and broken a hip or just left there to die by children that couldn't be bothered with them any longer. Deanna thought the place smelled like disinfectant and old people.

They wheeled her into the home's dining hall and positioned her at a round table, across from a little Vietnamese girl named Kim-Ly. She waved a free hand toward Deanna as she talked to an old man that gummed his food.

"We'll take your things to your room. You can get acquainted with Kim-Ly and have a little lunch." The aide patted her on the shoulder and disappeared before Deanna could object.

"Dina", the young girl said. "I wait for you. Nurse tell me you come today; I wait all morning." Her dark almond eyes twinkled in the harsh fluorescent lights and her hair cascaded down her tiny little back in a raven-black waterfall. Five years younger than Deanna, only eleven years old, Kim-Ly had been there for six months before Deanna arrived.

Deanna pulled the stocking cap farther down on her head to cover the prickly right side of her head. "How could you . . . know I . . . coming today?" She tried to snap at the little dark-haired angel but the words came out stilted and slurred.

She had so much pent-up anger; even Kim-Ly's smiling face was not exempt from her scorn.

"They tell me friend come today, they tell me last night. So I wait and wait for my new friend, and now here you are. I am Kim-Ly. You are Dina."

Kim-Ly reached her hand across the table to Deanna and smiled, showing perfect straight white teeth. The old man next to her dribbled water down his front and an aide came by and helped dry him off with a towel. He didn't acknowledge the aide. He watched Deanna eye up Kim-Ly.

Deanna did not return Kim-Ly's outstretched hand. "Dee— Ann— A, not Dina." She shook her head at Kim-Ly. Slowly, she formed the syllables. "My name is Deanna. Dee —Ann— AAA." She wanted to ask how she knew her name, but the words which had come earlier now jumbled in her mouth.

"Good to have girlfriend instead of old men that drool." Kim-Ly cocked her head to the side in the direction of the man beside her. But she smiled at him and patted his hand, gently massaging the old gnarled knuckles.

Deanna didn't want her sympathy, or anyone else's. And especially not from someone who could just get up and walk out the door, free of disabilities. "Are you . . . a child ther—a—p—p—ist? Should I be happy? Your ch . . . cha . . . char . . . ity work— not wel . . . come. Go play w . . . with . . . your . . . friends and leave me . . . alone!" When upset, her words tangled on her tongue, making her more frustrated with the situation.

Kim-Ly looked at her quizzically. She didn't understand what Deanna was talking about. "Go? Go where? I no go Dee-hanna. I stay here with you. You see. I no go. We be good friends."

She wheeled her chair around to the other side of the table. Deanna flinched when she saw Kim-Ly didn't have any legs. Both legs had been amputated well above both knees. A strap around her waist kept her from falling out of the chair. The stumps of her legs were covered in heavy dark knit stocking caps like Deanna's brother used to pull down over his face in the snow.

Deanna felt foolish about her charity work comments but she still didn't want or need a new friend. Kim-Ly's injury was more severe than Deanna's, but she wasn't complaining. She only wanted to be Deanna's friend.

Kim-Ly and Deanna were the only patients under the age of sixty, so they assigned them to room together. Over Deanna's bed, a hand painted poster read "WELCOME" in bright primary colors. Over Kim-Ly's bed, dozens of posters of American pop idols, Shawn Cassidy, Leif Garrett, and The Brady Bunch covered every square inch of the wall.

Before Deanna was even settled in bed, Kim-Ly wheeled into the room, slapped a high-five to the aide and pulled her chair up beside Deanna.

"Hey girlfriend. Why are you in bed? It's not bedtime."

"Leave me alone," Deanna grumbled at her. She rolled to her side, away from Kim-Ly's smiling face.

"You no like my sign I make for you? I want my new girlfriend be welcome."

Deanna heard the disappointment in her voice but she didn't turn back to face her. Kim-Ly's cheerfulness only made her think of Daniel. Deanna pleaded silently. Please just leave me alone. I don't care about you or this place... or anything. Just leave me alone.

One night as they lay in bed, Kim-Ly heard Deanna crying. To distract her from her own sorrows, she told her the story about what happened to her village in Khanh Hau, Vietnam.

"The American GI's, they all left when I was very little. Even deep in the Mekong Delta, we knew they no come back. The planes no fly over our village anymore. The North Vietnamese soldiers came instead. They come into our village and tell us there a new Vietnam, a united Vietnam. Anyone who did not agree to their demands was shot. They took Papa-san and brother with them; make them join the new Communist Vietnam army. Mama-san and I stayed in the village, hoping and praying they would let Papa-san come home. Only old men, women and children were left. The soldiers used the villagers to scan the mine fields that were left from the war. Nobody knew where the mines were. One day they pointed at Mama-san and prodded her with their bamboo spears. I was so afraid. I knew she no come back. She kissed me on my head and told me to be a good girl and listen to Auntie Su. It shames my Mama-san to cry in front of soldiers so I try hard to be brave. I follow her to the edge of village; never take my eyes off of her."

Deanna listened to Kim-Ly talk, feeling her own shame for how she had initially spoken to her new friend.

"Mama-san comes back, but she wrapped in a shroud cloth. The mines took her. The first time I walk the mine fields I was six years old. I take a step, and then wait so hear the click of the mine before it explodes. The birds screamed over my head. I try hard to listen for the click, but it no come. The soldiers cheer when I make it across. They no cross the field, but they clap each other on back and laugh anyway. The second day, they send me into the fields again. I made it out again. They called me Lucky, they think if they always follow me, they no get struck by mine, but I not no so lucky. One day it happened. I heard the click and froze. I tried not to breathe; hoping I could stop what I knew was coming. The mine exploded at my feet. At first, it no hurt. My ears rang from the sound. Then it was so quiet. I lay there thinking I had missed being hit. Looking up at the sky, I saw the birds fly from trees in beautiful dance. When I pull up on my elbows to get up, I see all the blood and the tiny bits of my pajamas on the ground. Then the pain start . . . before everything go black. I not know how I get out of mine field. I have no memory. I woke up in

Auntie Su's hut. She tied strips of cloth tight around the tops of my legs. The pain so bad but she give me broth. Make me sleepy and the pain go way. Later Auntie Su carry me for many days. Sometime I wake up and scream. Mostly I sleep. We go long way. She put me in small boat and pay man to take me with him."

Deanna sucked in her breath. "Where did he take you? Was he a good man?"

"Yes, yes, good man. He take me down river and cross to hospital. He said we in Thailand now. Missionaries work in hospital. They very nice to me. They help me get strong. Then one day, they tell me I go to America. The missionaries did this for me. I very grateful and honor them by being strong and no cry when I leave." Kim-Ly stopped talking, her dark eyes staring out into the darkness.

Deanna wondered if she was thinking about her missionary friends or her family.

Kim-Ly snapped out of her melancholy memory and broke into a broad smile. "Then I come here. And now I have new friend, Dee-Aaa-Na. And I am going to get new legs. Kim-Ly very lucky now."

Instead of wallowing in anger and self-pity, Kim-Ly was the light that shone brighter than any star. She raced down the hall in her wheelchair; she spun wheelies in the lounge and taught Deanna how to balance on the back two wheels. "Let's race Dee-Aaa-Na. I beat you in wheelchair race!" She made the old residents laugh. Even Deanna laughed when all she wanted to do was cry or curl up in a ball and give up. Kim-Ly never gave up. "Movies tonight Dee-Aaa-Na, let's go see old movies in lounge tonight. Wanna play game Dee-Aaa-Na? Wanna play Scrabble?" Kim-Ly was relentless.

English was Kim-Ly's second language thanks to the Baptist missionaries at the hospital in Thailand.

Every week Deanna received another letter from the prison. Kim-Ly pleaded with her to open them. Deanna did the same as she always did, tore them in half and dropped them into the trash can beside her bed.

Kim-Ly raised her eyebrows and looked in the trash can. "Who write you nice letter you tear up?"

Deanna groaned. "You don't understand. My mother did this." She waved her arm across her lap. "It's her fault I'm here, her fault I'm a cripple. She killed my little brother."

"I know you have Mama-san and I don't. I be so happy to get letter from Mama-san. Maybe she sorry. Maybe she no try to hurt you or brother?"

Deanna turned her back on her new friend so she wouldn't see the sadness mixed with anger in her eyes. You just don't understand. My mother is the last person I want to hear from. I will never forgive her.

Esther and Nils came once a week to visit. They tried to cheer her up with word from Susan, that her mother was doing well and missed her very much. Deanna stiffened at the very mention of her mother's name. One week they brought Reverend Olson from the church. "You remember Rev. Olson, from the church, don't you?"

Rev. Olson ran his hand through his thick blonde hair and extended it out to meet her small delicate one. "So very nice to see you, Deanna. We have kept you in our prayers at the church." Deanna did not return her hand so he rested his hand on her head, offering his blessing.

Deanna squirmed as his hand lingered a long time on her head. With her head bowed, she didn't know if he was silently praying or what. She felt herself flush at his touch. Wow. He is really cute, too cute to be a minister, even if he is old enough to be my father.

"Reverend Olson was the youth pastor of our church when your mother was a child." Nils offered a smile to the minister. "He was your mother's private tutor for many years. We are very grateful for the help he offered her."

Uh, didn't do much to keep her from being a drunk, did it? Maybe she spent too much time staring into those blue eyes instead of praying.

Rev. Olson's hand slid from her head and cupped her chin in his palm, raising her head to look in his eyes. She caught the scent of peppermint as he spoke. "That's right, Deanna. Would you like me to tutor you as well? I have a teaching degree besides being a clergyman." He nodded his head at Deanna, expecting her to follow suit.

His question caught Deanna off guard. She was preoccupied with his good looks and fabulous physique. "Ahh, I don't know. We have a tutor here. Maybe. I'll ask them if it is okay."

Kim-Ly looked at Deanna, confused by Deanna's reaction. "We have teacher, good teacher, teach English and history and numbers." Why you want a new teacher?

Deanna didn't know how she felt about this whole idea. Maybe it would be fun. He is soooo cute. I'm not sure how I would ever concentrate on my studies if I was looking at him the whole time.

Esther's brows creased together. "Very well, we will speak to the staff here and see about your studies here. That is very gracious of you to offer, Reverend Olson."

"It would be my pleasure Esther. You know how much this family means to me. You have always been dear to my heart.

Deanna mumbled a weak "Thank You" but did not look up into his eyes.

Nils bend down and kissed the top of Deanna's head. "Well, fine then. We'll see what we can do for our favorite granddaughter. Kim-Ly, you keep after her. I know you'll help her get her strength back."

"Yes sir, Mister Papa-san. I make her work very hard."

The pastor and her grandparents left the girls alone.

"Why you want that teacher, Dee-Aaa-Na? We have good teacher."

Deanna rolled her eyes as Kim-Ly. "Don't you think he is cute?" She is such a child.

"Oh, I see now. I too young for boys, and he is too old man for you. Why you like old man?"

"I don't know. Let's drop the subject. They probably won't let him tutor me anyway."

Kim-Ly got her "legs" two weeks before Deanna. She was so happy even Deanna couldn't help but be happy for her.

When Deanna finally received her first prosthetic, Kim-Ly clapped excitedly from across the room. Both fitted with "legs", Kim-Ly challenged Deanna to races down the hall, even though the "races" were wobbly at best. Kim-Ly always won. It was her constant energy and optimism that pushed her forward.

As much as Deanna fought it, she kept getting stronger, physically and emotionally. Her speech was almost back to normal as she approached the one year mark since the accident.

Chapter Eleven

Susan continued to write to Deanna. Some of the letters were returned unopened. Most were not. Susan held out hope that at least a few were being read and not simply thrown away.

The ward had a visitors list before anyone could visit. A corrections officer brought Susan an updated list. A knew name had been added to her list. Susan looked at the form in disbelief. Reverend James Olson's name had been added. He was requesting a visit. Susan crossed off the name, digging deeply into the paper tearing a whole in it. I don't need another person trying to preach to me. Thomas' Come-to-Jesus lectures are enough religion for anyone. And definitely not the great Reverend Olson!

She handed the form back to the officer. "Sorry I tore it. I don't want Reverend Olson to visit. I do NOT want to see him." She didn't mean to raise her voice, but other inmates looked up from their magazines wondering what the commotion was about. The correction officer shrugged her shoulders and moved on down the hall, the request tucked in a notepad she carried with her.

Susan began to write stories to pass her time. She bought paper with her money she earned in the kitchen and the shops. Gladys saw her writing in the library head and storing them in her foot locker.

"What you writing all the time?"

"Children's stories. Just something I like to do."

Susan's children were her inspiration. Her animated characters, Danny and Denny were squirrels that constantly got into one mischief after another. Regardless of their antics, Susan's little characters always came home to their loving mother, with a slight scolding and a big hug.

"Tell me 'bout dem." Gladys pleaded.

"Well, in one story, Danny jumped precariously from branch to branch looking for acorns until he was far from his nest high in the canopy of trees over Central Park. One jump too many landed him not on a tree branch, but on the terrace of a Fifth Ave. penthouse where he befriended a little boy, sequestered to his luxury apartment with a haughty grandmother and a soft hearted maid."

"What's precar . . . precare . . . and seques . . . seques . . . dem words your use?"

"Precariously means dangerously and sequestered means set apart, or confined."

"Like solitary?"

Susan smiled. "Yes, it's something like that."

Gladys tried to read a few of the stories but she stumbled over the words. Susan read them aloud to her. Gladys' dark eyes lit up and a melancholy look crossed her long angular face which was slightly out of place on her stocky body.

"My sisters would love dem stories. Dem lil' squirrels always find der way home. And dey had a mamma dat really loved them. I love happy endings."

Susan sighed as she thought a moment about what Gladys said. "Yea, so do I. Too bad we didn't get a happy ending, huh? Well, maybe someday, when we get out of here, we can have a happy ending too."

It gave her a diversion and some comfort, but it didn't take away the pain. The stories accumulated under the orange jumpsuits and sparse underthings in her foot locker. She dreamed of someday seeing her stories published.

But even with her stories, Susan knew she still needed more help. She finally joined the AA group and accepted she was powerless over the alcohol. That was Step One.

"Hello, my name is Susan, and I am an alcoholic."

"Hello Susan," the group repeated back in unison.

When it came her turn to speak, she choked on the words.

"I killed my little boy and another man. We were going to the mall. I don't remember drinking that day, but that's not unusual. Drinking was like breathing. I needed it." She paused and took a deep breath, suddenly feeling herself hyper-ventilating. Heat crept up between her shoulder blades, around her neck and flushed her face.

"Sometimes I couldn't find any," she continued. "Thomas would throw away the bottles he found. I thought I was fooling him. I'd told him I had quit. He would get so angry."

The others in the circle nodded their heads. They all understood. They waited patiently for her to go on.

"On April second everything changed. Mom and I had been rather distant for the last few weeks. I think she was struggling with talking to me about my drinking and vowing never to interfere. I thought a little day trip to the mall might lessen the tension and give us some much needed time together.

There was a light rain. I kept adjusting the wiper speed, one was too low, and the next level up was too fast. The kids were in the back seat of our station wagon, playing some kind of game. Out of the corner of my eye I saw two little squirrels dart across the road in front of us. I swerved slightly to miss hitting them and sailed through the stop sign. I didn't even see it. I heard tires screech just before the impact."

Susan paused, gathering her composure so she could go on. Gladys gave her a slight smile of encouragement.

"I don't remember being thrown from the car, but I can still see the car in my mind as I crawled out from the ditch. Black smoke curled from the hood. I could smell gasoline. A man in a gray jogging suit grabbed me as I stumbled toward the car. I had to get the kids and Mom out. He wouldn't let go of me. He kept saying, 'It's gonna blow, ma'am, you can't go near it.' I fought with all my strength, trying desperately to tell him that my family was in the car.

"My mother, my kids . . . ." I hollered out, and then collapsed in his arms.

Someone must have called 911 for help. The smoke from under the hood of our mangled station wagon was getting thicker. Another car rocked on its hood upside down. There were all these people just milling around. I didn't know where they all came from. It was like an invisible line around the car. No one wanted to get too close, afraid of an explosion. Others were morbid curiosity seekers, the kind that chase ambulances but didn't have the stomach for seeing it up too close. I watched them all just standing there. Nobody was helping get my family out.

I heard the sirens blast through the still afternoon air, muffled slightly by the rain. The sedan that had been rocking on its top was still now. I thought I saw someone hanging upside down from the seat belt, wedged in between the seat and the released air bag.

A ladder truck careened to a stop. They quickly pulled a flame retardant from the truck, and the firemen extinguished the flames that had started under the crumpled hood of our car.

An ambulance arrived just seconds behind. Two EMT's ran over to the sedan. I didn't know at the time, but the man inside was dead.

Once the danger of fire was gone, the jogger let me go. I remember staggering toward the vehicle, screaming. "Get them out, get them out." At least I thought I was screaming, but it was only in my mind. I'm told the only sound the EMT heard was barely over a whisper.

The entire right side was just a mass of twisted steel and fiberglass making the car crumpled like an accordion.

I heard a very weak moan escape from inside the tangled pile of rubble. Firemen and EMT's heard it too and rushed to try to locate the source of the sound. From deep under the metal and fiberglass, they saw a small blond head.

Everyone seemed to be moving in slow motion. I needed them to hurry, that had to be Deanna or Daniel's head they saw.

A young fireman with muscular tattooed arms and a shaved head called out. "Don't move honey. Keep your head still. We'll get you out."

"I watched the Jaws-Of-Life rip away at the car, ever so slowly in my mind. I could see the top of her head then too. I used all my strength and to call out to her, "Deanna, Deanna!"

Someone pulled me away again. The fireman kept removing debris. Finally they reached her enough that the EMT's could check Deanna's vital signs and assess her injuries. They said her legs were still pinned under piles of steel and her pulse kept weakening.

"I saw the fireman with the tattoos give a huge pull on the metal and it gave way enough for them to slide her from the car. Suddenly, instead of slow motion, everyone was rushing around so fast I couldn't keep up with what was happening. They rushed her onto a stretcher, I heard someone calling out vital signs, and then the ambulance sped away, seconds after her release.

"A female paramedic tried to hold me still and put something on my forehead. I kept brushing her away. Where was the rest of my family? I suppose I was in shock. I called out for my baby, for Daniel, but the woman just kept telling me my daughter was already on the way to the hospital. No one understood. I couldn't get them to understand Daniel and Mom still had to be in there.

"Then a fireman shouted out from the front of the vehicle. 'There is another person here!' It was Mom. She was unconscious, her arm protruded through the windshield, blood dripping from a large wound and some serious burns from the hot metal. They hadn't seen her at first through the black smoke. Her body had been covered by the hood of the car that had collapsed on top of her.

"A second ambulance arrived on the scene just as they got her out. The driver jumped out and helped them put Mom and me on stretchers and into the vehicle with the two EMT's before they raced away. I wasn't in any real danger, but they worked hurriedly on my mom's arm, trying to stop the bleeding. She must have lost a lot of blood.

"Maybe they gave me a sedative, or maybe I was just in shock, I don't know, but I don't remember anything more until I woke up in the hospital with Thomas sitting by my bedside.

"Things were still very groggy but Thomas told me Deanna's leg had been wedged in so tight they almost took her leg off to get her out. Then he told me about Daniel and the man in the other car that died.

"A K9 unit scanning the surrounding area found Daniel. He had apparently been thrown from the car, landing head first on a rock. He was already dead."

Susan broke down and sobbed uncontrollably and sank into the chair. Gladys slipped her arm around her. The girl in the chair to the right of her reached over and squeezed her hand. Nobody spoke for a long time.

Susan struggled with Step Two in the Twelve Steps of Recovery. If there was a greater power, how did He let this happen? She blamed Him for her alcoholism and the death of her child. The

Twelve Steps hung on the wall next to Gladys' pictures. They gave her little comfort. Still, Susan would find herself staring down from her top bunk looking at them for hours.

The Twelve Steps of Alcoholics Anonymous

1. We admitted we were powerless over alcohol – that our lives had become unmanageable.

2. Came to believe that a Power greater than ourselves could restore us to sanity.

3. Made a decision to turn our will and our lives over to the care of God as we understood Him.

4. Made a searching and fearless moral inventory of ourselves.

5. Admitted to God, to ourselves, and to another human being the exact nature of our wrongs.

6. We're entirely ready to have God remove all these defects of character.

7. Humbly asked Him to remove our shortcomings.

8. Made a list of all persons we had harmed, and became willing to make amends to them all.

9. Made direct amends to such people wherever possible, except when to do so would injure them or others.

10. Continued to take personal inventory and when we were wrong promptly admitted it.

11. Sought through prayer and meditation to improve our conscious contact with God, as we understood Him, praying only for knowledge of His will for us and the power to carry that out.

12. Having had a spiritual awakening as the result of these Steps, we tried to carry this message to alcoholics, and to practice these principles in all our affairs.

Chapter Twelve

Gladys got her parole in November. Juanita replaced Gladys. Word on the quad filtered down to Susan that this was Juanita's third placement. She made trouble wherever she went.

Barely five foot two, what Juanita lacked in height she made up in breadth. Huge muscular arms strained against the short sleeves of her jumpsuit. Her shaved head proudly displayed a tattoo of a tiger. Craters from a severe case of acne in her youth covered the olive skin of her square face. Across her upper right forearm, the word, 'Tigresa', tattooed in red letters conveyed the message. Even without understanding Spanish, Susan knew it meant 'Tiger Lady' or something similar. Susan couldn't tell her age but guessed her to be in her mid-forties.

"Move your sheeet", Juanita barked to Susan in a strong Latino accent as they clanged the door behind her in the cell. "The top bunk be mine."

Juanita started pulling the things off the top bunk and tossing them on the concrete floor before Susan could grab them off the bunk. Susan picked them up, hugged the bedding against her body and retracted as far back into the corner of the cell as she could go. She wanted to stay as far out of the way as humanly possible in an 8 x 9 cell.

Quivering with fear, "Sure, sure, whatever you want."

Juanita threw herself onto the top bunk with a hefty leap. The springs creaked and sagged under her weight. Susan hoped the springs would hold and not crash through to the bottom bunk and suffocate her in her sleep.

Susan knew all about her by the gossip, but Juanita never introduced herself or asked Susan her name. Juanita had also heard about Susan. She called her "Asesina de bebes, Baby Killer."

The first night they shared a cell, although it was too dark to see, Susan could almost feel the sagging springs just inches from her nose, as she listened to the deep guttural snore from the bunk above her. It took several nights before she slept, relatively certain the bunk would hold.

Trying to be quiet and unassuming around Juanita, Susan took on extra laundry and kitchen duties. She increased her hours in the flag room and the metal shop. She did anything, just to be someplace other than sharing a cell with her. Instead of writing her stories in her cell, Susan limited her writing to the library. Being too close to Juanita usually meant trouble.

"*Asesina de bebes*, you work the kitchen. Cop me some extra oranges. I like oranges." Juanita licked her lips and almost smiled at the thought. Thinking better of it, she scowled down at Susan from the top bunk.

"Sure, okay, I'll try." Susan stammered from the foot locker where she sat trying to read. The space between the two bunks was so small; Susan could not sit up on her bunk when Juanita was above her, weighing down the springs.

Drugs were easy to get at 'The Farm'. Juanita had a bad coke habit. When stoned, she didn't know her own strength. She tore the two shelves off the wall in a fit of anger when she was denied a visit due to her outbursts. At dinner call, four girls on the quad crossed her path while she was high and ended up in the infirmary with broken arms.

Juanita stirred the Latina gang into a frenzy so she could take the rule of the quad and the drug traffic away from Georgia and her white gang. Georgia had ruled the quad for close to fourteen years and although others had tried to oust her before, no one ever succeeded. It got ugly. Juanita and her Latina girls jumped Georgia in the laundry room on a Sunday afternoon.

Susan was at the visitor center with her parents at the time. The next time she saw Georgia, ugly red burns on her face and arms confirmed the rumor Juanita had tried to shove her into one of the huge dryers. Georgia's girls had come to her defense. It resulted in a total lockdown. Juanita spent two weeks in isolation.

When she came out of isolation, Juanita's had been moved to a different cell on the ward but she still ruled the Latina in the yard. Constant fights between Juanita's gang and Georgia's girls resulted in everyone losing their free yard time. This didn't set well with any of them, and the inmates took their frustration out on the correction officers. Susan tried to stay neutral and not associate with anyone. Georgia still protected her and on more than one occasion interceded when Juanita overstepped her boundaries.

The inmates found ways to make weapons out of almost anything. During mail call one day, Juanita twisted the elastic sleep bra she had into a tight rope and strangled a guard right between the bars because she didn't have any letters from her man.

Eventually they were granted yard time again, and Susan especially steered clear of Juanita's gang. She watched them beat someone into a bloody pulp over a gesture or a sideways glance. The Latinas ruled by fear.

Georgia's girls controlled with less violence. For them it was a matter of supply and demand, functioning as the contraband supply store. If someone wanted something, Georgia could always get it, at a price. Susan was glad she had her as an ally instead of an enemy.

Life existed for Susan as a strange oxymoron. Most of the time, she went to work, ate her meals, spoke with friends, and lived a strangely normal life. On the other hand, the barbed wire fencing around her constantly reminded her where she was, and the fear of crossing paths with Juanita or so many of the other dangerous inmates became a way of life.

Chapter Thirteen

Deanna was making great progress with her rehabilitation. The one thing she abhorred was changing her bandage on her stump. The swelling had gone down and the tight elastic bandage had to be re-wrapped several times a day after they applied more healing suave to the raw skin around the stump. The nurses said she had to learn to do it herself if she was ever to go home. The site of her stump just below her knee still made her stomach quiver. The flap of skin they used to pull over the end was tight and raw. The stiches were mostly on the underside of what was left of her calf. They said she was lucky to still have her knee. Lucky was not a word she associated with anything having to do with her anymore.

As she struggled applying the ointment to the raw skin, Reverend Olson walked in. Kim-Ly was down at the lounge area playing Canasta with old Mrs. Withers. Deanna hastily pulled the sheet across her stump.

"Deanna, don't feel you have to hide anything from me. I am here to help you." Reverend Olson offered a broad smile, showing gleaming white teeth. He wasn't dressed like a minister. He had on soft worn blue jeans, a white polo shirt and sockless dock-siders.

"No, no, that's okay. I need to learn to do it myself." She tried to back away from him but there was nowhere to go in the small arm chair beside her bed.

Reverend Olson pulled up a stool beside her, making himself eye level with Deanna. "That's silly. Let me help you?" He reached for the sheet that covered her leg and swiftly pulled it away.

Deanna gasped in surprise at his sudden movement.

"Now, that's better." The Reverend reached for the ointment beside the chair and squeezed a little into the palm of his head. "Is it better if I warm it up a little?"

Deanna nodded her head, unable to say an intelligible word.

Slowly he applied the ointment to the end of her stump. He worked slowly, making sure every inch of the raw skin was covered. "Now, what's next . . . the elastic bandage?" His blues eyes penetrated hers and she gulped in response.

She shook her head and nodded toward the cotton cap that absorbed the extra ointment. He slipped it effortlessly over the stump. "Now shall I do the elastic?"

Deanna tried to take it from his hands. He brushed her hands away and started to wrap the bandage around and around. She had to admit he was doing a much better job than she could have ever done. It was neat and just the right amount of pressure.

When he finished the wrap and secured it with two silver clasps, he rested his hand on her knee. "There, now that wasn't so bad, accepting some help now, was it?"

She shook her head, aware of the heat from the palm of his hand. Oh My God, he's got his hand my knee. Should I pull away? She looked up at him.

His smile caused a dimple on his left cheek to flash in and out and he inched his hand two inches above the knee giving her leg a quick squeeze before he released his grip.

Part of her wished he would put it back. Her skin felt the cool breeze from the overhead fan, empty after his warm touch.

Deanna stuttered, trying to think of something to say. Her mind was blank except for the over powering presence of this man. Kim-Ly came flying through the door on her new legs.

"Wow, I beat them again. First Mrs. Withers, then I beat old man Kri . . . ." She stopped when she saw Reverend Olson sitting in front of Deanna, their knees almost touching. "What— what? Are you okay Dee-Aaa-Na?"

Deanna's face burnt scarlet with embarrassment. Can everyone read my thoughts? Reverend Olson stood awkwardly and turned away from both girls.

Deanna finally found her voice. "Yes, I'm fine; Reverend Olson helped me change my bandage." Why do I feel dirty? I didn't do anything wrong. "Isn't that right Reverend Olson?"

Rev. Olson turned to smile at Deanna. "Yes, she is all fixed up now. I must be going Deanna. You take care and wrap it just like that. I'll see you next week. Goodbye Deanna. Goodbye Kim-Ly."

Kim-Ly eyed her friend closely. She noticed Deanna was trembling. "What going on, friend? I no like him. Why you face turn red when he here."

Deanna pressed her hands to her face. She couldn't explain why she felt so drawn to this man. A man, not a boy. This was her grandparent's pastor. "It's nothing. I just couldn't look at the stump. You know how I hate to look at it. Reverend Olson just helped me out. You startled me when you rushed in here so fast." She looked away from her friend, afraid her eyes would betray her true feelings she didn't understand herself.

Chapter Fourteen

Pauline replaced Juanita as Susan's cellmate. She introduced herself as Pauly. She was a welcome sight in spite of her bizarre full body tattoos and large holes from extreme piercings in her lips and ears. It presented a slightly mutilated look to what could have been an attractive girl. Her once spiked hair had been dyed a florescent blue, but with the roots grown out nearly three inches, the effect was a strange striation of blue and black. In spite of her twenty-one years, Susan perceived her as young and too naive to be a hardened criminal. Susan felt neither young nor naïve anymore.

Pauly put on a tough act in the yard, but when they were alone, Susan could see the real Pauline as a frightened young girl with nowhere to turn. The orange jumpsuit strained against Pauly's expanding belly. Susan soon realized Pauly was pregnant.

"My baby-daddy is going to take her. When he comes and sees me popping with his kid, he'll take her. You wait and see."

Susan doubted Pauly's boyfriend would ever come for her child. With Pauly in prison, odds were that somewhere, he was serving time too. Not one visitor came for Pauly.

Pauly's jumpsuit got tighter and tighter around her middle until she couldn't close the Velcro anymore. When days turned into weeks with no visitors, she began to face the truth; that no one was coming for her child.

"What are they going to do with my baby?" she cried to Susan. "Will they take her away from me? How am I ever going to be able to take care of my baby in here?"

'The Farm' may be one of the oldest reformatories for women, but was very progressive for the eighties. It opened its doors to the new nursery quad a year before Pauly's arrival. Minimal and medium security inmates that were pregnant at the time of intake and serving short term sentences of twenty-four months or less qualified for the nursery quad. Pauly would be transferred there by her eighth month. They had already begun her prenatal program of nutrition, vitamins and childhood education.

Susan tried to reassure her. "It'll be fine, Pauly. You'll get to stay in the nursery with your baby, and you will learn all about taking care of her properly. Then when you get out, you'll be ready."

Susan was sad to lose Pauly as a cellmate. In the few months they were together, she became almost a daughter to her.

Pauly loved her pre-natal classes and began to look forward to being a mother. Susan visited her often at the nursery, impressed with the care and the facility itself.

Susan arrived early in the day, and Pauly met her in the social lounge. Mothers and children gathered together in a colorful room of primary colors, children's toy's scattered around and babies in various bouncers, strollers and pack-n-plays. The expectant mothers hovered over the new babies, all ooh and aahs, they were excited about their own soon arrivals.

The atmosphere was light and happy, a strange oxymoron in a facility designed to punish or reform the transgressors of society. In the quad, it was easy to forget these were prisoners. The TV played Sponge Bob Square Pants cartoons and the smell of baby powder and clean, precious babies filled the air.

"Pauly, you look wonderful," Susan exclaimed. Pauly had that glow that only comes from being a healthy, happy expectant mother. Only tips of the odd blue hair remained and her natural dark hair shined healthy and groomed.

"I'm really getting excited. I know she'll be here soon, about four more weeks."

Pauly took Susan back to her room, which she shared with another girl about the same age who had just given birth. Two little cribs along the one wall matched the twin beds with simple, but colorful bedspreads. A changing table and a double dresser for each girl gave her room to put her own clothes in one side and the baby's clothes in the other. Pauly introduced Susan to Daisy, her roommate. Daisy proudly offered her nine pound strapping little boy for Susan to hold. She wrapped the child snugly in his blanket and cradled him in her arms. Susan thought back to Daniel when he was first born. She had to conceal the sadness she felt so as not to steal the joy from the room for Daisy or Pauly.

"What's his name?" Susan asked, gazing down at his big round eyes looking back at her. She ruffled his full head of soft black curls.

"Tyrone", said Daisy. "After his daddy."

"Well, hello little Tyrone, it's nice to meet you." Susan took his tiny little hand as his fingers wrapped around her pinky.

From that day on, Susan's visit to the nursery quad became the highlight of her day. Even if it was only to drop in and say hello, she never missed a day.

Chapter Fifteen

A calendar supplied by the Southern Baptist Women's council hung on the concrete wall by masking tape. It didn't adhere well to the block wall and Susan had to constantly put it back up in the morning when she found it on the floor. This day as she was re-affixing the calendar, the next day without a hash mark jumped out at her. April 2, 1983. Susan stared at the date for a long time and let the calendar slip from her fingers and slide back to the floor. It was the one year anniversary of the accident.

One Year! Was that all? I feel like I have been in here forever. How could thirty seconds change everyone's life so completely? If I would have been going a little faster, or a little slower, I would have missed that car. If I had seen the stop sign, if it hadn't been raining. If I hadn't been drinking

Susan sank onto her bunk, paralyzed by grief. She had been doing so well, until she looked at the calendar. It was open floor time and all the cell doors were open for the inmates to walk freely about the quad.

Juanita appeared at Susan's cell door with a sneer on her face. "Hey *Asesina de bebes*, you gonna die today. I hear you snitch. I hear you tell the guards about my little visit with Georgia in the laundry."

Susan jumped from the bunk, looking to see if there was a way to position herself between the door and Juanita, but she held her ground blocking the way. "No, no, I didn't even know about it until after it was over. I didn't tell anyone, honest."

Juanita threw her head back and bellowed. "Honest? What? I'm s'pose to just take your word? The word is you gonna die." A glint of something shiny caught Susan's eye as Juanita lunged toward her. Behind her, two Latina inmates blocked the doorway.

Susan jumped back but with nowhere to go, she crossed her arms across her face. The first slash cut her forearm, blood instantly gushed from the fleshy part of her skin. Juanita swung again and caught her side. The tearing sound of fabric ripped through the air as the shank connected with more fabric than skin. Susan was cornered with nothing to protest herself. In a flash through her mind, she saw Daniel's face. Was this the day she would meet him again?

A formidable force threw the two Latina women away from the door like rag dolls. They stumbled in either direction and landed on the floor of the hallway. They didn't get back up. Huge tattooed arms grabbed Juanita by the neck before she could turn around. A giant hand squeezed around Juanita's windpipe until she dropped the shank. "Who's gonna die today bitch? Maybe you?"

Susan found her voice. "Georgia, don't! Don't kill her! She's not worth it."

Inmates started gathering at the door, screaming at her to finish the job. They chanted "Kill the bitch, kill the bitch!" Juanita was slipping into unconsciousness by the time Georgia came to her senses and released her grip. The limp body slipped to the floor.

Susan stared at Georgia. "Go, get out a here before the guards get here. Go!" She grabbed a thin towel from over the stainless steel sink and wrapped it around her bleeding forearm. "Go!"

Georgia hesitated for just a minute. The other inmates stepped out of the way and covered her escape with their bodies. By the time the corrections officers got through the maze of inmates, only Juanita, still slumped on the floor holding her throat and Susan, with her arm wrapped in a towel were there to face the wrath of the officers.

"What the hell's going on here?" A burly female corrections officer with a crew cut and huge biceps stumbled through the cell door. "Juanita do dat?" She motioned with her head toward Susan's arm.

Susan quickly surveyed her options. If she admitted the attack, it would only mean future retribution from either Juanita or one of her girls. She glanced around to see if the shank was still on the floor for evidence. Someone must have picked it up as everyone scrambled away. She pulled her arm in close to her body so the guard would not see the cut fabric of her jumpsuit. "No, no. I cut it on the corner of the bunk. You have to do something about these conditions in here. I could have got hurt bad. Juanita just came by to get something she left in her foot locker. Ain't that right Juanita?"

Juanita looked up at Susan from her position on the floor and gave a cynical smile through crooked teeth. A red ring around her throat told another story, but the guards didn't really care what had happened, as long as it was over. Rarely did they get involved in the inmates squabbles. The guard glanced back and forth between the two inmates. *It's a lie, but who cares? Let 'em kill each other for all I care. Just don't mess up my record here. If I report this, it means tons of paperwork and putting the bitches in lockdown. I don't really give a shit.*

She pointed at Juanita. "Get back to your cell, spick! And don't give me no trouble. And you," she nodded toward Susan, "get down to the infirmary and put a bandage on that before you drip blood all over this floor."

Juanita got up from the floor and gave a nod of approval in Susan's direction before heading out the door. The officers followed behind her, rapping their billy-clubs on the bars as a reminder of what would come if anyone crossed them.

Susan knew it would take more than a Band-Aid to stop the bleeding on her arm. She slowly pulled the towel back and looked at the gash. It was laid open about a quarter inch and looked to have hit an artery. Blood continued to spurt out until she wrapped the towel like a tourniquet above the gash. She checked her side and saw only a surface cut pierced her side. She was lucky there. That could have been bad. She clumsily changed into another jumpsuit so the doc wouldn't see the tear. She fumbled getting both feet in the legs with only one hand and maneuvered the jumpsuit onto her shoulders, grateful for Velcro instead of buttons or zippers. By the time she was changed and heading toward the sick bay, she was beginning to feel a little woozy. The adrenalin running through her during the attack had blocked any pain, but now the throbbing in her arm pounded throughout her whole body.

The doc at the infirmary didn't buy for a minute that it was a cut from the metal bunk bed. He had seen many knife wounds in his ten years at The Farm and this was a classic case of a crude instrument made out of something smuggled in through the many corrupt officers. He really didn't care. It took twelve stiches to sew up her arm.

***

The date didn't pass Deanna by unnoticed either. She had spoken to Esther and Nils about this day. On the day Daniel was buried, she had still been in a coma. For this somber anniversary, her desire was to go to the cemetery to say good-bye to her little brother. The rehab center had agreed she could leave after her physical therapist approved the expedition.

She was nervous and Kim-Ly gave her some privacy to deal with her feeling. *How will I feel looking at his headstone? Can I do this? Yes, I HAVE to do this. For Daniel.*

Nils pulled the late model Chrysler Impala into the circular drive. Esther stayed seated in the passenger seat, but offered a smile toward her grand-daughter as the attendant wheeled Deanna out through the double doors. She clutched the two metal crutches on her lap. The weather had made a quick change to blue skies and billowy cumulous clouds. Daffodils bobbed their little yellow heads toward her and she caught the scent of another spring flower. Hyacinths, she looked around, and tucked under the daffodils where blue and lavender hyacinths, their sweet fragrance wafting up through the gentle spring breeze.

Nils put the car in park and came around to the passenger side and opened the rear door for Deanna. "What a beautiful day for a ride in the country. How is my little *flicka* today?" He planted a kiss on Deanna's cheek and winked at the attendant. "We won't kidnap her, promise; we will bring her back safe and sound."

"Hi Gramps." Deanna offered up a nervous smile. With the help of the arm of the attendant, she pulled herself into a standing position and let Nils take the crutches from her grasp. Turning, she plopped down less than gracefully into the back seat. She straightened her prosthesis in front of her and reached back to put on her seat belt.

"Hello sweetheart," Esther greeted her over her shoulder. "Are you ready for this?"

"Yea, no... I don't know. I'm kind of nervous. Silly, huh?"

"Not at all, dear. Gramps and I think you are being very brave. Don't feel like you have to say or do anything. Just take your time. This is a big step." Esther reached across the seat and patted her husband on the thigh. It was a big step for all of them.

Nils chatted about the weather and his first purchase of trays of impatiens and begonia's from the local greenhouse. "They're all hot-house flowers, pretty but not as sturdy as the ones we grew in the big garden back when. They'll never make it if there is another sudden frost. It's been known to happen as late as May."

Deanna wasn't listening. She watched out the window as the city streets slowly spread out into rural roads. Street lights were replaced with old stop signs and the size of the postage stamp city lots expanded into suburban sprawl. She knew the cemetery was on the other side of her small home town and sat on the crest of a hill, even if she couldn't remember the name of the road. She had gone with her grandfather many times to plant fresh flowers before Memorial Day at all the family headstones.

The last time I was there, Daniel and I had played hide and seek among the headstones while Gram and Gramps planted and weeded. Gramps had scolded Daniel when he leaned on an old stone and it fell over. Gramps had carefully reset the stone on its cracked foundation, and apologized for being cross with Daniel. He knew a small boy couldn't break the stone by himself. It had already been cracked and his weight had simply tipped it over. Now we are going to visit his stone. How strange is this? It doesn't feel real.

The car slowed and turned right through two large wrought iron gates, left open so they could enter unhampered. The narrow road in the cemetery snaked around in figure eights, each section marked with a large alphabetical sign. They passed some of the newer sections recognizable by the color and texture of the headstones. Nils pulled the car close to the metal sign with the capital letter C on it. It was one of the oldest sections in the cemetery, evidenced by the old headstones, some worn so thin and weather-beaten, the writing no longer decipherable. Some were written in German, others in Swedish, Norwegian and a few Irish. The Lundgren plot was large, encompassing room for twenty of more graves. A huge granite stone sat at the top of the plot with LUNDGREN etched deep in the smooth grey surface. Ten headstones of varying size and age were scattered in front of the family marker.

Deanna stared through the car window up the hill. She knew Daniel's grave was up there somewhere, but she couldn't find it from the car. "Where is it, Gram?"

"Second row from the top," Esther nodded toward the top of the hill. "Are you sure you want to do this? We can plant the flowers for you. You can stay in the car if you want."

"No, I have to do it myself. If Gramps can just carry the flowers for me while I use the crutches."

All three car doors opened simultaneously and they stepped out into the warm sunshine. Nils handed Deanna her crutches and handed the potted lilies to Esther to hold. He wanted his hands free to assist Deanna if she stumbled through the rough grass. Slowly the small entourage made their way up the hill. Deanna spotted her Uncle Ray's stone first. She had helped her grandfather plant flowers there every year as long as she could remember. She stopped and her thoughts drifted to her mother. You buried a brother here too, didn't you Mom? But he was a grown man, not a little boy. Still, a part of her understood the pain of her mother losing a brother.

Two spaces over a new stone looked too fresh, out of place among all the old stones of relatives gone long before he was born. Deanna stumbled just a minute when she recognized the marker, then she let her crutches drop to her side and she slid down into the cool grass in front of the stone. She read the words aloud. DANIEL THOMAS JENNINGS Born - June 8, 1975 – Died - April 2, 1982 Beloved son and brother. And brother, that was for me.

Nils set the pot of lilies and the trowel by Deanna's feet and stepped away, giving her some time alone. He clutched Esther's arm and they paused in front of some older graves, Ray's and Esther's parents who had been gone for more than twenty years now.

Deanna wanted to cry, but no tears came. What's wrong with me? Why can't I cry over my baby brother's grave? It didn't feel real, she realized. The name was correct, and the date of birth was correct, but she couldn't put together losing Daniel on a day she barely remembered. This isn't where Daniel was. His bright little smile and bundle of energy could never be contained under a pile of dirt and stone. He isn't here. I'll plant the flowers for Gram's sake, but Daniel isn't here. She stuck the trowel into the soft earth making a deep round hole and loosened the roots from the terra cotta pot. She slipped the plant into the hole and covered the roots with the fresh dirt. Glancing one more time at the stone, shook her head and rolled onto her good knee to stand up.

Nils raced to her side and helped her up, offering the crutches as support under her arms.

"Are you done?" He looked at her in surprise. He thought there would be a scene, tears, maybe heart wrenching screams.

Dry eyed, Deanna nodded at her grandfather. "I'm done. I didn't need to come here after all. Daniel's not here." She turned and headed back to the car, unaware how her grandparents alternated looking at her back walking away and at each other, trying to discern what she meant.

Chapter Sixteen

Reverend Olson started his tutoring in April, but limited the class time to religious training as the center insisted she continue with their state-approved teacher. Kim-ly was not a part of the private religious classes and would excuse herself to visit with the other residents during his visits.

"Where you attending church before the accident, Deanna?" Rev. Olson opened a Bible and placed it on the small night stand beside Deanna's bed. Deanna felt uncomfortable sitting on the bed and moved to the arm chair squeezed into the corner of the room near the foot of the bed.

"Yes, Reverend Olson, I usually went with Gram and Gramps. Mom and Dad didn't go to church."

He moved the small straight chair over toward where Deanna was sitting and sat down. The small room had little extra space and his knees were slightly brushing hers. "Why don't you just call me Jim, or Brother Jim, if you prefer. Reverend Olson seems so formal for our circumstances here."

What did he mean by circumstances?

"Alright, J—J— Brother Jim." She felt the back of her neck warm with embarrassment. Why does he have this effect on me?

The minister took her hands into his large palms and squeezed slightly. "Let's pray Deanna. Always best to start with a chat with the good Lord."

She bowed her head, hoping he could not feel the heat coursing through her body and into her hands that he grasped so firmly.

"Dear Lord, give us the strength to always do your will. Give us mercy for our sins and cleanse us of impure thoughts and deeds. Lead us in Your Word and direct us in Your Path. Amen."

Oh no, my impure thoughts? Can he read my mind? Can he tell what he does to me? This is so embarrassing.

Deanna hardly heard a word the pastor said. He read from the Scriptures and spoke to her about personal faith. She was only aware that his knee was still touching hers and the room was closing in even more, if that was possible.

"Deanna, are you listening to me?"

She pulled her head up suddenly, nodding her acknowledgment.

He rose to leave, first resting his hand upon her head as he customarily did as a blessing.

"See you next week?" He smiled down at her.

She nodded but wondered if this was really not a good idea. How will I ever learn anything when I can't pay attention to a single word he says?

When he was gone, Deanna sat quietly staring out the window. This is crazy. He is my minister, that's all. His touches are part of his job. Don't be such a silly child. He's not thinking of you . . . not like that!

Chapter Seventeen

On May 1, 1983, Susan went to see Pauly but she wasn't in her room. Daisy told her she was in the recovery room. They wouldn't let her in to see Pauly, but a corrections officer led her over to the window of the infant nursery and pointed out the round little boy who was Pauly's new son.

"Does she know it's a boy?" Susan inquired. Pauly had been calling the baby "she" throughout the entire pregnancy.

"Yes, she knows." The nurse beamed. "At first she looked a little disappointed, but the minute we put that child in her arms, those notions went right out the window. She is elated."

"And he is healthy? Everything is okay? What about Pauly?"

The nurse at the window nodded her head. "Mother and son are fine. Pauly and the baby will be back in their own room tomorrow. You can stop back then and see them."

Susan walked back to her quad almost giggling with joy. She couldn't imagine she would be any happier if it had been Deanna instead of Pauly who had given birth. She felt like a grandmother to the little boy. I wonder if Deanna will get married someday and have children. She can. I'm sure amputees do all the time, even if I don't know of any. Will she forgive me by then; and let me be a part of their lives?

The knitting group in the sewing quad had invited Susan to join in a few months prior and she kept busy working on a yellow and green baby blanket for the new arrival. Susan wrapped the blanket in soft tissue paper she bought at the prison commissary and put it in a bright gift bag with teddy bears and balloons.

Susan arrived at the nursery, and found Pauly sitting up in her bed, a beautiful boy suckling on her breast. Her eyes lit up when Susan walked in the door.

"Susan, oh look, isn't he beautiful?" She gently pulled him away from her body and modestly covered herself. She looked down adoringly to the baby who had fallen fast asleep, his little lips suckling the air.

"He is very beautiful, Pauly. Congratulations. I brought you a little gift." Susan handed the gift bag to her, careful not to bump the little head in Pauly's arms. He had light brown peach fuzz on his perfectly shaped head, and a tiny little pink nose.

"Oh thank you Susan. Do you want to hold him for just a minute while I open this up?" She looked up joyfully.

"Of course, let me at him." Susan laughed quietly so she did not wake him. He felt so warm and tiny in her arms. What a miracle of life. A rose among this thicket of thorns.

Pauly gently pulled the blanket from the bag and unwrapped the tissue paper. "Did you make this?" she exclaimed with joy.

"Yes, I've been working on it for a while. Do you like it? I did green and yellow because I wasn't so sure about your prediction for a girl."

Pauly laughed. "Yes, that turned out to be a good thing, huh? That was the plan, wasn't it? But how could I be disappointed in this?" She beamed at the baby boy in Susan's arms. Pauly spread the blanket on the twin bed and Susan placed the sleeping baby in the corner, swaddling him snugly like she had done dozens of times with Deanna and Daniel.

"What's his name?"

"Desmond, after my grandfather. He was the best man I ever knew."

"Well then, little Desmond, you are a very lucky little boy."

"Susan, I'm going to be such a good mother. When I get out of here, I'll never get into trouble again. I have a big responsibility here, and I'm not going to mess this up."

"I know you will, Sweetie. You're going to be a terrific mother."

Better mother than I was. I wanted to be a good mother, but the drinking always got in the way. If I could do it over again, I would never have taken that first drink, no matter what I was going through.

Forty eight hours after giving birth, propped up on pillows on her twin bed, Pauly felt much better. Her color was back. The once grey tattoos on both arms changed back to their original purple color. She wanted to talk and Susan was glad to listen. Susan and Daisy sat in the rockers, and Desmond and Tyrone slept soundly in their cribs as Pauly started her story.

"Joey had a heroin habit. We never had enough cash to feed his habit. He told me it would be easy. All I had to do is drive the car. I'd wait about a half a block away when Joey went in to get the cash. He promised me nobody'd get hurt."

Pauly sat up straighter on the bed and looked over at the little bundle snug under the green and yellow blanket. "We watched the store for a week so we knew when the shift change was. Joey said that just before shift change they had to count all the cash before the next person came on. So that was when he'd go in, wave a gun in their faces and walk out with enough money to shoot up for a few more days."

She paused and looked down at her trembling hands. Pauly reached out and took

Susan's hands and gripped them to steady hers. "I didn't know he had bullets in the gun. It was just supposed to scare them. It was supposed to be the young kid working the store, not the owner. He wouldn't give Joey the cash. Joey panicked and shot him. When he came running out of the store, I had just lit up a dooby, so I was moving a little slow. Joey was screaming at me to 'Go, Go, Go.' I heard the alarm from the store going off and I tried to get the car in gear. I stalled it out and Joey shoved me out of the way, trying to get behind the wheel.

"By the time he got the car in gear and raced down the street, a cop car came out from the side street and another one pulled in front of us and blocked us in. We didn't even get a full block away from the store. They took us in two different cars. The only time I've ever seen Joey again was in the courtroom."

Pauly stopped talking and wiped the tears from her eyes with the corner of her bed sheet.

"He screamed at me. He said everything was my fault and he called me a bitch." She got quiet and looked up at Susan, resignation dawning on her crestfallen face. "He's never coming for me, or my baby, is he, Susan?"

Susan shook her head. She hated to lie to her even though she was sure Joey was never coming. Word travels fast in prison and everyone knew Pauly's story. Joey had been convicted of first degree murder of the convenience store owner in the hold up. Pauly was lucky she had only been convicted of being an accomplice and sentenced to twenty four months.

"You don't need him, Pauly," Susan said. "You can do so much better. And with this little guy, you're going to be too busy to worry about him."

Daisy nodded her head in agreement. "Forget about that loser. I wouldn't take him back even if he did come back around."

Susan helped Pauly write letters to her mother telling her all about Desmond. Pauly had dropped out of school in the 6th grade and she could barely read or write. Life looked pretty bleak for her and Susan knew that she didn't have many good options without knowing how to read, even when she did get out. One of the nurses at the quad took a picture of Pauly and Desmond and printed two copies for her. Pauly mailed one with the letter to her mother and put the other on the dresser beside the crib.

Susan decided she needed to help Pauly improve her reading and writing so she could get a job when she got out. There were classrooms for her where she could study for her GED. Pauly resisted going to class, but with Susan's urging, she conceded. Susan used her own children's stories as reading material. She sat with Pauly as Desmond slept or nursed, and helped her with phonetics and grammar. Pauly was slow to learn, and barely reading at a second grade level when she said she had left school at the sixth.

"What happened, Pauly? How is it that you can't read?" Susan tenderly rubbed the back of Pauly's neck.

"Don't know. Nobody cared as long as I don't cause no trouble. They just pushed me on to the next teacher. My mama was just glad to see me go on. I never had a mama who loved me like Danny an' Denny, like them squirrels in your stories. I knew I wasn't like them other kids."

"Didn't cause any trouble," corrected Susan. "Didn't you ever ask for help?"

"Nah, I was too ashamed. I hated it when they called on me in class. The other kids laughed at me. So I tried to be quiet and most of the time nobody paid any attention to me. By the time I got to the sixth grade, I was so far behind, I just quit. Nobody ever questioned it."

"Well", said Susan, "It's going to be different now. I'll help you. You are going to work hard, study and get your GED. And that is not an option."

Susan laughed. She knew she was donning her "mother knows best" hat. Pauly laughed too, and nodded her head in agreement.

Chapter Eighteen

Esther regained most of her speech after the accident but her arm was useless. Nils had become an extension of her, even more so than ever before. Together, they got along fine. By the time Deanna was ready to be released from the rehab center, Esther was seventy years old. Nils was seventy-three. They knew in their hearts Deanna should come to live with them, but they sought the Lord for guidance. "*Må Din vilja ske*. Your will be done, dear Jesus. We are your weak and humble servants." Thomas was still Deanna's father. They invited him to their home to discuss the options for Deanna's care.

Thomas arrived at the old two-story house, hesitant to hear his ex-in-law's advice. He had filed for divorce from Susan six months earlier. He had moved on. Thomas was sure they would tell him that Deanna should come home with him. The small ranch house next door that had been the Jennings home had been sold to pay for Susan's attorney and bail bond. He had a new apartment in Canfield, a small town northwest of North Lima.

Nils showed him into the familiar front living room. "Have a seat, son. It's been a long time. Would you like some tea, or coffee?"

Thomas twisted his hands and accepted a seat in the old brocade settee under the window. "Coffee would be fine. Thank you, Nils."

Esther smiled as she approached from the kitchen. "Nils, can you bring in the tray from the kitchen?" She cocked her head toward the doorway of the kitchen.

"It's nice to see you Esther." Thomas stood and placed a peck on her papery thin cheek. He tried to avoid looking at the shriveled right arm that hung lifeless under the pink cardigan sweater than rested across her shoulders.

Nils carried the silver tray with three cups of strong black coffee and set it on the antique coffee table in the center of the room. He handed Thomas a cup, one to his wife and settled next to her on the green camel-back sofa opposite Thomas.

"Susan seems to be doing fine." Esther started the conversation. "We don't get to see her often but Nils writes faithfully every week."

"Um, yes, I'm not so good at writing. But I was there not too long ago to see her. She looks good . . . considering . . . ." His voice trailed off. What was good about life in prison?

Nils changed the subject. "Deanna is about to be released from the rehab center. She has made remarkable progress. Don't you think?"

Thomas didn't really know. He had only been to see her five times in the eight months she had spent at the center. He stammered, trying to sound like he knew more than he actually did. "Yes, yes, she's doing great."

For a few minutes, no one spoke. Thomas loudly slurped the strong brew. The tick-tock of the old grandfather clock in the corner made the only other sound. The clocked chimed. Thomas jumped at the sound.

"Son," Nils began. "Deanna is still your daughter. Are you planning on bringing her home with you now?"

Thomas fidgeted in his seat. He sat his coffee cup back on the silver tray. He wrung his hands. "The thing is, Sir." He hadn't called Nils "sir" since he was dating Susan, so many years ago. "The thing is, since I sold the house next door, well with the cost of everything... the attorney, hospital bills . . . the funeral . . . ." He stopped at the mention of Daniel's funeral.

"We understand." Esther tried to let him know they did not judge him, even though they wondered why he was so distant from his only daughter. "It has been a difficult time for all of us. We just need to know your intentions. We were thinking, well . . . ." She looked toward Nils to finish her sentence.

"We were thinking perhaps Deanna should come here." Nils explained. "She is familiar with it here, and you have a place she has never seen before. We thought she might be more comfortable here." Nils and Esther exchanged a smile. Their conversation flowed between them like one voice. Their voices almost sounded alike with their Swedish accents.

Thomas looked at them and thought about how people start to look alike after they had been together for a long time. Nils and Esther looked like matching book ends. Esther's thin grey sausage roll around the crown of her head matched Nil's Caesar-look with the silver ring around the back of his head. Over the years, they established identical stooping postures and matching shuffling gaits.

Thomas exhaled. He had feared he would have to tell them he didn't think Deanna should come home with him. Now he didn't have to. "I agree. She needs familiar surroundings. You are very gracious to invite her. Naturally, I wanted her with me, but . . . ." Thomas was off the hook and Esther and Nils knew it. But they knew that even before the little meeting. Deanna had told them he rarely visited and the relationship was strained at best.

Nils clasped his hands together. "It's all settled then. We prayed with Rev. Olson from the church about it. He agrees Deanna should come home to us. Would you mind helping to move some of her things from her old room over here?"

Thomas looked at them with alarm. "You spoke to Brother Jim, I mean Rev. Olson about Deanna? Has he seen her?"

"Well of course, son. He is our pastor. He's been to see her, and asked to see Susan too. He only wants the best for us. About those boxes, will you help?"

Thomas recovered from the initial shock. Nobody knew the truth except him. He had to keep Susan's secret. He'd take it to his grave. "Of course, all of her things are in storage. When the house was sold, I saved everything of hers. I'll take care of it all. It's the least I can do."

After Thomas left, Nils and Esther sat quietly on the sofa. "He didn't put up much of a fight for her, did he?" Esther spoke her thoughts out loud to her husband.

Nils patted his wife on the knee. "We knew he wouldn't now, didn't we? I don't know what is happening with him, but we'll just leave it in the Lord's hands. He has a plan."

Two weeks after the meeting, Thomas showed up in a U-Haul truck with everything from Deanna's room. He wouldn't let Nils lift anything with his heart condition and Esther was of little help with one arm. Thomas carried everything up the narrow stairs and set up the bed and hung the mirror and pictures on the wall. He stood looking at the boxes, wondering if he should unpack those as well.

"We'll take it from here Thomas." Esther assured him as she entered the room. "I'm going to wash these curtains and spread before I put the room in order. Thanks for your help. Nils never could have moved that furniture by himself."

"Not a problem," Thomas said as he backed out the door. He did not want to linger around. They made him feel guilty for not wanting Deanna with him, especially when they treated him with nothing but love and compassion.

Esther grasped Nils arm with her good one while they watched from Deanna's bedroom window as Thomas pulled out of the drive. She turned and looked at the stacks of boxes.

"We are not young anymore, Nils. Can we handle a teenager again? What are we getting into?"

Nils hugged his wife. "We'll be fine *flicka*. You know we will. Just trust in the Lord."

Chapter Nineteen

Deanna felt anxious about what was going to happen to her when they released her from the rehab center. The more she thought about it, her stress level increased. Her parents were divorced and her mother was in prison. Where will I go? Will they send me to live with my father? Where would that be? He doesn't seem interested in being a part of my life anymore. Will I live with Gram and Gramps? Deanna felt misplaced, like an old t-shirt. It had been thirteen months since the accident, over eight which she spent at the rehab center.

Esther and Nils came to tell Deanna the news. They sat in the lounge area, among the other patients in wheelchairs, most with blank stares or asleep, slumped over and secured by sheets knotted around their chests. The big screen TV blared in the background; no one paid any attention to it. Nils took Deanna's hand. "We want you to come home with us. What do you think of that idea?"

Deanna saw the love in their eyes. And she was grateful for them. But she pulled her hand away and turned her face away so they wouldn't see her tears. Why am I crying? Isn't this where I wanted to go? Of course it is. What about Dad? Didn't he want me? Deanna brushed away a tear and turned back to face them. She managed a smile. She didn't want them to know she felt abandoned, astray. She'd lost her brother, her mother and now, her dad.

They talked about school. Deanna had already missed so much school she didn't want to go back. Her sophomore year was just ending.

"With only a few weeks left, maybe Reverend Olson can home school me for the rest of this year? Then I'll go back next year, I promise."

Deanna looked toward Esther, expecting her to be pleased with the proposal. "Deanna, your grandfather and I think it is really important that you get back into school right away. Rev. Olson can still tutor your religious studies, but we want you with kids your own age."

Deanna's face dropped in disappointment. "I think I need time to adjust. I know I need to go back, but can't it wait till fall?" She gave her grandparents her most assuring smile.

"No, Deanna. We are going to be firm about this. You'll see. It is for the best."

Telling Kim-Ly she was leaving was the hardest part. Back in their room, she broke the news.

"Lucky girlfriend to go home", Kim-Ly said. But her smile was forced and she turned her face away so Deanna would not see the tears glistening in her eyes.

Deanna saw the pain. "We'll stay in touch. I'll call you every day. I promise." The words felt hollow. They didn't help the pain.

The day Deanna left the center, the girls cried in each other's arms, and for the first time, Kim-Ly didn't have a joke to lighten the tone.

When they pulled into the driveway, the hairs on Deanna's arms prickled and a wave of nostalgia hit her square in the face. The wood siding of the old farm house still needed a fresh coat of paint. She rolled down the window to breathe in the fresh country air. The rusty chains from the porch swing creaked as it swayed back and forth. Little blue crocuses poked their heads through the green lawn and yellow and white daffodils swayed in the breeze in the flower beds on either side of the front porch steps. Deanna leaned out the window and glanced up at the third floor attic window, and for a second she thought she saw a little boy with blonde hair waving at her. But the image faded as quickly as it came. Daniel was gone. Although everything looked the same, Deanna knew nothing would ever be the same again.

Nils opened the car door for her and Deanna sat there looking down at her new metal leg beneath her sweatpants. She took his hand as he helped her out but when he tried to take her elbow and help up the porch steps, she waved him away. *I am not a child anymore. I can do this. I can! I have to learn to do things for myself.* Deanna chastised herself for being such an unwilling patient for so long. The extra physical therapy would have paid off a lot. The three steps up to the wooden plank porch were easy, but when she opened the front door and saw the steep stairs to the second floor, she gulped with trepidation. She was in for a challenge. The staircase looked a mile high. It would be quite a job to climb them with her new prosthetic leg.

Esther saw her granddaughter staring up at the steep steps. "I'm sorry we don't have a first floor bedroom for you. You can sleep on the sofa in the front room for now if you want."

"Thanks, Gram. But I got this. I can do it." Deanna needed a room of her own, and the challenge of the steps was just one more thing she had to overcome.

"Kim-Ly wouldn't think twice of it. She'd gladly climb these stairs if she were here," she spoke out loud to herself. "Going down will be easy. I'll just sit down on my backside and take them sitting down for now." She tried to offer a reassuring smile to her grandparents.

It felt like an eternity for her to make her way up the stairs. Out of breath, she leaned on the railing before making her way to her room. The door was ajar. Most of her personal belongings from her room in the small house next door were there.

Esther waited for a reaction from her granddaughter. "Your father brought everything over for you. He wanted you to be in a familiar place with all your things around you." Esther wanted Deanna to know that her father had not forgotten about her.

Deanna looked down at her old twin bed with the rainbow bedspread and matching curtains. She eyed the pictures on the wall and on the old French provincial desk. A picture of her family sat on the night stand beside the bed. She picked it up and caressed the frame. They were all smiling, arms wrapped around each other. Deanna couldn't remember who took the picture. Perhaps Dad had asked a stranger to take the shot, because we are all in the photo. Turning it over, she read the inscription; The Jennings: Thomas, Susan, Deanna and Daniel. July 4, 1980. She remembered that day well.

We had driven to Columbus to watch the fireworks over the State Capitol building. We all got drenched in a sudden downpour earlier in the day. Even in the picture, Deanna and Susan still looked a little like drowned rats. I loved that day. Daniel screamed in delight at the fireworks and held his hands over his ears at the loud booms. Even Mom and Dad were happy. No one argued that day.

Deanna took the picture and laid it upside down inside her night stand. Days like that were gone for good. Better to get used to it. She glanced in the mirror over her dresser. Her hand picked at the short curls that were finally covering the right side of her head. Most people would never know the damage below those blonde curls.

She was not happy about going back to school for her sophomore year. Going back to school terrified her. *I'm a freak. They'll all laugh at me, or just stare at me. What will I say to them? That my mother did this to me?*

Not one single friend from high school came to see her after the accident. Even her soccer teammates did not come to visit. Deanna had never had very many close friends because she spent all her spare time with Daniel when she wasn't playing soccer. Leaving the rehab center and Kim-Ly behind, now she felt completely alone.

There were only a few weeks left of school before summer vacation. The first few days convinced Deanna she had been right. Kids gave her side glances but rarely spoke to her. Then one of the girls from her soccer team, Sandra, finally told her why they all felt uncomfortable. They all knew about the accident and since they didn't know what to say, they just avoided her.

Eventually a few of the students inquired about the accident and what it was like to live with one leg, but no one was mean or vindictive. With the help of Sandra, more of them started talking to her. Some even treated her like a celebrity, like she had been on a long romantic vacation. Deanna wore long pants all the time and other than a little limp, she blended in drawing as little attention as possible to herself.

Deanna missed Kim-Ly. When it came time for Kim-Ly to be placed in foster care, Deanna begged and pleaded with her grandparents to take her in. But they were concerned that taking care of one handicapped child was almost more than they could handle at their age. The idea of two overwhelmed them. They agreed to pray about it. Deanna was sure their prayers would lead Kim-Ly home to them.

The county took the decision out of their hands. They would not grant them foster care custody of a handicapped child at their age.

Deanna cried and protested to her grandfather, "But we will love her more than anyone else will."

Nils nodded his head. He would have taken her. He was as heartbroken as Deanna. They had all learned to love her over the past year. "I understand dear. But we can't go against the county. Kim-Ly is only eleven years old. They think we are too old, Deanna."

Kim-Ly went into foster care in a town sixty miles away. They stayed in touch almost daily at first, cranking up the long distance phone bills much to Nils's chagrin. But he didn't have the heart to tell his grand-daughter that she shouldn't talk to her friend.

Chapter Twenty

Deanna was surprised when a boy asked her to the senior prom. She was only a sophomore. His name was Brad Simpson. About three inches shorter than her, he was a book worm, with thick glasses and jet black hair cut a little too short for the late 80's. If he ever noticed her limp, he never let on. Ever since the accident, it never occurred to her that she would ever dance again.

She told Reverend Olson about it when he came for her weekly lessons. "What do you think, Brother Jim? A boy asked me to prom. I didn't think the church approved of dancing."

He frowned at her and was silent for a moment. "Our church has always had a strict policy about dancing. But they are getting more lenient. We need to encourage young people to join the flock and many are turning away instead. I think it is fine. I just don't like the idea of some young boy acting inappropriately with you." His frown turned into a smile and Deanna wondered if it was personal or religious reasons he didn't want a boy touching her.

Don't be insane, Deanna. Of course it is religious reasons. He only sees you as a child. You are the only one with these silly ideas of romance between us.

Before the accident, Deanna loved to dance around the house. Susan had none of the old fashioned ideas her parents had. Deanna would turn up the radio or cassette player and swing Daniel around by the arms. Sometimes she'd hold him on her hip and slow dance and even her Mom would join in. The three of them would sway back and forth and twirl around and around until they all fell down in a fit of giggles.

Deanna was shocked when Esther agreed with Reverend Olson and defied the rules of the Swedish church. She told Deanna she should go to the dance. She and Nils were determined to do anything to help her acclimate to her new life.

Deanna curled her stump of a leg under her good leg on the living room sofa as she listened to her cassette tape play her favorite melancholy tunes. She had recorded them by putting it up to the speakers of Gramps's old AM radio. Static muffled the tunes and between the songs, a snippet of the DJ's voice chirped in where she didn't hit the stop button fast enough.

When Elton John's 'Blue Eyes' came on, Nils got up from his chair and stood before Deanna on the old oval braided rug. He extended his arms with a twinkle in the eye on his weathered face. "Would you like to dance, Blue Eyes?"

Deanna knew her grandfather had never danced a step in his life. He never would have gone against the wishes of the church. The idea of her grandfather dancing made her burst into a fit of giggles. She knew she shouldn't, but she couldn't control herself until she hiccupped and tears streamed down her face. But he stood there, arms extended until she strapped her prosthetic to her stump and he pulled her up from her seat.

Together, in the middle of the living room, Nils and Deanna learned to slow dance together. Because of him, Deanna finally got the courage to try. They stumbled over each other's feet. Her leg didn't always cooperate with the turns, but they laughed and started over when the tape skipped to 'Hopelessly Devoted to You' by Olivia Newton-John. Deanna tried to teach Nils to fast dance when 'I Love Rock N Roll' came on, but he drew the line in the sand there.

"Be a good girl darling and none of those gyrations. Be a good Christian girl and stick to slow dancing, at a good arms-length away." He sounded stern, but she caught the twinkle in his eyes as he led her back to the safety of the arm chair.

Esther took Deanna shopping for a prom dress. Deanna wanted it to be a happy occasion and she tried to put a good front for her grandmother, but silently, she wallowed in self-pity instead. She didn't want to admit it, least of all to herself, but she missed her mom. *Why can't I have a normal life, with a mom to go shopping with me, to do my hair, be here for me? All the other girls have their mom. All I have is Gram.*

Esther tried to comfort her granddaughter and did her best to fill the void in Deanna's life. But she knew there was only so much she could do. Together they found a beautiful long silver gown that flared softly at the hips so Deanna's prosthetic leg was not noticeable at all. Still, Esther knew it was Susan who Deanna longed for at that moment in her life. She watched as her granddaughter got dressed and did her hair and makeup. Deanna struggled with her hair, trying to get it twisted in a knot, the length not quite long enough to hold it in place.

Esther tried to help, but with only one good arm, it was a futile attempt. "It's okay, Gram, I can do this," Deanna exclaimed. She pulled the pins from the knot and tousled her hair, letting it fall loose around her face. In the end, even Deanna had to admit she looked pretty as she slowly made her way down the stairs somewhat gracefully in an upright position.

I wonder what Brother Jim would think of me in this dress. Oh stop, Deanna!

"I'm glad I still don't have to go down the stairs one step at a time on my butt. Boy would that be embarrassing," Deanna laughed out loud. Esther and Nils looked on with pride.

When Brad arrived at the door in a powder blue tuxedo with a pleated shirt, Deanna was a little taken back and had to fight the urge not to burst out laughing. Powder blue tuxedos were incredibly out of date and this one was far from a perfect fit. Nils whispered in her ear that he thought it was probably borrowed from an older brother.

"More like his father's." She whispered. "And I was worried people were going to stare at me. At least the focus is going to be off my leg."

As Deanna and her other friends watched her grandparents wave away the limousine, she felt a pang of guilt that she had wanted her mom there instead of them. Gram and Gramps were the best. They don't deserve the anger and frustration I take out on them.

At the dance, Deanna saw one of the popular jocks snickering at Brad's blue suit. There were always a few who thought they could have fun at the expense of other's feelings. Brad and Deanna moved close to them on the dance floor. Deanna turned and gave the guy a swift kick in the shin with her prosthetic foot. The shock and pain that registered on his face satisfied her as she smiled sweetly at him and murmured a lame apology. Brad tried to say something to him, but Deanna pulled on his shoulder and moved him away from any confrontation.

Chapter Twenty One

Deanna stood in front of the mirror. She smoothed the front of her flared jeans with her hand, analyzing her look. The light blue baby-doll top matched her eyes and her hair had grown back even thicker and curlier than before the accident.

No one can even tell I am wearing prosthesis with these jeans and boots on. Not bad. I'm far from beautiful, but not bad.

She leaned forward and applied some light mascara and lip gloss.

I wonder if Jim, I like calling him that instead of Reverend Olson or even Brother Jim, I wonder if he thinks I'm pretty. She gave one last smile to herself in the mirror and made her way down the stairs for her seventeenth birthday party.

Several of her friends from high school had already arrived. They made a fuss over Deanna's new outfit and she glowed in the limelight. She kept watching the door for another guest to arrive. *I invited him, surely he will come.*

The doorbell rang and Deanna jumped to answer it. Thomas stood at the door with a young blonde on his arm that looked to be about Deanna's age. Giving Deanna a short awkward hug, he introduced the woman as his fiancée, Janice. Deanna was mortified he would take this opportunity to spring this news on her. *No warning. I didn't even know he was seeing anyone.* Janice complimented Deanna on her outfit and made a big fuss about how she liked her hair. Deanna could tell she was trying to a make a good impression but being only five years older than Deanna, it was an uphill battle. The conversations were stilted and even Deanna's friends whispered among each other and avoided Deanna's father and guest. When the doorbell rang again, Deanna beat her grandmother to the door.

Reverend Olson stood at the door with a bouquet of daisies in his hand. "Deanna, Happy Birthday! I am sorry I am late. And you look lovely."

Deanna blushed as she accepted the flowers and ushered him into the living room. The teenage girls all looked on, mystified that this older man would cause such a reaction from Deanna.

Thomas met the minister half way across the room. His eyes bore into the man and his body language spelled aggression. He physically moved between Deanna and the minister.

"Rev. Olson, what are you doing here?" Thomas didn't even attempt to be civil.

The senior pastor clapped Thomas on the shoulder, offering a wide grin. "Thomas, it's so good to see you. How are you? I am here to help your little girl celebrate her birthday. I've been tutoring her, didn't you know that?"

Thomas shrugged his shoulder removing the hand. "No, I did not know. And I don't like it." He muttered under his breath. "Stay away from her, Jim. We don't need you or your kind of prayers."

Reverend Olson knit his brows. "Whatever are you talking about? Esther and Nils both agree she could use my counseling. If I recall, you and Susan didn't give her much instruction in her faith."

Thomas leaned forward and whispered into the minister's ear. "I'm only going to say this once — " But before he could get another word out, Janice arrived at Thomas side, unaware of the tension between the two men. "Hey Baby, Deanna is about to open her gifts in the other room. Coming in?"

Thomas pointed his finger close to the minister's nose and gave one final dagger look at him before he whispered under his breath. "Stay away from her. She is my daughter, and I don't want you near her. Got it?"

The coffee table was full of brightly colored presents and the teenage girls clustered around on the floor. Sitting next to Deanna on the sofa was Kim-Ly, giggling with excitement for her friend. Esther and Nils observed the girls with amused delight as Deanna tore into the gifts of the latest fashions, the latest albums of the 80's and practical gifts like mittens and scarves knitted by her grandmother. Rev. Olson gave her a white leather Bible with her name engraved on the cover. Deanna felt her cheeks flame red when her eyes met his as he leaned in the doorway of the room. Thomas and Janice had a card with cash. Slightly impersonal, but Deanna understood that he hardly knew her anymore and this was the best he could do. One more gift was left to be unopened. It didn't share the bright colored wrapping but was taped together with brown paper. Deanne noticed the return address and wished she could toss the package in the trash without causing any attention. She glanced at Kim-Ly who understood her dilemma. Kim-Ly nodded her head for encouragement and prodded Deanna to open the gift.

Deanna placed the palm of her hand over the return address so her friends could not see the address of the Marysville Correctional Facility. They all knew her mother was in prison. It was a small town, but the less attention she could draw to it the better. She slipped her fingers under the tape and broke the binding. The brown paper fell away and exposed a small, loose stack of type-written pages along with a note, hand-written and folded in half.

She opened the note and read the words to herself, ignoring the pleas of her friends to tell them who it was from and what it said.

My lovely Deanna,

Today you turn seventeen. You are no longer a child, but a young woman. I was hoping to be there to share this day with you, but my heart is there with you even if my body is not.

I realize you are too old for these. They are children's stories. But I wrote them for you, and your brother Daniel. As you will see, the characters are named after each of you, and unlike me, the mother of Danny and Denny in these stories never let her children down, never leave them to feel lost and alone and never let anything terrible happen to them.

I hope your day is wonderful. I am so proud of you. Your grandparents tell me how you have become so strong and are walking and talking just fine. I know it has been a difficult time for you. Please know how much I love you and how pleased I am that you are doing so well. I hope to hear from you soon. I have never stopped loving you.

Love always,
Mom

Deanna sprang from the sofa, the papers slipping to the floor at her feet. She had to get out of there before she broke down in front of all her friends and family. She stumbled over the legs of one of the girls as she hastily tried to make an exit. She felt herself begin to fall as strong arms grasped her by the waist and pulled her away from the tangle of legs and bodies around the coffee table. She looked up as Brother Jim scooped her up and planted her safely on the round braided rug. His hands lingered on her waist as she fought the tears that pooled in her eyes. She shook herself free and clamored for the stairs.

Upstairs she sunk onto her rainbow colored bed and buried her face in the pillow to muffle her cries. *How could she do this to me? On my birthday, she ruined my birthday and embarrassed me in front of all my friends.* In spite of her tears, she could still feel his touch around her waist where the pastor had saved her from falling flat on her face. *He saved me. But he also saw me lose it, like a little girl, having a tantrum. What must he be thinking of me?*

Chapter Twenty Two

It was a beautiful Friday afternoon as Deanna climbed down the steep steps of the school bus with as much grace as she could muster. She was two months into her junior in high school and things were beginning to look up. It had been a good day at school. She took a deep breathe. The air had a sudden crispness and she could almost smell snowflakes lingering in the clouds. She had promised to help Gramps rake the leaves which had started to accumulate under the big oak trees.

Nils sat in his favorite chair, looking out the window as the leaves trailed down in autumn cascades of colors. Esther was in the kitchen getting him some coffee. She called to him when it was ready. He didn't answer. Esther could only carry one cup at a time. She chose to bring his into the living room first. From across the room she could tell something was terribly wrong. Nils' body was slumped over to one side of the armrest. At first she froze in place. His favorite coffee cup slipped through her hand and exploded on the hardwood floor. She screamed for Deanna.

Deanna rushed into the room. She first noticed the broken cup and began to tell her that it was okay; one broken cup was nothing to get upset about. Then she saw the stricken look in her grandmother's eyes. The blood drained from her face and a chill ran down her back. She looked toward her grandfather, and stumbled as she rushed to his side. She checked his pulse. She put her head against his chest, trying to listen for his heartbeat. Nothing! She called 911. Esther sunk quietly to the floor next to Nil's chair. She knew the good Lord had taken him. She took his hand, but he was not there. His eyes were open, but he wasn't looking at her. His soul had already left his body. This was not the man Esther had loved for over fifty years. This was just his shell. He was gone. It was November 2, 1983. *Gud välsigna hans själ.* God Bless his soul.

Deanna brushed her hand over his eyes and closed them. She heard the siren as the ambulance approached. She slumped onto the floor beside her grandmother and rested her head upon her shoulder. Another one gone.

The funeral was large. Everyone in town had loved Nils. The receiving line went around the vestibule of the church out into the yard. Deanna brought Esther a chair and tried to make her sit down through the endless receiving line, but she wouldn't sit. She said those people had come to show their respect for Nils, and she was determined to make it through standing up. It was the last thing she could do for her beloved Nils. Rev. Olson offered the eulogy. They laid him to rest right between Daniel and Ray.

When it was over, Esther asked Deanna to host the guests at the house. No tears escaped her eyes until she lay down on the bed they had shared for fifty years. Looking over and stroking his pillow, she knew she would not see him again until they met alongside Jesus. Just for that brief moment, she questioned the Lord's will, wondering why she had to live here without him. Then the tears finally came. It was time for her to learn to survive without Nils.

Rev. Olson met Deanna at the bottom of the stairs after she had checked in on her grandmother. He reached for her and pulled her into an embrace. A few relatives offered a sympathetic smile, appreciative of the minister's compassion for Deanna.

Deanna let him envelope her with his big strong arms. *See, he does care for me. I am not imagining this. I know he love me.* But when he pulled her close, she felt the bulge in his pants pressing into her thigh. She twisted out of his arms, embarrassed to look him in the eye, knowing that she felt the same urges.

"I'm here for you, you know that don't you?"

"I know. Rev . . . I mean, Jim." she whispered where no one could hear.

As she moved across the room, Thomas noticed Deanna's flushed cheeks and assumed it was about her grandfather's death. He strode across the room and enveloped her in his arms. "I'm sorry, sweetheart; I know how much you loved him."

Deanna nodded rested her head on her father's shoulder but her eyes remained on Rev. Olson as he made his way around the room, offering condolences and words of comfort. He loves me. I know he does. He'll take care of me someday. Look how good a man he is. Look how he takes care of Gram. Age doesn't matter, not when you are in love. Not with us.

As the weeks passed, Deanna tried to do the things for Esther that Nils had always done. It was an awkward dance; her not knowing how much help Esther wanted or needed; Esther not knowing how to ask when Nils had always just known.

Chapter Twenty Three

Deanna didn't want to do it, but her conscience got the best of her. *I know I need to tell her. It's the right thing to do. Gramps was her father, and I know she loved him.* Marysville was only a three hour drive, and she debated about going in person. In the end, she just couldn't muster the courage to face her. She took the coward's way out.

Nov. 8, 1983
Dear Mom,
I am sorry to have to tell you that Gramps passed away last Friday. He died sitting in his chair looking at the fall leaves he always loved so much. The doctor said his heart just gave out. He had a good life and Gram says that if everyone could have a life as fulfilled as his, everyone would die with smiles on their faces. Gram is holding up like a trooper, as I am sure you can imagine. Reverend Olson gave the eulogy. There were so many

people at the funeral. Everyone loved him. We buried him between Daniel and Uncle Ray.

I guess you know I am now in my junior year of high school now. Don't worry about Gram. I'll stay with her after graduation and help take care of her until you get out.

Sorry I have not written.

Sincerely,

Deanna

She knew the letter was lame, especially since it was her very first letter. But she still harbored a lot of anger about the accident, and her mother's drinking. She really wasn't sorry for not writing, and coming up with more than that was impossible. It was the best she could do at the time. She sealed the envelope and dropped it into the mail. When Esther asked if she had informed her mother, at least she didn't have to lie.

***

At the prison, mail delivery was late again. The last mail for Susan was from her Dad over two weeks ago. She still held out hope for a letter from Deanna. She knew it was wishful thinking, but if she could exonerate her, Susan told herself she could even live with prison.

Mail always created a big stir in the house. For most of the inmates, the mail could make or break the whole day. A good day meant a letter from someone who hadn't forgotten about them. A bad day would be no letter at all, or even worse a "Dear Jane" letter, which were all too common.

Long before they could see her, murmured voices and shuffling of feet let the inmates know the matron was making the rounds. Except for the occasional mumbled thank-you and the squeak of bunk springs, it was quiet on the quad during mail call. Everyone became consumed with their own thoughts. Sometimes Susan heard cries or moans and knew someone had received bad news. Occasionally there was a whoop of delight.

Wheels turned slowly on the concrete floor making creaking noises as the matron moved the mail cart forward, handing out magazines and very few letters. Anticipation mounted as the matron stopped and fumbled with the precious contents in front of Susan's cell.

Susan stepped back away from the cell door and waited for the matron to put the mail through the slot. One lone letter floated from the slot to the floor and landed in front of the bunks. For a moment she didn't pick up the letter, savoring the moment. Stooping to pick it up, she recognized the return address but not the handwriting. Her dad's handwriting was small and neat. This was large and flowing. Could it be from Deanna? She shook the envelope to drop the letter to the one side and carefully tore the other end. Her heart started to pound. Perhaps Deanna finally read one of her letters. Maybe she liked her birthday gift of the children's stories and her note and finally understood. She sank onto the bunk and started to read quickly, then slowed down, and read it again, her heart breaking with every word. — I am sorry to have to tell you . . . . It was from Deanna, but the news was bad. Her dad was dead. She curled into a fetal position and clutched the letter to her chest. Her dad had been the most loving and gentle person she had ever known in her entire life. *What is Mom going to do without him? What am I going to do without him? Even in here, just knowing he was there, loving and supporting me, gave me comfort.* Like a sinking ship, her mind and body succumbed to the grief. She was glad she was without a cellmate. Nobody was there to see her crumble, paralyzed by her sorrow. It wasn't until hours later that she could think straight enough to realize she had a breakthrough with Deanna. She had written. True, it wasn't good news, but at least she took the time to write and tell her. *Surely, she must feel something for me if she was willing to do that? Didn't she? Maybe there is still hope for a reconciliation . . . and forgiveness.*

Chapter Twenty Four

The first holiday without Gramps was almost more than Deanna could bear. She and Esther attended the traditional Christmas Eve service at the church. The scent of the pine wreaths that hung from each of the stained glass windows filled the air. Candles adorned the altar and flickered in the dim light. The choir sang beautiful carols in Swedish accompanied by the bell choir and a huge pipe organ.

In the pew in front of them, a large family filed in, taking up the entire row, a mom and dad, four kids, and two grandparents. Deanna looked at Esther to her right and realized her family had been reduced to just the two of them. *Why do they get to have a whole family when we have lost everybody? Did God love them more than us? Gramps is gone, Daniel is gone. Look at Gram's arm, or my leg. I don't even have my parents. Dad's off with his little tramp and Mom's rotting away in prison. I am alone. Everyone has abandoned me.*

It was insufferable. Deanna tried to be quiet but trying to stifle it only made it worse. She cried uncontrollably through the entire service. At home, things weren't any better and it produced a teary, mournful Christmas. Esther pleaded with Deanna to get some help. As much as she did not want to admit it, Deanna knew she was right. Her body literally ached from tip to toe. Lumps formed in her throat and her stomach twisted in knots. She cried from Christmas Eve until after New Year's Day.

Deanna knew there was only one person she could go to for help. Brother Jim opened the door to the chapel office before Deanna even raised her hand to knock. He was shocked by the sullen look and dark circles that surrounded her blue eyes. The luster had gone out of them and he took her into his arms without saying a word.

Deanna breathed in his scent. It was manly and smelled slightly of musk. It had been weeks since she was last at church or had met with him for Bible study. He arms felt strong and she laid her head upon his chest. His heart beat strong and steady beneath the white dress shirt.

"What is it, Deanna? Are you alright?"

Deanna pulled herself away and moved to the moss-green chenille sofa in the corner of his office. She curled her good leg up underneath her hip and propped her prosthetic leg across the cushions and hugged a throw pillow to her chest.

"I'm so lost." Deanna sighed. "I don't know where to turn. I've lost everything. Mom's in prison, Dad has basically deserted me for his new bride . . . even Kim-Ly is gone, and now Gramps is dead too."

"That's a lot of stuff. Why don't we take one thing at a time and see if we can sort through it. Okay?" He smiled gently at her and slowly, he helped Deanna sort out her feelings. He sat down beside on the sofa and casually draped his arm over the back. His fingers lightly stroked the nape of her neck. Somewhere outside a car horn went off, blaring incessantly, like the security of a car had been breached. Deanna could feel the sweat begin to trickle under her arms and seep through her blouse.

"Let's start with your Mom. Why are you so angry with her?"

"You think I should forgive her, don't you?"

"I didn't say that. Who do you think your anger is hurting the most? Her or you?"

Deanna shrugged her shoulders and let out a deep sigh. She knew she was a long way from understanding, and had her doubts she ever would.

"You have feelings you have not even admitted to yourself yet. Perhaps understanding your mother will release some of that pent up anger, and your feeling of loss." His arm slipped from the back of the sofa to her shoulders.

"Why should I forgive her? It's her fault, all of it. If it wasn't for her . . . for her drinking, Daniel would still be alive, and I wouldn't be a cripple, and Gram would have a good arm. Dad wouldn't be marrying that little bitch, Janice." She gulped when she realized she had gone too far.

"Sorry", she mumbled.

He smiled at her and rested his hand on her knee, above her stump. "That's okay, you are upset. But hating her is not going to bring back Daniel or your grandfather, or even keep your father from being with Janice."

Deanna didn't remember anything else they discussed that day, but she left his office with a smile on her face. *He loves me. I know he does. Look how gentle he is with me. Even if I don't have Daniel, or Gramps, or Dad, I have him. I don't have to worry. Someday he will be mine.*

Chapter Twenty Five

Christmas after her father's death sank Susan into a depression deeper than anything she had ever experienced. It made no sense to her. She had been through so much; her youth, the alcoholism, the accident, going to prison. *Why now? Why can't I move on from this? It feels so helpless.* When Georgia offered to get her something to help her sleep, she grabbed at the contra ban. But the pills didn't help her sleep. She tossed and turned, seeing her father's face in every twist of her body. So she took two more, then two more again.

When they found her, she was unconscious on her cell floor. They moved her to the infirmary and pumped her stomach. Later, they moved her to a padded, suicide watch cell.

Doc, the house physiatrist visited her every day for two weeks. Doc frequently ran her fingers through her short salt-and-pepper hair. She usually dressed in tailored slacks and blazer but sometimes she wore big hoop earrings and a long peasant skirt. It made her softer, more vulnerable. Susan liked the look. Doc was easy to talk to. She spoke firmly but gently to Susan. "It's time for you to forgive yourself. Have you ever considered writing a memoir? It may be the way to deal with the pain that has been building in you for years. And sharing that pain with your family will release it. It will no longer have power over you. Trust your family. They love you, even Deanna, even if she doesn't know it yet. I see you can express yourself well in writing. Your children's stories were a good start, but those are all fantasy. It is time for you to deal with the facts."

Susan talked a lot about her Mom, Deanna and Thomas. Doc told Susan she could have a good life when she got out and she still had time to rebuild the relationship with her daughter. Susan wanted to believe her, but was afraid to hope after so many returned or unanswered letters.

Some days Susan thought she actually could forgive herself. When things were going smoothly she even forgot about it for a day or two. But for the most part, the guilt had become a part of her now. It defined her.

"It doesn't have to be that way," Doc spoke gently to Susan.

"I decided I am going to try it," Susan finally admitted in one of their sessions. "I'm going to write my memoir and tell Mom and Deanna about it. There are things that need to come out at last."

A broad smile, showing straight white teeth in a wide mouth, lit up Doc's whole face. "I'm proud of you Susan. This is a huge step." Susan had told her almost everything by now but she suspected there were still things Susan was holding back.

***

Susan calculated it would take three days for the mail to get to Esther and Deanna. They had probably received their letters by now. She was nervous and excited. She was going to tell her family what she was about to do.

She began to doubt her motives. *Is it really going to solve anything to reveal the past now? Isn't it water over the bridge? Will telling the truth hurt Mom more than ever? Deanna might still hate me. But, if I am going to write this memoir, I think I'll write it by hand. I'll ask Thomas to bring me a notebook or a journal next time he visits. Since Dad's death, Thomas has been my only visitor and he comes less and less since his marriage. I appreciate any visits, even as they become more and more infrequent.*

I don't blame him for moving on. Divorcing me was the best thing for him. I can never let him know that I still love him. Always have, always will. Even though he "found Jesus" and a new woman, there will always be that tug at my heart. Thomas saved me when my life was falling apart at nineteen. And he had stood by me even when my drinking continued to escalate, even with all the arguing.

On Sunday, Susan waited at the booth for Thomas to sit down. He looked good. His dark hair was cut short. The ponytail was gone. He had put on a few pounds and it suited him. Shortly after the accident he had lost a lot of weight. Susan knew it was from the stress. Thomas always gained weight when he was happy and lost when he was stressed.

He gave Susan an uneasy half smile and picked up the phone on the other side of the glass divider. Susan followed his lead.

"How's it going?" He looked through the glass divider with those big brown eyes that Susan loved. "Have you been outside much? It's going to be a hot summer I think."

"You look good Thomas. I like the haircut."

Thomas nervously reached for his ponytail and smiled at her when his hand came up empty.

She noticed he seemed to be rambling but he no longer twisted his hands in the old nervous gesture. She couldn't deny that something had changed him.

"I'm good, Thomas, well as good as I can be, I suppose. My tomato plants are doing well. Thanks for bringing me those plants. Everyone in the yard is watching them grow."

Thomas interrupted her. "I read a great verse this morning while doing my devotions. Can I read it to you?"

He pulled a small black Bible out of his breast pocket. He looked so hopeful.

Susan rolled her eyes at him. "Thomas, please don't start. You know I don't want to hear any of that crap. Can't we talk about something else?"

"It's not crap, Susan. I know you had a bad experience with the church Susan. But this is real, Susan. It will give you eternal life. And make your life here full."

"You call this a bad experience?" Susan laughed motioning around her to the booths and guards standing nearby. "You have got to be kidding!"

"But eternal life is waiting for you. Here, just let me read a few verses. . . **For the wages of sin are death . . .**"

"Stop, Thomas." Susan could hear herself raising her voice. The officer stood up and peered over the divider. Susan lowered her voice into the phone.

"I want to talk to you about something. It's important to me. Okay?"

Shaking his head, he put the Bible back in the breast pocket of his jacket. "What is it, Susan?" he asked.

"I need you to bring me something to write in, a journal or at least a nice notebook. I am going to write my memoir. What do you think?"

Thomas eyebrows raised in a look of surprise. He couldn't imagine why she would want to recount the whole sordid story.

"I'll see what I can find for you. I can't come next week. We have a church picnic. I am handling the set-up of all the table and chairs. It's going to be so nice. We have a missionary coming to speak and . . ."

His voice trailed off when he saw Susan's pained expression.

"But I'll come the following week and bring what I can find."

She nodded her head and tried to be polite even though she didn't really want to listen to his church talk. She made a special point to always ask about Janice.

"How's Janice?"

"She's good. Thanks for asking."

"Have you been to see Deanna lately?"

Thomas bowed his head and shook it slightly. It pained Susan that Thomas had shut Deanna out of his life shortly after the accident. It was not Deanna's fault. Susan thought his "come to Jesus" awakening would have made him want to amend some things between Deanna and himself. Susan had a feeling his new bride did not want any reminders of his past life with Susan and Deanna . . . or Daniel.

***

The Sunday visit two weeks later, Thomas held something under his arm. Susan watched in anticipation as he spoke to the officer. The corrections officer looked through it, fanning the pages to make sure he was not smuggling in something forbidden. Then she handed it to another officer on her side of the glass wall. Susan held her breath when he handed it to her. The quality of the journal was amazing. She was surprised Thomas went through so much trouble to get her such a nice one instead of an inexpensive composition book from the drug store. She held the book in her hands, turning it over and over, relishing the feel of the soft, tan leather. Faint blue lines covered each page and when she closed it, the edge was gilded in a gold patina. Inside the front flap, Thomas had inscribed "To Susan, May the Lord Bless You And Keep You, In God's love, Thomas" Susan looked at Thomas through the glass, tears filled her eyes.

"Thank you, Thomas. This is beautiful." She was at a loss to what else to say. She could hardly wait to get back to her cell and start writing.

"You're welcome Susan. But, I can't come see you anymore. Janice says I need to put my old life behind me. I'm sorry."

"But," Susan began to protest, and then nodded her head in resignation.

Susan knew it would come to this. But now she could write about her life. Some of it would not be pleasant. But it was important for Deanna know the truth.

Chapter Twenty Six

Susan had been released from the suicide watch and had just returned from visiting Pauly and the baby on the nursery quad. Mother and son were doing fine. Six month Desmond had smiled at her as he nestled into her arms. A beautiful child with big dark eyes, soft curls framing a perfectly shaped head, and a firm grip on a lock of her hair.

Susan watched as a letter slipped through the slot during mail call. She gingerly grasped the letter between her fingers before it fell to the floor. The return address was from her mother, but the hand writing was Deanna's. She shook the envelope to drop the letter to the one side and carefully tore the other end. She sat on the bottom bunk curling her legs under her Indian style. The cell felt larger since she was back and without Pauly. Despite the overcrowding, they had not assigned a new cellmate to her yet.

January 10, 1984

Hello my darling Susan,

I was surprised to receive your letter and that you are writing a memoir. Perhaps it is good. I always believe the Lord has a purpose to everything, and for you, if the memoir brings you some peace, I am all for it.

Life is hard since your father's passing but Deanna does a wonderful job helping me out. Between the two of us, we get along just fine. She is a dear sweet child and the joy of my life at this time with Nils gone. We so look forward to the day you can come home.

Reverend Olson has been a real blessing. He tutors Deanna on matters of our faith, just like he did for you. He has always been such a comfort to the family, hasn't he?

Take care of yourself and know God has a plan for you.

Forever my blessings and love,

Mother (and Deanna)

Susan flinched at the mention of Reverend Olson's name. *Why did he always have to be in the picture? I wonder if Deanna objected to being called a "sweet child" I am sure she thinks she is quite grown up at seventeen. How I wish she was not still so angry with me. Still, she had written it down, word for word, just as I imagine Mom had dictated it. Susan could hear her voice in the words. Will the memoir really help me heal? Will it bring Deanna back to me?*

It was quiet on the quad, eerily so. Susan feared it was the calm before the storm. Things had been brewing for quite some time. A new arrival was vying to take Juanita's place among the Latina Queens. Alliances were being formed. It was just a matter of where and when the challenge would take place.

She brushed the palm of her hand over the soft leather cover of the journal. The florescent light in the ceiling cast a shadow from the upper bunk across the pages. Doc had been right in suggesting this. It felt healing already, just thinking about writing it down.

How do I explain how I got from there to here? Most people probably cannot pinpoint when their downhill spiral began. But I can. I know the year, the month. I even know the day and the hour it all began. I was fifteen. It was a Wednesday, August 10, 1962. It was almost three o'clock in the afternoon. Wait, before I get to that, I must start at the beginning.

She picked up her pen and started to write.

***

I was born Susan Gerda Lundgren into a wonderful loving home on February 14, 1947. I grew up in the mid-west in the small rural town of North Lima, a few miles south of Youngstown, Ohio. Most of the families in North Lima were farmers or blue collar workers.

Home was an old two-story farm house my grandfather had built himself when my mother was ten years old. It had been my home until I married Thomas. The old house creaked from wide plank flooring that expanded and contracted with each change in weather. On warm summer nights we propped the windows open with books when the rope sashes broke. We weren't really farmers. Dad was a banker. But from the window in the bedroom, I could look out over the neighbor's corn fields and Dad's massive garden that had once been farm land. Tall pink and purple gladiolas towered over the blue iris in the summer or yellow daffodils in the spring. They waved in the wind creating a dancing rainbow. Beyond the garden, a new subdivision had sprouted up where Dad had sold off most of the maple orchard.

The flowers were Dad's passion, but they also supplemented the family income. He sold his flowers to the funeral homes and florist shops in town. You could get lost in the corn fields or in the gladiolas. As a child, I spent countless hours running between the stalks, playing hide-and-seek and tag with my big brother. Ray was two years older than I. I adored him. Even when we went through that awkward stage when he didn't want anything to do with his little sister tagging along behind him, I only wanted to go where he went, do whatever he was doing, hang out with his friends.

Besides the church and our good Lord, Mom's passion was polo games. In the summer after church, we went to the polo matches. They didn't have a real polo field, just part of somebody's farm. But everyone pulled their cars in a long rectangle, three hundred feet long and formed the correct length around the field. They pounded goals into the ground at either end and we sat on the hoods of the cars to watch the games.

The sounds echo in my mind still. The pounding of hooves, the snorts of the ponies as they raced by, the hard smack of the ball with the mallet . . . even the cheer of the crowd. Closing my eyes, I can still see it clear as day. Oh, the sights and smells; the sweat that glistened off the ponies backs, freshly churned dark soil kicked up by hooves, even the faint smell of cornstalks in the next field linger in my dreams.

Mom always said I was a natural with horses. At about five or six, I walked Curly's pony to cool him off between chukkers while the adults stomped the divots on the field. It never dawned on me to be afraid of the ponies. Even when my head still fit under the belly of the beast, I walked along holding the reins in my little hands. Only a handful of children, myself included, were trusted to cool the ponies.

Mom and Dad were strict Christians and members of the Swedish Congressional church. At least twice a week we crossed the threshold of the stark white building with the huge steeple. Before every service, prayer meeting, wedding or funeral, the bells rang from the steeple casting beautiful mournful tones throughout the countryside. If there was an event at the church, the whole town knew by the ringing of the bells.

Even though my parents were strict, I always knew how very much we were loved. Most of our social life had centered on the church; pot luck dinners, bible studies, craft fairs, baptisms and funerals. Even most of the polo players, like Dad's friend, Curly Kirkson, were members of our church. Being the only girl in the family, I went with Mom to all the women's things like sewing bees, bake sales and mother-daughter banquets. I was a tomboy and longed to play with the boys like Ray. At picnics, that was not an option. I was expected to stay with the women. Since Mom was also an only daughter, you'd have thought she understood my desire to play with the boys. None-the-less, I had a very happy, but sheltered childhood.

Every meal was prefaced by the traditional Swedish prayer. *Gode Gud, välsigna denna mat som vi är på väg att äta. I Jesu namn, Amen.* Dear God, Bless this food which we are about to eat. In Jesus name, Amen. I still silently say that prayer before a meal, without even thinking about it.

Yes, life was good. Right up until the summer following my fifteenth birthday.

***

Susan smelled it before she saw or heard anything. There was a fire on the floor with the putrid smell of burning plastic. A blaring alarm sounded in sharp piercing tempo. Cell doors were put on automatic lock down. They closed on their own, locked into place. The bang of each door jarred the senses. Susan closed her journal, tucked it safely in the foot locker across from the bunk and peered out through the window in her door to see if the fire was near to her. Inmates started to yell, and bang anything they had against the cell doors. It created more of a diversion than out of fear. Any commotion further complicated the shift change for the correction officers, which only encouraged more noise and chaos.

Word traveled down the halls quickly. The new contender for the leader of the Latina gang had started a fire inside of Juanita's cell, blocking her exit. When the alarm sounded, the door automatically closed and locked her inside with the fire. The acrid fumes of burning plastic swiftly traveled through the air.

As the officers struggled to get the door open and extinguish the fire. Black smoke caked the inside of the Latina Queen's nose, eyes and ears, causing her to panic. When she opened her mouth to breathe, she inhaled the toxic black smoke that choked off her breathing. In less than five minutes, she was unconscious on the floor of her cell.

The guards moved her quickly to the infirmary. Other correction offers moved Susan and the other inmates into the yard as they brought in large fans to remove the smoke from the quad. The inmates were nervous and paced like the caged animals they were. Everyone understood how quickly a fire could become a death trap for all of them, even with the huge sprinklers designed to prevent just that. Georgia's girls blamed the Latina gang for starting the fire and they in turn blamed it on Georgia's gang. They responded by threatening with shanks that appeared out of nowhere. Georgia moved her gang to the far end of the yard, away from the Latinas and a sure confrontation.

Chapter Twenty Seven

After surviving the fire and recovering in the infirmary, Juanita was transferred to another quad. The Latina inmate who started the fire spent three weeks in solitary confinement. Upon her return to the quad, she successfully took Juanita's place as the leader of the Latina-Americans.

Susan made a conscious effort to avoid her as much as possible. Georgia still controlled both the white and the Afro-American gangs. She and Susan maintained their unusual friendship.

Susan absent-mindedly tapped her foot on the cement floor, anxious about what she needed to include in her journal. She wanted to be honest with herself, but she would have to reveal things she had never said out loud to anyone except her ex-husband. And not even Thomas knew it all.

With a shaky hand, she began the hardest part of the journal. She wrote about three pages and couldn't breathe. Susan placed the journal on the bunk and paced in her cell. The doors were open and although she was free to go down the hall, she didn't want to talk to anyone at the moment. She wiped her sweaty brow and the back of her neck. The pounding in her heart drummed out any other sound on the quad.

Come on, Susan, you can do this. Just pick up the pen and write it down. No one can hurt you anymore. Not ever again.

She poured water into a paper cup from her corner aluminum sink. She drank it slowly, attempting to gather the courage to continue. She took a deep breath, picked up the pen and started again. She wrote for hours, pouring out the details she had kept hidden from everyone for so long. The floodgates were opened. Once Susan started writing, she couldn't stop. The words tumbled from her mind onto the pages quickly, building strength with each word.

The corrections officer called lights out on the quad. Susan was glad to stop writing. But she also felt release, as if a burden had been lifted from her shoulders. She lay back, and stared into the dark springs of the top bunk.

I'm okay. I wrote it down and I'm okay. I can do this. Amazed at the sudden feeling of relief that washed over her, she slipped into her most restful sleep in forty years.

Susan continued writing for days on end. She didn't visit Pauly or attend any of the workshops. She wrote about her marriage to Thomas and

Deanna's birth. She poured her soul out onto the pages, not mincing any words or covering up the truth. She was more honest to herself than she had been for thirty years.

Just before they called lights out on the quad, they called a cell-check. Susan quickly tucked the journal next to her mother's letters, under her uniforms in the foot locker. She knew it wasn't really hidden or secure. Everything was open game to the correction officers.

"Cell check. Move back away from the door." The new correction officer chewed on wads of peppermint gum, mouth wide open, exposing yellowed teeth and swollen gums.

Susan shivered and moved against the wall, face first, and placed her hands high on the concrete blocks, per standard procedure. Susan watched over her shoulder as they went through her few belongings. They helped themselves to a half-pack of cigarettes on her bookshelf. They tipped over the jar of coins and a few dollars Susan used to buy deodorant and candy bars. They spilled onto the floor. Pocketing the paper bills, they pulled apart the bed and searched between the sheets and blankets. They flipped Susan's mattress over and left it upside down on the floor.

They opened the foot locker. Susan held her breath. They rummaged around, picking up and examining things that might contain contraband like drugs or weapons. One of the officers opened a letter from her mother, determined it was boring and dropped it on the floor. One of them briefly began reading the latest adventures of Denny and Danny Then the officer saw the journal. She picked it up and thumbed through it.

"Looky here," she said with a grin. Susan didn't like the way she took the time to read some of the entries. These were Susan's personal thoughts. She had no right to read them.

"That's private," Susan spat at her, immediately regretting her outburst.

Big mistake! The new officer liked to throw her weight around and prove she had control. She raised her Billy club before Susan could duck out of the way.

Pain shot through the small of Susan's back as the blow of the billy-club made contact. Susan fell to her knees and was struck again, across the shoulder blade.

"Nothing is private in here, bitch! What is yours is mine. I think I will just take this. Maybe it will make some good bathroom reading. Do I get to hear all about your little love nests in here? I know how you girls are, after you have been here a long time. Need a little pussy to keep you satisfied these days?"

Susan was used to hearing comments like that from the inmates, but hearing it from the officer repulsed her. "I'm sorry. I shouldn't have spoken up to you. There isn't anything exciting in there. It will only bore you. Maybe I can get something more interesting from one of the other girls. I have been here a long time. I have connections."

"No, no, I think I'll just take this." She grinned at Susan and gave her one last kick in the stomach before walking out. The cell door slammed shut, echoed domination.

Susan stayed on the floor on her hands and knees until they were gone. Her back throbbed and began to welt up. To no avail, she fought off the convulsing from the kick in the stomach. She crawled over to the steel commode and she threw up the little bit of food she had left in her stomach.

All Susan wanted was to get her journal back. *What was the use of writing it all down if now some sleazy new correction officer was going to read it, and tell all the other officers her secrets? She may burn it or just throw it away.* All that time lost. She climbed onto her bed and collapsed. Her body throbbed from the pain. She knew tomorrow would be worse, once the swelling and bruises started to show.

Chapter Twenty Eight

Deanna looked up from the sink under the kitchen window and called out to Esther. "Gram, I see the mail lady coming down the street. Got anything that needs to go out?" When Esther did not answer, Deanna draped a jacket across her shoulders and headed down to the box, just as the mail truck pulled away.

She watched as two small boys played soccer in the yard across the street. The ball rolled into the street and one boy darted after it, forgetting to look for cars in the street. Luckily, the road was empty. It reminded her of Daniel. He did things like that, running into the street without looking. She always kept an extra eye on Daniel at the park or the playground.

I wonder what Daniel would be like if he was alive today? He'd be ten years old now. I bet he would be tall, like Gramps. Would he have gone to college some day?

Have a great job? Who knows what he could have become.

She kicked the ball back across the road, triumphant in her ability to still land a good shot. Boy, it's been a long time since I've done that. She smiled to herself as she carried the mail back into the house and sorted through it. A brown package was addressed to her. It was from the Marysville Correctional Facility. *It looks like something from my mother. The memoir she mentioned? Did she mail me her journal? Well, I don't want it. If that is what this is, I am not reading it. She can't make me.* She ran her fingers around the edge of the package, wrapped in the same brown grocery store bag as her birthday present, cut and taped to fit around a book or something. The name above the return address said Ms. Pauline Wilson. Deanna did not know a Ms. Wilson.

It's not from Mom. Maybe she died and this is all she had left. Why else would someone at the prison send something to me? How would I feel if Mom was dead? Deanna's stomach turned, making her queasy and she could feel her heart racing. She sank into the chair and stared at the brown paper. Why am I afraid to open this? Something told her that whatever was in the wrapper, it couldn't be good.

"What's this?" Esther asked as she dropped a laundry basket she had resting on hip on the floor next to the counter.

"I don't know. It's from somebody at the prison. What if it is bad news?"

"I'm sure we would have heard from the authorities if something bad had happened to your mother. I guess you are not going to know until you open it. Do you want some privacy?"

Do I? No, I want Gram right by my side if I'm going to find out my mother is dead.

"No, please stay with me. Let's open it together. Want some coffee?"

"I'll get it. Don't get up."

Deanna watched as Esther reached for two china cups.

She placed the coffee in front of Deanna. Inhaling the rich smell of fresh brew, she cupped both hands around the delicate teacup. She lifted it toward her face, and let the steam and the aroma warm her hands and face.

Esther didn't say anything. They sat there in the silence, quietly sipping their coffee. The sound of a talk show host carried from the TV in the living room. She nodded her head in the direction of the package, gently prodding Deanna to open it.

Setting down the cup and moving it aside, Deanna turned the package over and slipped her fingers under the tape. She caught herself holding her breath and didn't know why. With shaky fingers, she slid the contents out of the wrapper.

She caressed the soft tan leather journal with the palm of her hand. The edges were gilded and the corners were just a bit worn. With it was a letter, neatly folded in thirds. Deanna looked at her grandmother for reassurance. She shrugged his shoulders. Deanna opened the first page of the journal. It had "Susan Lundgren Jennings" written in the middle of the page. The second page contained addresses, this address and the address of the rehab center she had recently left. The next page had an inscription. "To Susan, May the Lord Bless You and Keep You, In God's love, Thomas"

"It is my mother's journal," she said softly, more to herself than to her grandmother. "Why didn't she send it herself? Do you think she is dead?"

"No dear, I do not. Read the letter, Deanna. Your answer is in the letter."

She unfolded the letter and began to read:

May 1, 1984

Dear Deanna,

I hope this package gets to you. I had to smuggle it to Georgia, queen of our quad, to get it out of here. She can do anything.

Your mother was my roommate for seven months until I moved to the maternity quad to have my baby. Susan told me I am just a few years older than you. She's been like a mother to me since I got here.

While we shared a cell, she talked about you a lot. She misses you so much and hopes every day to hear from you. I am sending this to you because I believe you need to read what is inside. It may be personal but I am sure she really wrote it on your behalf.

A new corrections officer took it away from her during a cell check. She told me how they stole it from her but I was surprised when I found it in the dumpster behind the kitchen. It is very precious to her.

I confess; I read the journal. I probably should have given it back to Susan, but after reading it; I think it would do the most good in your hands. I think you'll understand after you read it. Then you can give it back to her in person.

She is not a criminal. She had a terrible secret she hid behind the bottle. We all have secrets . . . and regrets. Give her a chance Deanna. She loves you.

Sincerely,

Pauly Wilson

Deanna placed the letter on the counter and fingered the edges of the journal. She didn't know what to think. Part of her felt compelled to read it, and yet, fear gripped her. "Gram, what kind of secret is she talking about? What could possibly justify what Mom did, to me, to you, and especially to Daniel?"

"I don't know, Deanna. I guess you will just have to read it."

Deanna was surprised by the surge of anger welling up in her. "Who is this woman and how dare her tell me what is best for me, or for my mother, for that matter? She's comparing herself to me? I remember Mom writing about a young girl who had her baby in prison. I guess this is her."

Esther shrugged hers shoulders, took the teacup, and refilled it with coffee. Bringing it back to the counter, she wrapped her good arm around her grand-daughter. "Whatever it is, I know she still loves you, even if you don't believe it."

Throwing the brown wrapper in the trash, Deanna tucked the letter inside the front cover of the journal. She decided she should eat something first, even though she wasn't really hungry. *You're just procrastinating. Either read it or not. No one is forcing you.*

She opened a can of chicken noodle soup, and popped the contents in a bowl to heat it in the microwave. She kept glancing back at the journal sitting on the table. It was good quality leather with gold gilded edges and felt soft and supple in her hands. She noticed it was only half full of writing.

Isn't it a shame that someone's life can fit into half a journal? Maybe she left out the hard parts, the parts I need to read for myself about the accident? Maybe she hadn't finished it before it was taken away from her? Why did this girl think I should read it? I have more questions than answers. I guess I'm not going to get them answered until I start to read.

Deanna forced herself to eat the soup, and made a point to rinse the bowl and put it in the dishwasher before she sat back down at the table with the journal. She was still stalling, and she knew it. She took the journal and headed slowly up the stairs to her bedroom. She turned the reading light on over the soft floral chaise lounge by the window. She removed her prosthetic and leaned it against the chair. Then she pulled a soft chenille throw over her stump and her good leg. It was her favorite reading spot. Finally, she opened the pages and started to read.

The early pages of the journal were interesting, but not especially eye-opening. Her mother's life with Gram was not much different from her own. Gram was the same loving mother to Susan as she was a wonderful grandmother to Deanna. She smiled about the polo games. *I never knew Gram loved polo, or horses.*

Then she got to the year Susan turned fifteen. Deanna read the first few paragraphs, unable to believe what she was reading, and went back and read the same words over and over again.

Chapter Twenty Nine

We loved church camp as kids. I looked forward to the two week reprieve from cooking and sewing, knowing I'd be doing the things I loved best, camping, hiking and horseback riding through the woods.

A single campsite consisted of eight two-person tents with wood platform floors circling a center fire pit. Ten campsites spread over several acres, encompassing the main mess hall, sick bay and chapel. The younger children stayed in a large dormitory with bunk beds located behind the mess hall.

Behind the chapel, a sparkling blue lake shimmered in the summer sun. It was here that we all took swimming and canoeing lessons. We had archery, horticulture, riding lessons, and of course, Bible study. Church camp was the highlight of our lives for many hot summers.

Brother Jim was the youth pastor the year I turned fifteen. It was 1962. With platinum hair that curled out from under a Chicago Cubs baseball cap, broad, tanned shoulders, and slim hips poured into skin-tight jeans, he didn't look like a minister. His penetrating blue eyes twinkled with mischief and a single dimple on his left cheek danced in and out when he smiled.

***

Wait! Deanna's mind raced and she counted back the years. *Brother Jim? Does she mean MY Jim, MY Brother Jim?*

***

When the girls at church found out he was going to be our camp counselor that year, they could not get signed up fast enough. Once there, the older girls rolled up their shorts to expose more of their long tanned legs and flaunted their voluptuous bodies in front of him at the lake. Their strict Christian parents would have been appalled if they saw their daughters throwing themselves at him like that.

As hard as they tried, Brother Jim didn't seem interested in any of those girls. When he started to pay extra attention to me, it confused me. He chose me first to learn a new craft, to demonstrate a new swim stroke, or mimic the correct way to paddle a canoe.

At the archery post, he wrapped his arms around me to demonstrate the right way to hold a bow. I remember the strength of his muscles across my back and the scent of peppermint on his breath close to my ear. When he wrapped his fingers around mine, the warmth of his hand rippled up my arm. Perspiration trickled down my blouse and I wondered if the other girls noticed how flushed I had become.

At the lake the next day, his hand brushed against mine under the water. I was certain it was accidental. When it happened again, he winked at me. He winked! Can you believe that? What was a fifteen year old girl supposed to do when a twenty-four year old pastor of your church makes passes at her?

***

Deanna quickly did the math in her head. That would make him forty-seven now? *Can this really be the same man?*

***

I had to admit I was excited and scared at the same time. I couldn't figure it out. Why would he pay any attention to me? I was a late bloomer. The other girls were far more mature than I. And they were falling all over him. I told myself that I must have imagined the whole thing.

***

Just like me. Deanna thought to herself.

***

The one part of camp we all hated was prayer hour. After a busy day of swimming, playing ball, and hiking through the woods, prayer hour was torturous. The staff believed an hour on our knees in prayer to bring our transgressions to the Lord would cleanse our souls.

Outside, crickets and frogs began their evening songs and the wind whipped the flaps on the tent in a soft thumping sound. The first ten minutes weren't too bad. By twenty, my knees were hurting and my legs were going numb.

Some of the girls broke the rules and sat on the floor of their platform until Brother Jim or one of the other counselors poked their heads in the tent to make sure we were still on our knees.

Brother Jim went from tent to tent, standing before us while we prayed. He placed his hand upon our heads to bless us. After this blessing we were allowed to lie on our cots while we waited for the others to be finished. Everyone hoped they would be first to receive the blessing so they could get off their knees.

One evening during prayer hour, my tent-mate, Connie, was sent to sick bay. I didn't really think she was sick but Brother Jim said she looked pale. Connie shrugged her shoulders at me as she left. She wasn't going to complain about spending an hour on a soft cot while the rest of us were kneeling on hard wooden floors.

It took forever for Pastor Jim to get to my tent. My legs had gone numb, and I couldn't concentrate on my prayers. I just wanted to get off my knees. When he finally arrived, he tugged the ties on the flap and let it fall into place. The little bit of light from the dusky sky was blacked out by the fabric.

For a moment, I thought it was an accident, and I wondered if I should get up and tie it open. But Brother Jim steadied me by pressing his hand firmly upon my head. He softly mouthed a prayer for forgiveness of my sins. The scent of peppermint filled the tent. As he did this, he took both his hands and cupped them over my ears and pulled my head forward.

I tried to lurch back as my face brushed against his jeans. But he held me firmly, with my head pressed against his body. I could feel his arousal begin to strain against the material. I couldn't move and I was too shocked and afraid to cry out to anyone. It felt like an eternity before he released his grip on my head. He gently pulled me to my feet. It was dark in the tent. I could barely make out his shape. I couldn't see his face but I felt his fingers pinch my chin, and ever so gently, I felt his lips brush against mine. Then he was gone.

I lay down on my cot, trembling, as I tried to catch my breath. What had just happened? The kiss was gentle but the pressure of my face against his erection frightened me. Tears marked my face as I wrestled to make some sense of it. It must have been an accident. He couldn't have meant anything by it. Nobody would believe me if I told them.

***

Deanna paused in her reading, recalling the feeling of his bulge against her stomach when he held her tight at her grandfather's funeral.

***

When Connie came back, I wanted to tell her. She was my best friend. I needed to tell someone, but what would she think of me? I decided I couldn't take the chance.

Once everyone was done with their prayers, they lit the big campfire in the middle of the campsite and we all gathered together. Normally, this was one of my favorite times of camp. Our voices were lifted in off-tune verses of "Michael-Row-Your-Boat-Ashore" and "Kumbaya". The smell of roasted marshmallows and melting chocolate joined with the smoky scent of pine and oak. Everyone stuffed themselves with s'mores and popcorn. I didn't have an appetite.

I watched for Brother Jim. He did not come out of his tent. One of the other girls asked where he was and another counselor said he felt the need to stay in prayer that night.

Sleep eluded me and I was still awake when the light of dawn peeked between the ties of the tent flap. Throughout the night I wrestled with what had happened. Had I been the one that rested my head in his crotch? Maybe he didn't do it, maybe it was me. It had to have been an accident. My heart raced at the thought of seeing Brother Jim at morning prayers. I was horrified he would say something to me about being immoral and having unclean thoughts in front of the other girls. Did he really kiss me or was that my imagination too?

I did not see him at prayers but I spotted Brother Jim at the craft table showing the eight and nine-year olds how to make bird feeders out of orange peels and peanut butter. He didn't look up when I crossed the field toward the mess hall.

Breakfast consisted of me choking on a bagel. My throat closed up tight, I could barely breathe, let alone eat. Someone came and gave me the Heimlich maneuver. After making a complete spectacle of myself and retreating into a corner with a glass of OJ, I decided it was all a bad dream. I must have imagined the whole thing.

We went through all the normal activities, but I don't remember any of them. I dreaded evening prayer hour to start, but nothing unusual happened. Brother Jim came into our tent first, rested his hand gently on my head, did the same for Connie, gave us our blessings and left the tent. He never looked me directly in the eye the entire day.

Two days later, padding our way barefoot through the cool stream that fed into the lake, I twisted my ankle on a slippery, jagged rock and fell into the water cutting a slice into my skin. I went down hard. The water wasn't deep, maybe only six or seven inches, but getting out of the water on one leg was impossible on the slippery rocks.

Brother Jim swept me up into his arms and told the girls they could continue their hike. He said he was taking me back to the sick bay. I felt horrified. Soaking wet from the waist down, my ankle throbbed, and there I was, in his arms, being carried like a child.

He walked until we were out of the hikers' sight. He placed me gently down on a soft mossy bank, and assessed my injury. My ankle was swollen but there was little bleeding from the cut. He took his shirt off, dipped it in the stream, and wrapped the cool garment around my ankle. I tried not to look at him, with his blonde chest hairs glistening in the sunlight. I didn't want to be attracted to him, but I was.

"How does it feel now?" His hands patted around the cloth. He sat down next to me and rested his body on one arm. His other hand was still on my ankle. Slowly, I felt his hand move up my calf, then to my knee, then to my thigh. I think I closed my eyes because I don't remember anything but light through my eyelids.

When he pressed his hand between my legs, I tried to scoot away from him. His body rolled on top of me pinning me down. He pressed his lips tightly against mine and forced his tongue in my mouth. It tasted of peppermint. I tried to turn my face away so I could scream, but his lips stayed locked on mine. This was not gentle or beautiful.

***

"No, no!" Deanna called out to herself. "Don't let it be! Don't tell me! No, No, No!"

***

I was afraid. I fought him, I swear I did. But he was much stronger than me. He tore my blouse when he reached under the hem, grabbing my breast. I don't know how he got my shorts off. Bright flashing lights burst before my eyes and I felt a searing pain when he entered me.

When it was over, he held me, and caressed me like a child. I was crying and when I opened my eyes, I saw he wept as well. He mouthed inaudible words. No, he was praying. He had just raped me and now he was praying!

I wanted to run as far away from him as I could. I tried to get up, tried to pull together the torn part of my blouse and pull my soggy, water-logged shorts back up from around my right ankle. My shorts were tangled in his shirt that was still wrapped around it. I tripped and fell. Grappling with his shirt, I managed to untangle it from my leg and throw it in his direction.

I tried again to walk, but I couldn't put any weight on my ankle and fell back to my knees. Twigs and pebbles dug into my knees and palms of my hands as I frantically tried to crawl away from him. He didn't stop me. He knew I wouldn't get far. He looked at me with pain in his eyes like it was him who had been assaulted.

"What's wrong with you?" I shouted at him. I didn't care who heard me. I wanted someone to hear me. "Look what you have done to me? You are my pastor!"

He looked at me intensely with those big blue eyes. His voice was smooth and steady, like he was giving a blessing. "It was an accident. The devil won this battle, but he won't win the war. This must stay between just you and I. Don't you see, Susan? I could not abstain my yearning for you. The serpent is a crafty, devious creature. We must seek forgiveness from the Lord. Let's pray together. This is between Him and us. It must stay that way".

I couldn't believe my ears. He was quoting the Bible and telling me I had to seek forgiveness. He stood up, adjusted his clothing and reached down and spryly picked me up. "I'm going to take you back to your tent to get dry clothes. Then we'll go to sick bay to have the nurse take a look at your ankle. I will stay with you to make sure you are okay. You will not say anything about this to anyone. I wouldn't want to have to call your parents and tell them you made sinful advances toward me. Now would I?"

That is how it all started. He was always sweet after. He always held me gently. But it was rape nonetheless. I knew he didn't love me, no matter how many times it happened or how often he told me. Love is what my Mom and Dad had. I know they had sex, but I could not imagine it was ever anything like that— holding me down, forcing himself. I never had a choice. And it was no accident.

**

Deanna got up from the chair and hobbled to the bathroom. She dropped beside the toilet and vomited, with heart wrenching tears and mucus running from her nose mingled with her afternoon lunch as she hurled into the porcelain bowl. *Oh my God, Oh my God! She was raped, by Jim, MY Jim! Oh my God! Oh no, why Jim, why did you have to do it?*

Chapter Thirty

Deanna took a break from her reading. She needed time to think. *Maybe she egged him on. She's the slut, right? He didn't do it. It's her fault.* But she knew in her heart she couldn't blame this on her mother, not this time. *It was Brother Jim's fault. It was all his fault; the rape, her drinking, the accident, losing my leg, even Daniel's death. Wasn't it?* Her head spun.

She picked up the journal.

***

I couldn't tell anyone what happened at camp, least of all my parents. I was so ashamed. In the fall, Brother Jim convinced my Mom that I needed extra help with my bible studies and my schoolwork. He offered to be my tutor. My grades had taken a nose dive. Mom thought it was so nice he took a special interest. When I resisted going for extra studies at the parsonage, she thought I was being resistant to the Lord's will and ungrateful for his help. I wanted to tell her. I almost told her a thousand times.

Mom and Dad wanted to pay him for tutoring me. He refused and said if I would clean the parsonage once a week; that would be payment enough. So after every assault, I stayed and cleaned his house as well.

He did help me with my schoolwork, teach me the Bible and pray with me. Our lessons always started at his dining room table, with an open Bible and my textbooks between us. They always ended the same way, on our knees in prayer at the foot of his bed, praying for forgiveness for our sins. He said the serpent tempted him with the desires of the flesh, something he could not conquer.

My skin crawled from his touch for hours after I left. But I didn't fight him anymore. I blamed myself for being too weak. He told me the Lord was testing my faith and I needed to continue to pray for forgiveness for my sins.

I had my first drink that summer I turned fifteen. I caught my cousins, George and Joe drinking something and smoking cigarettes behind the church when everyone else was in a prayer meeting. I watched where they hid the bottle in the hollow of an old tree. When they were gone I sat down on the grass and pulled the bottle from its hiding place. I took a big gulf. It was horrible. My throat burned and I almost threw up. As it burned my throat, it felt like a penance for my sins. After a while I didn't choke anymore. Instead, a warm feeling started in my stomach and traveled up my body. My skin quit crawling. The fog in my head made it easier to face the world, and Brother Jim.

George caught me once and laughed when he saw me drinking but Joe wanted me to stop. I pressed them to tell me where they got it. A shop keeper in town didn't card anyone, even when he knew they were minors. It was so easy. All I had to say was my parents had sent me to the store for them. Had he known my parents, he would have known they had never touched a drop their entire lives.

On Sundays and Wednesdays, during church and prayer meeting, Brother Jim cleverly found ways to touch me. He brushed his arm against mine or pressed his hand upon my head for blessings. I fought my impulse to shrink away. Otherwise, my parents would have known. I couldn't bear to let them know.

I decided I needed to bring my grades up, at least enough to graduate from high school. If I could get away from town, I'd never come back. I dreamed of living somewhere warm, perhaps going to college in southern California. But my grades never came up enough. No college acceptance letters came for me.

I took a job at the local grocery store, first as a bagger, then eventually as a cashier. It gave me time away from the parsonage and away from Brother Jim.

Still he pursued me. By then, my self-esteem was so low, I believed whatever he told me. I was an immoral sinner and no one would ever want me. He threatened to expose me if I told anyone and being a pillar of the community, he convinced me no one would ever believe me. So I continued to go to the parsonage, endure his advances and clean his house. He was paying me for my housework, but I felt like he was paying me for sex. I felt no better than a common prostitute.

I met Thomas at the movie theater in town. Dad didn't like me going to movies, but by then I was eighteen and he knew he could not isolate me altogether from all earthly things. Thomas lived with his older sister, Catherine. Their parents had both died in an automobile accident when Thomas was only ten years old. At first they lived with a distant great aunt neither one of them had ever met before their parents' death. When Catherine turned twenty-one, the courts gave her full custody of her little brother. She tried to take care of him herself but he ran pretty wild and was easily influenced by the wrong crowd. I don't think he ever had a real male role model.

Thomas' long black hair rested on his shoulders and coffee colored eyes twinkled with mischief. The very first night on the way to the movie theater, he offered me some beer from the back seat of his car. It was such a relief to have someone who was not always judging me. He didn't expect me to live up to the perfect life of my parents. Soon we became a steady item, although I didn't bring him home to meet my parents for a long time.

Thomas and I always had things to talk about. He didn't ask me to pray or study the Bible. We talked about baseball and who was going to win the World Series. We talked about the war in Vietnam where my brother, Ray was serving in the Army at the time. We talked a lot about politics and the war. We didn't always agree, but the heated debate was part of the fun.

We drank a lot, smoked a little weed, and went to movies and college frat parties on campus with his buddies. For the first time in my life I felt comfortable with who I was. I didn't have to hide . . . much.

When we got drunk, Thomas wanted to have sex. He thought I was still a virgin. He was gentle, so completely different from Brother Jim, but when he put his hands on me, my skin crawled and I pulled away. He thought I was holding out until we got married.

Thomas asked me to marry him in December of 1965. I agreed if he would to take me away, anywhere away from North Lima. Even though the encounters with Brother Jim had lessened over the years, he still called me to the parsonage from time to time. And I still went, blackmailed by my own sins.

Thomas agreed to take me away, so it was settled. I knew I'd have to tell him sooner or later I was not a virgin. I hoped he wouldn't care since I surmised he was already experienced when he met me.

That same December, I missed my period. At first I blamed it on stress. When I couldn't hold my breakfast down in the mornings, I suspected the worst, yet hoped for the best. I knew the time had come to tell Thomas the truth. It was the hardest conversation I ever had.

We finished off a six pack on the couch in his living room. His hand slipped under my blouse reaching for my breast. I pushed his hand away.

"Thomas, we need to talk," I said.

He groaned and twisted his hands in front of him like he always did when he was nervous. "I know, I know, you want to wait until we're married. But I can hardly stand it anymore. You're driving me crazy."

"I know and I'm sorry. I need to tell you something, something awful. You may not want to marry me when you hear."

"Really?" he laughed. "I seriously doubt that. I've been waiting a long time for this." He reached his hand between my legs.

I recoiled from his touch. My mind flashed to Brother Jim. I didn't like being forced.

"Listen, you need to listen to me!" I choked on my words. I felt my cheeks flush red. The room was suddenly very warm, and my hands trembled.

Thomas sat up straight and wrapped his arm gently around my shoulder. His gentleness only made it worse as my tears soaked his shirt. "Okay, Okay, I'm listening. What could be so terrible?"

"I'm not who you think I am. You think I'm this good Christian girl who just drinks a little too much once in a while. I'm not. I'm not a nice person, Thomas. Not a good girl at all."

"I can't ever think anything bad about you. I love you, just the way you are. What is it? Just tell me."

I took a deep breath and started to hiccup through my tears. "I'm not a virgin, Thomas. I've had sex with someone else." I buried my face in my arms and collapsed in another burst of tears.

Thomas didn't answer right away. I felt his body stiffen. He squared his shoulders and jutted his chin out. His words were shaky, but he was determined to sound strong. "Is that it? Hell, that doesn't matter. Sure, I would have liked to have been your first. But when did this happen? Before we met? I'm not a virgin either you know. I've been with quite a few girls, before I met you, I mean . . . not since I met you . . . honest."

"No Thomas, there's more. It wasn't willing sex. I didn't want it. I hate him! I hate him so much! I wish he was dead!"

Thomas got up and paced the room. He pulled his long hair back and wrapped it in a rubber band at the nape of his neck. "Whoa! Whoa! Are you telling me you were raped? What the hell? Who did that to you Susan? Did you call the police? Why didn't you tell me before? No wonder you pull away from me. I am so sorry."

He didn't hate me. He understood. I didn't know how to tell him what I feared the most. I knew he would find out sooner or later. And there was no one else to turn to. "It's bad, Thomas. There's more."

"What do you mean more?" He sat back down beside me, taking my hands in his. "Tell me, Susan. What's going on?"

I couldn't look him in the eyes. I looked down at our hands clasped tightly together. "He said he'd tell my parents and I'd be the disgrace of the family. He would tell everyone that I seduced him. Nobody would believe me."

I looked away from Thomas. "I can't even look you in the eye. You don't believe me. You think I'm horrible."

Thomas gently took my chin and turned my face so I had to look him in the eye. "You're wrong." He said. "I do believe you! This is just a lot to take in all at once. Who did this to you Susan? You've got to go to the police."

"No, no, I can't. There's more. Thomas— I missed my period . . . I think I'm pregnant."

"You are pregnant from the rape? Oh God! Who, Susan, who? You have to tell me."

"Why do you need to know, Thomas? Isn't it enough that I had to tell you this? I just want you to take me away, away from here, away from him. Let's just go Thomas. Can't we just go away?"

He tugged on the elastic band, freeing his long hair, his ebony locks falling over one eye. He stood up and headed out of the room. I thought he was walking out on me. But he came back with two beers in his hand.

I looked at the beer. I really needed a drink. But I already had too much to drink. If I really was pregnant, I didn't want to hurt the baby. I placed the bottle on the table. "I need to know for sure, Thomas. Will you take me to the doctor? We can pretend we are already married."

"Okay, Okay, I'll take you. But I need to know Susan. Who is it? Who did this to you?"

I said it so softly he didn't understand until I said it again.

"Jim Olsen, Brother Jim."

"The pastor did this?" He sprang back up again, clenching his teeth and pounding a balled fist into his left palm. "That bastard! I don't get it. Where? When did this happen?"

I couldn't tell him how long it had been going on. I let him think it was just the once. He didn't need to know any more. I just shook my head. Thankfully, he didn't push it any further.

***

Thomas took me to the doctor in a different town. I signed in as Mrs. Thomas Jennings. It sounded nice. The young female doctor called Thomas into the room to deliver the news to us.

"You are very lucky young people. I am happy to tell you— you are going to be parents in

August. Everything is fine. Mommy and baby are fine." She beamed at Thomas. "And you are going to be a Daddy."

Thomas looked at her like she had just announced he had cancer. He dropped into a chair and buried his face in his hands. She misunderstood his emotion for happiness and said she would leave us alone. She gave me instructions for a return visit in thirty days, vitamins for me and the baby, and a pamphlet which said, **"So we're going to have a baby!"** And it showed a smiling couple on the front. She closed the door quietly behind her.

"So? Now what?" Thomas looked as me in my paper gown, the most undressed he had ever seen me. "Are you going to keep it?"

"I guess so," I murmured. "I don't believe in abortion. And he . . . or she . . . is still my baby. I can't imagine giving her away."

The ride home was quiet. Neither one of us knew what to say. I cried most of the way. Thomas concentrated on the roads, glassed over with black ice. He gripped the steering wheel tightly. I noticed his knuckles were white.

What was I going to do? How was I going to tell my parents?

"Let's go Thomas," I finally said. "Let's leave here. Get married right away. We could move to California. Could you love this child? It's mine too, not just his. If you really love me, let's just go, now."

He nodded silently in agreement.

We didn't run away as planned. Thomas told me it just wasn't right. He asked my dad for my hand in marriage and he reluctantly said yes. I know Mom and Dad had hoped I'd marry a Christian boy. I think Mom was hoping that after all the time I spent at Brother Jim's, I'd fall in love with him. How little did she know?

Mom assumed we would have a long engagement and she wanted us to be married in the Swedish church. I didn't want any part of that church. And we needed to get married right way.

We were married on January 3, 1966. We settled on the living room of our home instead of the church. Mom asked me if I wanted Brother Jim to officiate. I thought I would vomit. We agreed on the senior pastor.

The holiday decorations were still up, so we left them all in place. Lit candles shimmered with red and green Christmas lights adorned the house. The scent of magnolia from the mantle arrangement filled the air. My wedding dress, simple ivory chiffon with long tapered sleeves, soft and flowing from the empire waist, made me feel almost like a normal bride. My hair, redder and darker in winter was pulled into a simple French knot at the nape of my neck. I carried my grandmother's *Näsduk* (handkerchief) with my simple bouquet of red roses. I was the third generation to carry the handkerchief that stayed wrapped in tissue in Mother's cedar chest waiting for the next Lundgren girl to get married. The ceremony was perfect. No one except Thomas knew I was pregnant.

Thomas was sweet and understanding as I cried in his arms on our wedding night. We didn't consummate the marriage. Thomas was patient with me and didn't force himself. It was a long time before I could let him touch me without recoiling.

We planned to tell my parents we were moving to California right after the wedding. Then in a month or so, we'd announce the baby long distance.

The surprise was on us when they surprised us with a wedding gift Thomas could not decline. My parents gave us a piece of land right next door to my parents' house and the funds to build our own home. I didn't care about the land or the money. I just wanted to get away, before anyone knew I was pregnant.

Thomas had never owned anything in his life. It meant a great deal to him to have this land. He couldn't turn down their generosity even though he knew how I felt about it. I knew living next door to Mom and Dad meant I would constantly be running into Brother Jim and the other members of the church. Was I never going to get away from him?

Chapter Thirty One

After the wedding, Thomas and I stayed with Mom and Dad in the old house until our new home was complete. The second month, we broke the news that there was a baby was on the way.

Mom was ecstatic having no idea the baby was not Thomas'. The construction time frame escalated to have the house completed before the baby was born. Dad and Thomas worked fervently on the home, day and night.

Once the morning sickness passed, I felt much better, trying to set aside the memory of who the baby's father was. I never told Brother Jim, and he left me alone since the wedding. I hoped he had not moved on to another young victim.

The occupancy permit on the house came through on July third. As Thomas and I were busy putting away multitudes of kitchen items from the high-stacked boxes, Mom and Dad tapped lightly on the door of our new home.

I could tell something was wrong by the look on their faces. Mom told me to take a break and sit down. She put the tea kettle on and settled down beside me. She took my hand. Thomas seemed uncomfortable. I wondered what on earth it could be.

"It's Brother Jim, dear," Mom said. "Pastor Erikson found him this morning. When he didn't show up for men's Bible study . . . He's in the hospital. He tried to commit suicide. Pills, it looks like he took a whole bottle of somebody's pain medication. We don't know where he got the bottle."

She watched me carefully. Thomas was watching my reaction. What did they know?

"Did he write a note?" was all I remember asking. Thomas came over and rested his hand on my shoulder. I was afraid of the answer.

Dad nodded his head. "Pastor Erikson said it was something about a girl. It's such a shame a girl could ruin a young man's life. A man of God."

Thomas and I exchanged knowing looks but shook our heads.

"What did it say?"

Dad set the note on the table, amid the boxes and crumbled newspapers we used for packing. I just sat there. The tea kettle whistled in the background. Mom got up and turned it off, but she didn't make the tea.

Thomas moved some of the boxes and paper out of the way. The small white note blended in with the white-painted table top. Only the black ink stood out in stark contrast to the table. Nobody said anything.

Finally, I picked it up. My hands trembled and the baby inside me kicked in protest. I had been holding my breath.

Thomas took the note out of my hand and searched my eyes for permission. I nodded. He read the note while I held tight to my mother's hand.

I have tried to fight the demons but the will of the flesh has won out. I am not strong enough to fight against the lust she draws from me. She is the snake bearing the forbidden fruit. It is time for me to depart this world, surely to be devoured by the fires of Hell for my actions. She tempted me and I became a victim. I can't live with her, nor can I live without her. I have wrestled with Satan long enough. I tried to save her soul but she took mine in exchange.

He called himself the victim. He took no blame for what he had done. Thank God he had not mentioned my name. I was glad he did not go into more detail.

I laid my head on the table. The wood felt cool against my flaming cheeks. How can I ever look my Mom and Dad in the eye again? I felt so ashamed.

My father shook his head in disgust. "Young women should not flaunt themselves in front of a man of God. I have seen how some of those young girls at the church flirt with him. He is only flesh and blood. He can be tempted. We will pray for him."

I couldn't lift my head from the table but my eyes focused on Thomas. I pleaded with my eyes at him. Please don't tell them Thomas. He looked away. I wondered if he figured out there had been other times. He never asked and I didn't volunteer.

My only reprieve from the guilt was the bottle. Thomas and I never spoke of it again. Brother Jim recovered, but was sent to another church to squelch the gossip that was beginning to spread through our small town. I still couldn't set foot in the church. Thomas thought I'd quit drinking because of the baby. And I tried. I cut way back, to just a small glass of wine, or a little sip of brandy. I thought I had it under control.

***

Deanna bolted from her chair in the living room. She couldn't read any more of this in the same room with her grandmother. "I'm going to take this to my room, where I can take my prosthesis off and relax on my bed."

Esther looked up from her knitting. "That's fine dear. I'll call you when dinner is ready."

Deanna's mind raced as she climbed the stairs. *She drank to hide the pain, but she kept going back there. Why didn't she just tell Gram?* Then the words sunk in. *That baby was me. Oh My God! Deanna gasped out loud. Am I a rape baby? And that bastard is my dad? I thought I loved him, like . . . that and he is my own birth father? This is sick, just sick.* Deanna reached the top of the stairs and sunk quietly to the floor beside her bed, the journal clutched to her chest. She needed time to think. This changes everything. Slowly, she opened the soft leather cover and continued to read.

***

The baby inside me was so small I hardly showed at all during most of the pregnancy. My water broke on the 20th of August, 1966, while I was visiting Mom and Dad in the old house. They thought the baby was a month early.

The pains were light and we made it to the hospital in plenty of time. Two hours later, six pound four ounce Deanna Florence Jennings arrived on the scene, limbs flaying, with a full set of lungs. When they brought her to me, I unfolded the blanket, counted all her little fingers and toes, and determined she was the most beautiful child on the face of the earth and for a moment I forgot who her father was. I didn't see any signs that showed ill effects from my drinking. I had tried hard to quit during the pregnancy, but I knew I had slipped up more often than I should have. Mom thought Deanna looked like her grandfather, very fair and light haired. No one suspected she was not Thomas'. It wasn't until months later that I saw the difference. Her hair started growing in, thick, with curly blond locks instead of thin and wispy like Dad's. When she smiled, a single dimple popped on her left cheek, just like her biological father.

***

Deanna held the journal in shaking hands, allowing everything she read to soak in. Unconsciously, she fingered her left cheek. She had often wondered why she was the only one in the family with that dimple. *I always thought the dimple made me special. Now I'll hate it. I got it from my father, the rapist, Brother Jim.*

***

Deanna was a sweet little child, always singing and dancing around the house. Her winning smile lit up everyone's life. Her dimple flashed as a constant reminder to me of who her birth father is.

Mom and Dad took her to church on Sundays and Wednesdays. I knew in my heart the church was safe for Deanna, but it brought back too many bad memories for me. I couldn't bring myself to set foot in there.

Deanna liked to play over at Mom's a lot and when she did I would take a break from my housework to have a glass or two of wine. I thought I had it all under control. Life moved on, and sometimes I could almost forget. But when the demons reared their ugly heads, I always had a hidden bottle somewhere to chase them away.

Just before Deanna's seventh birthday, on the 8th of June, 1975, Daniel was born. The doctors said he had FASD, Fetal Alcohol Spectrum Disorder. Obviously my drinking was hurting more than myself by now. Daniel weighed barely five pounds and was sickly from the very beginning. We had to wait to see what the lasting effects would be, but they suspected he would at the very least, have some learning disabilities, or worse, brain damage.

Devastated by what I had done to my baby. I tried again to stop drinking, but the baby would cry, or I'd run into someone from the church at the market, or I was just depressed and I thought; 'just one more glass of wine, or a quick shot of vodka before Thomas came home, just to take the edge off.' The demons just wouldn't go away. Each time I said, "Just one more, then I'll stop."

Thomas no longer wanted to share happy hour with me. He told me countless times I was out of control. So I started to hide the bottles around the house where he would not find them.

Unlike Deanna that was born outgoing and demonstrative, Daniel was shy and introverted. Deanna spent more time with him than I did. She learned to give him a bottle when she was still a little one herself. Deanna adored her baby brother. She sat with him and made up stories to the words she did not know in the books for hours. They built play forts out of blankets and chairs. I was sure Deanna would eventually grow tired of having a little tag-along, but she never did. In many ways, she was more of a mother to him than I.

***

Deanna fingered the words in the journal gently, her mind on Daniel. *He had been such a sweet boy. I'm not completely wrong about my mother, am I? The rape didn't change the fact that she drank too much.*

She couldn't even look at me without thinking of my real father, or having a drink. I have to tell someone. He is doing it again. Now he is after me. Part of me still wants to hate her, but for the first time in my life, I can't.

Deanna didn't even hear her grandmother when she quietly knocked on the door. "Deanna, dinner is about ready. May I come in?"

Deanna quickly closed the journal and struggled to her feet. She opened the door and offered her grandmother a weak smile.

"Tough reading, I take it?" Esther returned her smile.

"Uh-huh." *How much of this does Gram know?* "That's an understatement. I am still trying to absorb it all."

"Want to talk about it?"

Deanna shook her head. "Not yet."

Esther nodded and turned toward the stairs. "Well, come down when you are ready. I have beef stew simmering on the stove."

"I will Gram. Thanks and oh, Gram?"

Esther looked back at her granddaughter.

"Yes dear?"

"Did you . . . Did Mom ever . . . Oh, never mind. It's not important." *I just can't do it. I can't ask her if she knew. It would break her heart.*

Later, in her twin bed, Deanna tried to quiet her breathing. But sleep wouldn't come. The ticking of the grandfather clock in the dining room quietly sounded in the background. It tolled a single mournful chime, then two, and again at three. It reminded her of the bell tower in Gram's church. She wondered if those chimes used to send chills down Susan's neck like the clock just did to her. She wondered if she could ever tell her grandmother her birth father was Reverend Olson.

Chapter Thirty Two

Deanna had made her decision. She sat at the breakfast table, waiting for her grandmother to wake up. She had gone over the words a thousand times in her mind.

Twenty minutes passed, then thirty. It was not like Esther to sleep in so late. Deanna was beginning to get worried when Esther finally arrived, her housecoat askew.

"Why, I never sleep this late. I don't know what has gotten into me. Here it is, half passed eight, and I am just getting moving. Deanna, I think your Gram is getting old." She chuckled to herself as she put the coffee on to brew and sank into a chair beside Deanna.

Deanna watched her settle in. The thin wisps of her hair were tangled in the collar of her floral housecoat. Deanna reached over and brushed them off her grandmother's neck, giving a light squeeze to her shoulder as she pulled away. "Gram, I have to tell you something. It's something real bad." *It's only right that she knows the truth. Unless she already does. I have to find out.*

"What is it darling?" Esther reached over and patted Deanna's hand.

Deanna crumbled into tears. She had it all planned. She knew exactly what she was going to say. But now it stuck in her throat. She couldn't get the words out. "It's Mom's journal. In Mom's journal it says some terrible things happened to her when she was fifteen."

Esther sat down her cup and fumbled with a handkerchief she pulled from her pocket. "What did she say, Deanna?" Esther tried to sound nonchalant but a shiver ran down her spine. She had seen the change in Susan that summer.

Deanna took a deep breath. *Just say it, if you are going to.* "It says she was raped Gram. Didn't you know something was wrong?"

Esther's body recoiled at the word. She hung her head. A tear dropped on the tablecloth, causing a round circle. She had known something was wrong. But she and Nils and brushed it off as puberty. Now she wondered how she could have missed it. She hesitated, carefully choosing her words. She spoke softly, her eyes cast down at the cup in her hand. "I asked her if something was wrong. She was acting so strange. But she said everything was fine. I didn't know."

Esther began to connect the dots. It was the summer she turned fifteen, right after church camp.

She had been so different. Could it have happened there? At church camp? She could barely say the words. "Did she say who did that to her?" Esther held her breath, not wanting to know but needing the answer just the same.

Deanna didn't hold back. "She said it was Brother Jim, Gram. Isn't that what they called Reverend Olson back then? Before he became the senior pastor?

Esther's body collapsed onto the table. She nodded her head. This was too much to bear.

"Where? Where did this happen?" Not only was her daughter raped, but by the one man she had trusted most in the world, next to Nils. She shook her head.

"At camp Gram, it happened at the church camp." Deanna watched her grandmother visibly shrink before her eyes.

"No, no, that can't be right. Not Jim Olson."

Deanna hated hurting her grandmother like this. It broke her heart. Did she dare go on? "Gram, there's more. Do you want to hear it all?"

Esther pulled herself upright and looked at her grand-daughter. *How could there possibly be more?* She nodded as she dabbed at her eyes with a white handkerchief.

"The journal says he kept assaulting her for three years. Right up until she got pregnant— with me. I am his daughter, Gram. My dad isn't my biological father. I'm not who you think I am, or who I think I am. I don't know who I am anymore!"

The shock on Esther's face said it all. "Three years? And she didn't ever come to me?"

Deanna shook her head. "I couldn't read anymore. I had to stop. That's when she started to drink. It wasn't her fault she drank, Gram. It was the only way she could endure what he did to her. She blamed herself. She was only fifteen, and with him being her pastor, she felt dirty and ashamed. He made her pray with him for forgiveness after he raped her. What a sick bastard!"

Esther cringed at the foul language but didn't chastise her. "Did your father know? Before he married her?"

"Which father? Thomas?" She whispered, almost unable to say it.

She nodded her head. "He knew she was pregnant, and married her anyway. They covered it up. But it doesn't sound like he knew about all of it, when she was younger."

Esther looked at Deanna. Her face was drained of all color. In those few minutes, Deanna thought she had instantly aged ten years.

"Is there more? I don't think I can take anymore." She recalled the suicide note Jim had left. Was Susan the girl he had mentioned in the suicide note?

"Yes, but I haven't finished it. I'll read more later. I have to know, about later, after they got married, when I was little, about the accident. I don't even know if she remembers what happened that night.

Esther could barely breathe. She mustered all her courage to keep talking. "I find this so hard to believe. But Susan has no reason to lie. I wish Nils was here. I need his strength. And to think it went on and on and she didn't feel like she could tell anyone, not even me, her own mother. I failed her."

Deanna put her arms around her grandmother's shoulders. They were both trembling. "I am sure she doesn't blame you, Gram. She was just too ashamed. Maybe it is time for me to go see her? I hope she hasn't given up me. Will you go with me Gram, to see my mother?"

Esther raised her head slowly and looked at her grand-daughter. Tears coursed down her cheeks and she made no attempt to brush them away. "Of course I will Deanna. We will go together. I can't recall the procedure. I'll call and make an appointment." Esther let out a deep sigh.

Chapter Thirty Three

The corrections officer stood over Susan, watching her maneuver the metal press. She formed the tin sheets into license plates for the Department of Motor Vehicles. The officer waited until the machine slowed and Susan turned it off.

"You have got a visitor, Jennings."

Susan stared at the officer in surprise. She opened her mouth to ask who it was, but the officer had already turned her back and walked away. Thomas had not been back since he brought the journal. And Esther had been there only once since Nils had died. She washed her hands in the sink, cleaning off the slivers of aluminum that stuck to her arms and hands. She followed the officer to the visitor's room in the next building.

She sat at the booth along with several other inmates, anxiously waiting for their Sunday visitors.

Visitors lined up on the other side of the high bullet-proof wall at the doorway as the corrections officers verified their identification and administered the pat-downs. All bags or purses were held until their visit had ended.

A scruffy looking black man entered first, tall and gaunt, looking like he should be the one behind bars. Next, an elderly priest, his clerical collar protruding through a paisley cardigan sweater, shuffled his feet through the metal detector. As the third person in line came into view, Susan let out a gasp.

A lovely young woman with blond curly hair, loosely drawn back into a low ponytail, fumbled with the clasp on her bag as she handed it to the officer. She said something Susan could not hear, turned, and walked toward Susan's booth, a slight gimp to her right leg.

Deanna sat down hesitantly across the bullet-proof divider. She did not make immediate eye contact with her mother.

Susan motioned to the telephone hanging on the wall of the booth and picked it up, watching as Deanna followed her example.

"Hello Mother," Deanna barely whispered into the speaker. She looked through the glass into her mother's eyes for the first time in two years.

Susan tried to speak but nothing escaped her lips. Her throat had a lump the size of an apple. Tears blurred her vision. *Could this really be happening? Deanna is here? Sitting across from me... in the flesh?*

She heard Deanna speaking into the receiver. "Say something, Mother. Do you want me to leave? Perhaps this was a bad idea." She stood up to leave.

"No, no, don't leave." Susan finally found her voice. "I am just so surprised to see you." She took in every inch of her face, the soft curve of her cheek, the blonde curl that escaped from the pony tail, the tiny diamond studs in her ears. She had grown up so much. She was so beautiful.

"I know, I should have written to you first, to ask if you even wanted to see me. But, I had to come."

Susan felt a sudden panic. Her voice raised in alarm. "Has something happened? What's wrong? Is it your Gram? Did something happen to her?"

"No, no, Gram is fine. She is outside. She's waiting for her turn to see you. She forgets things all the time now, but she's fine. It's you, Mom, and it's me. I blamed you for Daniel's death. I was so angry about Daniel, about my leg, about Gram's arm." Deanna hung her head, tears streaking down her face.

"It's okay baby. It was my fault. I was a drunk. But I never wanted anything bad to happen to you or your Gram." Her voice became a whisper. "And especially not Daniel. I had problems, things I had trouble dealing with, but I never meant to hurt you."

Deanna peered into the glass, compassion evident on her face. "I know, Mom. I understand now. I know all about it. I have to ask. Why didn't you tell someone? Why didn't you go to Gramps? I don't understand."

Susan looked at her daughter, shocked at what she heard. "What do you mean? Tell them what?" By the look on her daughter's face, she knew Deanna already understood the truth. "How do you know what happened to me?"

"Your journal, your friend with the baby, Pauly something, she sent it to me. I brought it back to you. They took it at the door, but they said they'll give it back to you."

Susan's mind raced back to the day of the cell check when the correction officer took the journal and left her beaten on the cell floor. She couldn't figure out how the book got from the officer's hands to Pauly's and now to Deanna's. She spoke her thoughts out loud.

"How did Pauly get my journal? The officer took it. So, you read it?" She dropped her head in shame. "I'm sorry. I am so sorry for what I did to you. I'm sorry I wasn't the kind of mom you needed me to be. I wanted to be a good mom. I really did. I love you, loved you both so much. Can you ever forgive me?"

Deanna matched her mother's tears with her own.

"I want to. I really do. But it is hard to just set aside all this time. So much has happened. I need some time. But I'm trying. I wanted you to know that. I have to know something though. Is that man, Brother Jim, really my father?"

Susan startled at the question and slowly nodded her head. "Yes, he is. But Thomas will always be your Dad. He loves you. He always has, even though he has been somewhat distant since the accident. The accident changed everyone. I know it was not easy for you. I wish I was there with you when you woke up. I am so sorry about your leg. It must have been awful. And I wasn't there for you. I'm sorry."

Susan saw Deanna start to smile, the dimple in her left cheek popping in and out. "We have to agree to stop saying 'I'm sorry,' she said. "We have so many more important things to say."

"Agreed," smiled Susan through her tears. "You've grown into a wise and beautiful young lady." The bell rang above their heads, signaling visitation time was almost over. Deanna and Susan pressed their hands together on either side of the enclosure, visually joining hands.

"Gram is waiting. She wants to say hello before it's too late. Let me trade places with her." Deanna got up and hurried out the door.

Susan watched as she walked away, noticing the limp that reminded her of the accident and her daughter's handicap. She choked back a sob.

Esther came in next. Her left arm hung lifeless at her side. "Susan, my Susan, are you alright?"

"Yes, Mama, I am now. Isn't she beautiful?"

Esther knew she was talking about Deanna. "Yes, she is. She is a blessing. She read your journal.

She told me what it said. Susan, why—why didn't you tell me?"

Susan hung her head. "The church is your world Mama, how could I let you know something so terrible was coming from there. I was young, and so scared. He said he would blame me. I'm sorry, Mama. I wish I had told you. I started to—so many times."

The corrections officers rang the bell again, reminding the stragglers visiting hour was over. Susan stood and watched her mother disappear behind the heavy metal door. Her heart jumped for joy. This was the best day of her entire life. She had her daughter back.

Susan made her way back to her cell in a daze. So many emotions coursed through her mind. *I can't believe she really came. But now she knows. Did I want this? Pauly shouldn't have given her the book. She had no right. Still, if she hadn't, Deanna wouldn't be here. She had to know. It was the only way she would ever forgive me. How did she get it in the first place? Did the officer throw it away? I have to ask Pauly . . . Deanna was here! I can't believe it. She looked so good.*

The day after Deanna's visit, one of the corrections officers brought back Susan's journal. The cell doors were all open since it was free time for most of the inmates. The officer tossed the journal onto her bunk, totally disinterested in its contents. Susan gave her an appreciative smile. The corrections officer shrugged her shoulders and sauntered down the hall.

Like meeting an old friend, Susan embraced the book, and realized that by putting her life in ink, Doc had been right. It had helped her heal. It bridged canyons between her and her daughter. She skimmed through the pages, reaching the last page with any writing on it. She had made it past the rape, and past Deanna and Daniel's birth. Now it was time to write about the accident. She propped herself against the cool concrete block wall, sat cross-legged on the bunk and let the words flow; afraid to stop, fearing that if she did, her courage, like a dry pen, would end her ability to let it out. She wrote it all down just like she had explained it to the inmates in the AA meeting. It brought back a flood of memoires. She could see the smoke of her mangled station wagon. She saw the car rocking on its hood. Two years later, the pain was the same as the day she woke up in the hospital and realized she was responsible for the accident and the death of her little boy.

Chapter Thirty Four

Deanna sat in her favorite spot by the window in the kitchen nook. She tried to piece together her first memory after the accident. Her grandmother told her she had been in a coma for three months. She was lost in an old memory. Somewhere, deep within her mind, there was an image that passed quickly before her. We were in the car. A look on Daniel's face, a look of surprise or dismay, his little mouth gaping open.

She shook her head, trying to clear the image from her mind. She thought about her time in the rehab center and how Kim-Ly gave her the will to go on.

She needed to talk to her friend. She had to tell her about her mother. She wandered into the living room and picked up the photo of two young girls showing off brand new prosthetic limbs. Their miniskirts were hiked up in a provocative pose. Their heads were pressed together, one blonde and curly, the other dark and shining. Deanna ran her finger around the frame, smiling affectionately at her old friend. *Was that only a year ago? It feels like ten. I wonder what crazy things she is up to now?*

She wandered into the living room and found Esther sitting in Nils' favorite chair, lost in thought. Deanna sat down on the floor beside her and recounted the many memories of the days she and Kim-Ly shared at the center. Esther had heard most of the stories before, but it was good to hear Deanna laugh. It was impossible to talk about Kim-Ly without putting a smile on her face.

"I'm going to call her right now." Deanna reached for the phone on the stand beside the chair.

Kim-Ly picked up on the first ring. "Hops!" she exclaimed, her familiar laughter spreading through the phone. "I saw you on the caller ID and thought, Can this be my one legged friend?"

"Look who's talking, Snake. How have you been? I've been thinking about the center, and you, and have some news I know you will want to hear."

"Well, the center wasn't all bad. We had some good times there, didn't we?"

"Yes, we sure did. How are you doing? Is your foster family good to you?"

"Yes, they are great. I have two sisters and a little brother. I am very lucky. How about you? What is this big news?"

"You won't believe it Kim. My mom! I went to see her in prison. She had her reasons, awful things happened to her. I'll tell you someday, but

I've forgiven her." She looked up at Esther and gave her a big smile.

Deanna waited for a response. The phone was quiet on the other end, but she could hear slight murmuring.

"Kim, Kim-Ly, are you there?"

Finally her voice came back on the line. "I am so happy for you. I knew someday you be a happy family again with Mama-san." They chatted for over an hour, typical teenage girl talk; what boy was cute, who was seeing who, catching up on the latest gossip. Deanna felt rejuvenated by the heartfelt talk with her dear friend. She pulled herself to her feet, and stretched.

Chapter Thirty Five

Warden Fisher had retired the year after Susan arrived. The new warden, a tall thin woman, perhaps in her fifties looked like she belonged behind a corporate desk of a law firm instead of the warden of a prison. Her pale skin, striking green eyes and coiffed hair looked out of place in this environment. In fact, Warden Cooper had been a practicing lawyer, then a judge, before she became warden.

"Miss Jennings, this is notification of your right to solicit the board for an early parole. Do you have an attorney?"

"No," Susan mumbled. The pathetic attorney, Herbert Miller, she had used two years earlier had abandoned her immediately after the trial.

"Hmm", Warden Cooper replied. "Is there someone on the outside who would speak for you, a sponsor?"

"I don't know Ma'am. I'll speak to my family." *The questions is, who? Deanna is too young and Thomas doesn't come around anymore. Mom is my best hope.*

"Very well, your parole hearing is set for 3 P.M. on October 1, 1984. Please have them here for the hearing. You are dismissed."

Susan made her way back to her cell, escorted by one of the officers. *The first is only three weeks away. Who could speak for me? Thomas quit visiting right after his marriage. Deanna is still a minor. It will have to be Mom or Thomas. I have to talk to Deanna and see if she can convince one of them.*

The following week dragged by. Susan counted down the days and the hours before Deanna's Sunday visit. When the day finally arrived, she took every second of her three minute shower to wash and condition her hair. The red tendrils were always hard to manage, but the grey ones sprung wildly without the control of a conditioner. Pulling it back into a chignon at the nape of her neck and giving one last inspection in the mirror, she headed toward the visitation area.

Visiting hours started at 10:00 A.M. Susan watched as other inmates waved greetings at their guests as they arrived and moved to the booths where they could share precious moments together. 10:10-no Deanna. 10:21-no Deanna. Susan's heart sunk. She was not coming. She couldn't tell her about the hearing.

At 10:33, Deanna burst through the door, showing her identification and sending an apologetic smile Susan's way. Once they settled in the booth, phones to their ears, they both spoke at once.

"I didn't think you were coming."

"I'm so sorry. Gram couldn't come. I had to get someone to ride along. Gram didn't want me to drive alone. They both stopped and started to laugh.

"Go ahead", Deanna said.

"I was saying I didn't think you were coming. I'm so glad you did." Susan took in the disheveled look of her daughter, her blonde hair loose around her face.

"Like I said, I finally got a friend to ride with me."

Susan smiled. "We don't have much time left, I am afraid. I didn't want to jump right into this, but I guess it's now or never. I need to ask you a favor Deanna, a big one."

Deanna's brows furrowed together. "A favor, sure. Is there something I can bring you, if they let me, I mean?" She was still uncomfortable with the institution. She felt sure she'd never stop jumping out of her skin whenever the clang of the doors locked behind her in the visiting area.

"A little bigger than that, I'm afraid. I am up for parole. I need someone to speak on my behalf, to agree to sponsor me. It's a long shot. You're not old enough yet, but if Gram or your father can speak for me. Maybe they'll let me out early." Susan pursed her lips and held her breath, waiting for Deanna to look up at her. She felt her heart pound in her chest.

Deanna raised her eyes to look at her mother, tears brimmed, ready to fall. She nodded her head. "I should have been more understanding, Mom. I hated you, because of Daniel, because I was a foolish child.

"Does that mean you'll try, Deanna? You'll speak to your father and Gram for me?" Susan's eyes lit up and her face relaxed.

Deanna nodded her head again and wiped away a tear that escaped down her cheek.

"I'll call Dad. He seems . . . ah . . . distant. But I'll call him. When is the hearing?"

"It's 3 P.M. on October 1st, in Conference Room B on the warden's floor. You will need to call ahead to register to attend."

"And your grandmother? You'll speak to her too?"

The bell rang, signaling the end of visiting hour. The phone in Susan's hand suddenly went dead in her hand. She pressed her hand to the glass, blowing a kiss to her daughter with her other hand.

Chapter Thirty Six

The ride home was quiet, save the blaring radio. Deanna's friend, Sandra had ridden with her for the three hour ride, but Deanna didn't want to share all the details with her. They cranked up the music on the radio, listened to their favorite tunes and kept the conversation to old high school gossip.

She waved good-bye to her friend and cleared the steps of the old porch in record time, letting the screen door bang as it pulled back from the wire spring. "Gram, I almost missed visitation time. Boy that place is creepy. Gram— where are you?"

She knocked on the bedroom door and when there was no answer, a feeling of dread washed over her. She rushed into the room and found her grandmother lying on the floor, her bed clothes and sheets jumbled around her.

Deanna stood shocked. The woman hardly resembled her grandmother. A disheveled look and a blank stare registered total confusion.

Oh my God. I don't think she recognizes me. What happened? "Gram, Gram, did you fall out of bed? Are you alright?" She was definitely not okay.

"Oh. Hello, Susan." Esther stared blankly at Deanna. "It's good to see you." She patted her grand-daughter's hand.

Esther opened her eyes wider and tried to focus. Her confused look denied recognition.

"I'm calling the ambulance. Gram, what's wrong with you?" Deanna was afraid to move her, not knowing if there were any broken bones. She untangled the sheets from around Esther's legs and pulled the comforter from the bed, gently placing it over her body.

"They're coming, Gram. Just try to relax." *What am I doing? Oh God. I don't know what to do? Stay calm, that's right. The paramedics will be right here. Oh, hurry, please hurry up. I'm scared.*

"Susan, I'm fine Susan. I just got twisted in my nightgown. I have to get Nils his breakfast. Help me up." Esther struggled to try to sit up.

Deanna pressed her hand on her grandmother's shoulder. "Gram, I'm Deanna. Please don't move. You might have broken something. Just wait. They'll be here in a minute." *Hurry, please hurry.*

Deanna heard the sirens as the ambulance approached. "I'm going to open the door Gram.

Please don't move. I'll be right back." She scrambled from the floor, tripping on her prosthesis as she went. She reached the door just as the doorbell rang.

"Come this way, quick. It's my Gram. She thinks she fell out of bed."

"When did she fall?" A young paramedic with a blonde crew cut followed a burly dark haired man twice his age.

"I don't know. I was gone. When I got home, I found her on the floor. I've been gone for hours. Oh My God! I never should have left her alone. Is she okay?"

The paramedics took her vital signs and checked for possible broken bones. Esther could not answer any of their questions. She was unaware of what year it was, or how long she had been on the floor. The older, dark haired paramedic called in her vitals on a two way radio. He looked toward Deanna. "We're going to take her in. I don't think there is anything broken, but she is not coherent. She may have had a stroke."

"Oh, no, what exactly does that mean?"

The young man gently touched her arm. "We'll take good care of her. What about you? Do you have someone else here? Someone you can stay with?"

Deanna had forgotten there was no one else. "No." She shook her head.

"How old are you, miss? We can't leave you here alone if you are a minor. We'll have to call children's services."

"I just turned eighteen last month. No, no, wait, my father. Let me call my father. He'll come and get me." I hope he will come and get me.

Deanna dialed the number three times, shaking as she hit one wrong digit after another. Finally the phone rang. She held her breath that he wouldn't let her down.

"Hello, Jennings residence." It was Janice's high pitched tone.

"Um, Janice, it's Deanna. Is my Dad there?" Her voice broke with emotion.

"Deanna, are you alright?"

"Please, is my Dad there?"

"Yes, yes, I'll get him."

Deanna heard Janice calling him from another room. The wait seemed endless. Finally, she heard him pick up at the other end.

"Deanna? What's going on? Are you okay?"

"It's Gram, Dad. She fell. The paramedics are here. They are taking her to the hospital. They don't want me to stay alone. Can you come and get me?" Her voice broke and she burst into tears.

The older EMT had finished strapping Esther to the gurney. "Esther, we are going to take you to the hospital now. Deanna can ride along with you and her Dad can pick her up there. Okay?"

Esther's wide eyes looked at Deanna with panic. "Where is Nils? I need Nils. Susan, tell your father to come in from the garden. It's time for lunch."

Deanna looked between her grandmother and the paramedic. She still held the phone in her hand.

Thomas shouted into the phone. "Deanna. Deanna. Are you still there?"

The younger man gently took the phone from Deanna's hands. "Sir, we will take her with us to Youngstown North hospital. You can pick her up there. Can we expect you soon? Our ETA is twenty minutes.

"Yes, yes," Thomas replied. "It will take me about thirty minutes to get there. Where will I find you?"

"I'll wait with her in the emergency waiting room. Please bring some identification."

Deanna held her grandmother's hand in the ambulance ride to the hospital.

The resident doctor checked over Esther and determined that although there were no broken bones, it was apparent she'd had a major stroke. It was unlikely Esther would be able to live at home without some long term care. They admitted her for evaluation while they made arrangements for her and Deanna's care.

It was recommended they transfer Esther to a nursing home where she could have the care she needed. A social worker met Thomas in the emergency waiting room, where they found Deanna and the older paramedic waiting.

Thomas fidgeted with his hands, never offering his daughter any comfort in his arms. "You okay?" He managed a weak inquiry.

Deanna nodded her head, her arms wrapped tightly around her body. She fought the tears that threatened to give away her false demeanor.

A tall thin black woman with a closely cropped head flipped through pages on a clipboard. "Mr. Thomas, do you have a place for Deanna to stay with you? She is eighteen but it says here Deanna has been in her grandparents care since her release from the rehabilitation center. And Mr. Lundgren has passed, is that correct?"

Thomas nodded his head. "We decided it was best for Deanna to stay with them since . . . since I got remarried."

"I see. But now Mrs. Lundgren has suffered a stroke and will not be able to care for her. Are you now in a position to take your daughter? Technically, she is of legal age to stay alone but I don't think she is in any shape to do that right now."

He hesitated just a minute. "Of course, yes, of course she can come home with me."

Deanna did not feel like he was very convincing and wondered how Janice would react to that decision.

He doesn't want me. Or at least Janice doesn't. I don't want to go there either. I want my Gram. I just want to go home. She burst into tears. She knew she was acting childishly, but at the moment she didn't feel all that grown up.

Chapter Thirty Seven

Deanna stood with the princess phone in her hand as she dialed the Marysville Correction Facility. She looked around at the sterile white furniture that was Janice's taste. Nothing in the house was warm or inviting. She waited as the corrections officer brought Susan to the phone. "Mom, it was just awful. She was on the floor and I didn't know what to do. One minute she knew me and the next she thought I was you. I called 911 and they took her to the hospital. I tried not to get upset but I had to keep repeating myself and I never did get her to understand. She wants to come home. I don't think she even knows where home is. "

Susan sucked in her breath. "Where are you? You can't be there by yourself, are you?"

"No, no. They called Dad and he picked me up at the hospital. They want to move Gram to a nursing home." She lowered her voice to a whisper so her father and Janice could not hear from their seat at the table in the kitchen. "I can tell Janice doesn't want me here. And Dad won't stand up to her. I don't know where I am going to go."

"I need to get out Deanna. You need to be with me, your mother."

"I know Mom. I tried to talk to Gram, but she just didn't understand. She got all upset, and then she reverted back into Swedish. I couldn't understand her at all."

Deanna hung up the phone. She missed the squeak of creaky old wood and the rattle in the windowpanes of the farm house. *I need to talk to my Dad, no matter how hard it is. I can't stay here. We have to get Mom out. If Gram can't be her sponsor, he is her only hope. Maybe Dad will. After all, he was her husband for longer than he has been married to Janice. I wonder how much Dad knows about the rapes. I don't understand him at all. Dad always pushes me away. Maybe it's because I am not his biological daughter. I don't get it. Maybe I remind him of the rape, and my real father.* She shuddered at the thought.

The following night Thomas arrived home from work fifteen minutes late. Not that it really mattered, but it irritated Deanna a little just the same. She offered him a light hug and asked if she could speak to him alone.

They went into the study and shut the door. The cushion let out a puff of air as Thomas dropped into the soft white leather chair. Deanna balanced herself on the corner of the desk. Pulling out the letter from Pauly, she said, "I want to show you something Dad."

He looked warily at her and took it in his hand. "What's this?"

"It's a letter from an inmate at the prison, Mom's old cell mate. It came with Mom's journal. I returned it the first time I visited her. There was some pretty heavy stuff in there. I've got to ask you, why didn't you go to the police about the rape? It said that she told you. Why did you keep it a secret?"

Thomas was slow to answer. He fumbled with the letter but didn't open it.

"What's this about Deanna? It was your mother's decision, not mine. She didn't want to upset your grandparents. She was ashamed. I think she blamed herself for letting it happen."

Deanna sprung to her feet. "She was raped! How could that have been her fault? She was only fifteen when it started. Oh how horrible!"

"Fifteen, no, no, you have it wrong. She was eighteen." Thomas set the letter down and rested his head in his hands. Deanna didn't know if he was praying or thinking. For a minute he didn't say anything. When he looked up at her, stress registered in his eyes. "What could I do? She was pregnant, with you. I had to protect her."

"No, Dad. It went on for three years. It just stopped when she got pregnant."

His body recoiled with her words. He spoke so softly she could hardly hear him. "Are you sure?

She never told me. Not ever. I thought it was just the once." He shook his head. "You are right. I should have called the police, regardless of what she said. She needed help and I didn't help her. I'm not a strong person, Deanna. I'm not good with confrontations."

"You were worried about confrontations, when she was raped? Like now, with Janice? She doesn't want me here and what are you going to do about it?" Deanna's voice hit an unusually high pitch. She stared at her father, wide-eyed, aghast at his words.

When Thomas spoke, he hardly noticed Deanna was in the room. He spoke his thoughts out loud. He shifted restlessly in the chair. His eyes remained downcast on the letter. "I know. I know. I'm weak. I had no idea what she had been going through. She didn't tell me about the rape until I asked her to marry me."

He stood and paced the floor. Finally he looked into Deanna's eyes. "She wanted me to take her away, away from this town and every memory it conjured up. Then she told me about the baby . . . about you." He waited for a reaction from Deanna. When she only responded with a blank stare, he continued. "Your grandparents gave us the house and land next door as a wedding gift. I was sure Brother Jim would leave her alone after that. And then he got transferred. So I thought she wouldn't need to drink anymore."

Thomas paused, caught in his own thoughts of remorse. "I was wrong. After we were married, I realized she couldn't stop. She was an alcoholic. I didn't know what to do. I'd find the empty bottles . . . and the open ones hidden all over the house. I hated it when we fought. So I just turned my back. It was easier to pretend I didn't know."

Deanna let him talk. Once he started, he had to let it all out. She moved from the desktop to the other arm chair. She could feel his pain as he spoke. His voice quivered with emotion. He twisted his hands in a nervous gesture and got up and paced the floor. Then he dropped back into the leather chair. He looked like such a little man.

Funny, I never thought of him that way before.

His ran his fingers through his pitch black hair. "I thought I took care of that bastard though. I did. I was sure he would never be able to hurt her again." His voice was barely audible but she could hear the disgust in his voice.

"What? What did you say? How did you take care of him?"

Shaking his head, she could tell he was not proud of the story. His whole body was trembling; perspiration beaded on his forehead.

"Your mother was having such a hard time coping . . . with the baby . . . you, on the way and still being around Brother Jim all the time. Even though we didn't go to church, this is a small town, and he was at your Gram's house often. Your mother was losing it. I didn't have a plan. I just went over to the parsonage to talk to him. I don't even know what I thought I was going to say. He was home alone, his Bible, a tablet and a pen were on the table, so I guessed he was studying. I told him I knew all about it. I knew what he had done to Susan. I told him the baby was his. That his rape produced a child."

Deanna waited for him to go on. She didn't realize she was holding her breath until she ran out of air and took a big gulp. The grandfather clock chimed in the other room.

"He was rambling. He didn't even acknowledge what I said about the baby. He said that the devil's temptation was stronger than his will. It was all such bullshit. He said he would pray for her to cleanse herself of the demons in her. I lost it. I couldn't hear anymore. He put all the blame on her, like he wasn't responsible at all. I was furious! I think it was the only time I have ever felt capable of violence.

"He had a bottle of pills on his desk. He was slurring his words and I realized he must have taken a bunch of them. I walked over to the desk and I looked at the tablet. He had been writing his suicide note. I bent down and read the whole thing. I was livid. Even while he planned to kill himself, he still lied. He didn't admit it was his fault. The only good part was that he didn't mention her by name."

Thomas ran a shaky hand through his hair. He twisted a few strands of his mustache between his thumb and forefinger. For a moment, nobody spoke.

Deanna looked at him. He looked so beaten, defeated by the burden he had carried for so long.

"He was dying. I knew it. I watched as he started to slip into a comatose state. He quit talking and his eyes started to roll back in his head. It felt like hours." Thomas got up and paced the room again. "I could have called 911, got him some help. But I didn't. I wanted him to die. I wished for him to die. Then I finally left. I just left him there, lying on the floor.

"The doorbell rang about 11a.m. the next morning. Your grandparents were standing at the door with a note in their hand. I was sure he was dead. But he wasn't. I acted just as surprised as your mother when I read the note to her."

Deanna needed a break. She went to the kitchen. Janice looked up from the paperback book she was reading at the kitchen table. Deanna didn't bother saying anything to her, poured two cups of coffee and headed back into the study.

As Thomas took the cup from Deanna's hands, she noticed how much his hand trembled. For a few minutes they sat in silence, the only sound was the slurp of hot coffee.

"Okay" he said. "I'll tell you the rest now."

Deanna curled her good leg under her in the chair. She felt sorry for him. He looked old all of a sudden. Lines in his face gave away his age. She was angry with him, for not fighting for her mother, for not fighting for her, for not being honest with her mother from the beginning. She understood now that not only did her mother have to live with the rape, she also lived with the thought she had caused his suicide attempt. And then there was the accident.

"She didn't know I ever went over there. She still doesn't.

"The church didn't want this big scandal, either the rape or the suicide attempt. They tried to play it as low key as they possibly could. The sooner the story went away, the better for them. They transferred him to a new church. I couldn't believe he wasn't thrown out. Your mother never told her parents the truth. I thought it was just that once. I didn't know. I swear I didn't. After a while, we all just stopped talking about it and went about our business like it never happened.

"Everyone that is, except your mother! She drank more than ever. I suggested AA. But she didn't want any part of it. She said it was God's fault. He didn't protect her and AA was all about God.

"We tried to go back to normal, but there never really was a normal after that. Your mother felt like an outcast. She was sure everyone knew it was her, even though he had not named anyone. The guilt was more than she could handle."

The letter sat forgotten on the desk. They both looked at it at the same time. They avoided looking at each other.

Quietly, Thomas asked, "Is that why wanted to talk to me? You wanted to know about Brother Jim?"

"That was part of it. Now that I know why she drank, I can't hate her anymore. I'm not sure whether I am ready to totally forgive her, but the hate is gone. But it's more than that. She could get paroled if she had someone to sponsor her. And then I could live with her in Gram's house. I think I am ready to start rebuilding a relationship with her. But she needs you to help her. I'm not old enough; I need to be twenty one. On the way home from the prison, before I knew about Gram, I was going to ask her to be Mom's sponsor. But now, well, that is not an option. She doesn't even know who I am. So you are it. Will you be her sponsor?"

He hung his head. "I can't Deanna. You know Janice would never stand for it."

Deanna jumped up from the chair. "What about you? Don't you have a say? What about me? What am I going to do? Janice obviously does not want me here. If you don't want me, then where will I go?

Thomas opened his mouth to protest, but could not come up with anything to say.

"Maybe you would rather I stay with Rev. Olson? He is my real father, after all. Not you. Maybe I should go live with him!" She turned quickly on her prosthesis and lost her balance, tumbling to the floor.

Thomas rushed to her side. "Of course I want you, but you don't understand. Someday when you are older you will." He reached for her hands.

"I'm eighteen, Dad. I'm not a baby. I just didn't want to be alone right now." Deanna pushed his hands away. "Don't. Don't touch me."

Thomas shrunk away, recoiling as if she had struck him. He stammered with his words.

"What Dad? Is there more? I don't know if I can take anymore."

Thomas cautiously reached out and took her hand. "I'm sorry. I haven't been much of a father. After the accident, I couldn't look at you without feeling responsible for what happened, to you, to Daniel, even to your mother. I had to get away from it all. I know you thought I was deserting you when you needed me most. I'm sorry. You probably don't believe it, but Janice really saved me. I was losing it. She helped me move on. I know it shouldn't have been without you, but she saved me. She brought me to the Lord. She showed me Jesus could forgive me for what I did. And he could lift my burdens."

Deanna covered her ears with her hands. She couldn't listen to any more of his excuses.

"I never told you, but I met Janice in AA when you were in the coma. That is when I stopped drinking all together. Your mother and I both had our secrets. I saw myself in her and didn't like what I saw. Together, Janice and I found the Lord. I am so grateful to her for showing me the way. We're all sinners, Deanna. I am not any better than Brother

Jim, for letting your mother drink, or my own drinking while I judged her. I know that now. The Lord has a plan for me and I am going to live the rest of my life serving Him."

Deanna waved her hand in front of her for him to stop. She didn't want to hear any of his sermons. *Without me, right? You say you're a sinner and pretend you are serving Him, but you are such a hypocrite. You are just a weak little man. You never told me the truth about my birth. You were running around with Janice while Mom was on trial for homicide. She needed you, and you weren't there for her . . . and now you claim to be saved. You are disgusting.*

"So I take it you won't help Mom?"

He shook his head.

Chapter Thirty Eight

Deanna called Susan and told her the bad news. There was no one to sponsor her. It would mean her parole would be denied. "I know this shouldn't be about me, but I don't know where I will go if Janice won't let me stay. What am I going to do Mom?"

Susan thought about it a minute. There was only one other person that could help her get out.

"Just hear me out a minute. I know this sounds crazy. It is a long shot, but if I can convince Brother Jim I still have an interest in him, he might agree to sponsor me. I'll tell him that I want us to be a family. I'll tell him you are his daughter. Surely he won't touch you if he knows that."

"What? Are you crazy? The man raped you? You can't possibly think that would work."

"What other choice do we have? He is a respected part of the community. Once I am out, we can work to expose him. But first I have to get out. And be with you."

Deanna shook her head in disbelief. *Could this get any weirder? The very man that caused all this mess being the one to get her out?*

Susan called Jim Olson on the phone as soon as she hung up from Deanna. He answered on the first ring. "Hello Jim, this is Susan, Susan Jennings. After some light non-descript conversation, she sprung the news on him. "Jim, I'm up for my parole hearing. It's been almost two years. To get out I need a lawyer, or a sponsor to speak for me. Not looking too hopeful here. My mother is ill. Thomas has moved on. Deanna is too young. But you could do it. You could sponsor for me." She held her breathe.

"Oh, I see." Rev. Olson responded. "When is the hearing? I'll have to pray about it. I've seen Deanna a few times. She is doing well. I didn't know about Esther. I will go see her at the hospital. Where did you say Deanna was now?"

Susan cringed at the thought of Deanna being near him. Was he making advances at her? Did he have any idea she was his daughter?

"She is with Thomas. But she needs her mother. The hearing is on October 1st, Jim. We could start over. We could be a family, you and Deanna and me. She is yours, you know. Deanna is your daughter." Susan dropped her chin to her chest. The very thought of being near him again made her skin crawl.

Brother Jim spoke quietly into the phone. "Are you sure? I'll pray about it. God Bless you, Susan."

The phone went dead in her hands. Susan dragged herself back to her cell, her heart heavy with what if's. *What if I can't convince him? What if he is abusing her right now? What if this nightmare had never happened? What if I'd never taken that first drink? What if . . . ? I have to get out of here. My daughter needs me. My mother needs me.*

Chapter Thirty Nine

October 1st started like any other day in the Marysville Correctional Facility for Women. Through the cross-hatch of metal over Susan's window, she saw a bus pull up to Quad One. New inmates were exiting the bus, their faces resigned to their fate. Roll call counted the current inmates, and Susan noted the correction officers' bored expressions as they started another day, secretly hoping the day stayed placid and uneventful.

Susan had been awake since 4 A.M. When they made shower call, she arrived first in line. Sharing a shower room with twenty other women, she wondered to herself what it would be like to have the privacy of single shower, of not having to watch over your shoulder for a gang-bang attack or a hand-made weapon. *It could be almost over. Today could change my life forever.*

The hours dragged until it was almost time for the hearing. Susan paced the yard ten times. She tried to make herself as presentable as possible for the commission. There wasn't much she could do about her attire, standard orange jumpsuit being the only option. She took extra care getting her hair clean and shiny. She pulled it back into a ponytail. Changing her mind, she took it out and brushed it into a side part.

She hoped she had convinced Jim of her sincerity. She hadn't heard a word from him since she sprung Deanna's paternity on him. Deanna had promised that she would keep trying to get Thomas to come to the hearing, but she had not heard a word from either of them.

Now, don't get too excited. You know the odds of being released are few and far between. And let's face it! Deanna just started speaking to you. Don't get your hopes up. You're just going to be disappointed.

No matter how much Susan tried to talk herself out of being excited, hoping against all hope that Thomas and Deanna, or at least Brother Jim would be there at 3 P.M., she still hung on by a thread.

At 2:45, the guards came to get her. They followed protocol and Susan offered her wrists out in front to be tie-strapped before leaving the quad.

"Knock 'em dead, girl," an inmate with a shaved head and huge swastika tattoo on her neck called out as Susan passed her cell. Susan gave her a tight-lipped smile. Her heart pounded loudly in her ears, pulsing through her whole body.

She entered the committee's office through the small door reserved for inmates. The parole committee's room was adjacent the warden's office. A heavy oak table with eight leather chairs dominated the room. A picture of the President of the United States and the Scales of Justice were the only adornment to the walls behind the eight chairs. The American flag stood in its post to the right of the Committee's table and the Ohio State flag stood to the left, followed by the warden's small wooden desk. There were two rows of folding chairs against one grey wall for witnesses and sponsors. Facing the committee's table was a small metal desk, with two chairs, for the inmate and her council. Four additional folding chairs directly behind the desk left room for other inmates and counsel to wait their turn.

Susan and two other inmates filed in and sat in the chairs behind the metal desk. She watched as six men and two women filed in and took their places behind the table. None of them made eye contact with the inmates. It was getting to the end of the day. Not the best timing for Susan. She suspected the committee had been at this all day and just wanted to get home.

Warden Cooper arrived through the door of her private office. She caught Susan's glance and offered a nod and a slight smile.

Susan thought again of how unlikely Warden Cooper looked for the job. Still extremely attractive, and with the polished look of a CEO, her navy-blue

Armani suite hugged her shapely body in just the right way to look both professional and feminine. She looked out of place in the shabby room with poor lighting and minimal amenities.

The bailiff called the hearing to order.

"The Commission calls the case of State of Ohio vs. Susan Jennings, File No.92-3178 FE."

Susan rose to her feet and stepped forward behind the metal desk.

"Ms. Jennings? Do you have a sponsor or a representative of counsel?" The Chair, James Q. McGregor, Ohio Parole Commission addressed her from the center of the table.

Susan's eyes looked about the small chamber. She scanned the faces in the small row of folding chairs against the wall. She didn't see a single familiar face. Her heart dropped.

"I . . . I guess not, Mister Chairman. I thought . . . I was expecting . . . ," she dropped her eyes to the wood slat floor. "No, Sir— I do not."

"Who is here that wishes to comment on behalf of Ms. Jennings?"

No one moved. The whirl of an old ceiling fan pushed stale air around the room.

A hacking cough from one of the inmates, sitting behind Susan, echoed throughout the room.

The Chair tapped his pencil pensively on the desk and turned to consult with the other eight members of the Commission.

From her seat, Warden Cooper watched Susan. She wasn't supposed to have a bias, but she had hoped someone would be there for Susan. She had been an ideal inmate. Other than having to defend herself occasionally from bad apples like Juanita from the Latina gang, she had actually helped to calm some of the gang tensions on 'The Farm'.

The Chair looked in earnest at Susan. He turned to face the warden. "Do you have a comment, Warden Cooper?"

Warden Cooper was silent for a long time. She looked down at the notes that lay on the desk in front of her.

Susan's mind raced through the last two years. *I feel like I've spent a lifetime here. Without someone speaking for me, I don't stand a chance. What happened to them? What happened to Jim? I thought I had him fooled. I guess I am the fool. Doc said she will talk to the commission. But she can't be a sponsor, and she's not here either.*

Warden Cooper opened her mouth to speak just as Doc came running through the double doors at the rear of the room.

"I apologize, Warden Cooper. I am late." Her short salt and pepper hair had been colored dark again and looked very much like when Susan first met her. Large hoop earrings swung at the sides of her head from running, and her long peasant skirt caught in the doorway as it closed.

"I do not look lightly on tardiness in my chambers, Dr. Waldron. This may be the committee's meeting, but this is still my house."

"I understand Warden Cooper." She loosened the skirt from the confines of the door. "I have new information to present to the committee."

Warden Cooper took off her glasses and set them on the desk. Eight pairs of eyes from the commission followed her gaze toward the door.

"What new information Dr. Waldron?" responded Chairman McGregor. "This is highly irregular."

"I have new character references and a sponsor for the inmate."

Startled by her answer, Susan looked up. She glanced over at the rows of seats. She still recognized no one.

Just then the double doors opened again and a man rushed in. Reverend Olson, perspiration dripping off his forehead, burst through the opening.

Deanna followed behind with a slight limp, barely giving away her handicap. Her thick blonde hair was pulled back in a messy French knot that escaped from the nape of her neck. She was dressed especially casual for a courtroom, blue jeans and a pullover fisherman's sweater. Susan smiled at her daughter. *At least she is here.* Unconsciously, Susan reached toward her, but the guard stepped forward blocking her path. Their eyes met and hung there. Susan tried to read Deanna's eyes, seeing love and forgiveness. Deanna smiled back, a dimple flashed in her left cheek.

"Mister Chairman", Doc addressed the committee and nodded in the direction of the warden.

"This is Susan's daughter and their pastor. They wish to request the early parole of Susan Jennings."

"I see." Chairman MacGregor responded, still frowning.

Deanna stepped forward with a slight gimp and spoke first, addressing both the commission and the warden.

Susan could not take her eyes off of her.

"Chairman, Sir, I am Deanna Hoffman, This is my mother." She looked over at Susan. "I apologize for being late. My grandmother was supposed to be here too, but she is sick."

Chairman McGregor creased his brows with concern. "Is your grandmother alright, Miss Jennings?"

"Yes sir. She would have wanted to be here, but at least she is stable, we hope." She looked around and rapped her knuckles on the wooden desk in front of her. "Thank you for asking. I know I am not old enough to be a sponsor, but I am eighteen. Reverend Olson and I are here to vouch for my mother's welfare.

Chairman McGregor peered out over thick black-rimmed glasses. "And where would Ms. Jennings live? Would she live with you? I understand you are one of the victims of the accident."

"We will stay in our house, of course. Gram's house actually, but she is in a nursing home now. And yes Sir, I was in the accident. Mom's been punished enough. Dr. Waldron said she goes to AA and everything. I believe in her sobriety. She is no longer a risk to herself or anyone else. You don't even have to give her a driving license. I can drive her."

Warden Cooper smiled slightly at the young girl and nodded her head in agreement. She turned her gaze toward Reverend Olson.

He let go of the table he was griping and approached the Chairman. He slowly scanned the faces of all eight committee members, adjusted his collar and stood erect, speaking in a clear, concise manner. "I am Reverend Jim Olson. I have known Susan her entire life. We acknowledge that a terrible tragedy happened when Susan caused the accident that killed her son and another man. But I will be her council, I will make sure she continues with her AA meetings and take personal responsibility for her."

The Chair nodded his head. The others followed suit. For a moment, you could hear a pin drop in the room.

"Is there anyone here to speak against the parole? Perhaps a family member of the other deceased?"

A little man in a tan suit stood up. Susan groaned openly, knowing what he was going to say. He must be the new attorney for the other victim.

The buttons of his suit jacket strained against his belly. He fruitlessly tried to fasten it until he finally gave up and let it gape open revealing his paunchy stomach and a short tie.

"No Sir," he began. "I am Attorney Maxwell, here representing the family of Mr. William O'Donnell. Previous counsel, Attorney Donovan, retired last year from our firm. The wife of the victim is deceased and her sons no longer wish to be involved. I am here to close the case for the estate."

Deanna and Susan exchanged hopeful glances. Susan wondered what had happened to the two sons. Rev. Olson gave Susan a "thumbs up" from his side, not undetected by the warden.

Susan's eyes were on Deanna. *Was she okay? Was Brother Jim making advances to her?* As soon as she was out, she could expose him. But not before. There was no one else to be her sponsor.

The clock in the back of the room ticked loudly while the committee spoke discretely among themselves. A note was passed to Warden Cooper. She read the note, nodded her approval to the Chair. Then Chairman McGregor addressed Susan. "Ms. Jennings?"

"Yes sir?" Everyone in the room held their breath.

"Under the circumstances of your exemplary behavior while incarcerated and with sponsors agreeable to assist you in your transition to the outside world, I hereby grant your request for parole. You understand you will still have to report to your parole officer every week, and you must register if you leave town. You will not be granted a driver's license and are further forbidden from leaving the state until your full term of sentence has passed."

Susan nodded her head in agreement. She tried to speak, but no words escaped her lips. Doc grinned at her. Deanna stood poised ready to spring, waiting for a nod from the warden to come rushing forward to wrap their arms around Susan. The bailiff glanced at the warden who nodded. The bailiff removed the wrist straps so Susan could embrace her daughter.

Susan rushed into Deanna's arms. Time stood still and the moon and the stars seemed aligned for one beautiful moment. There was so much she wanted to say to her daughter.

"What can I possibly say to make up for a ruined childhood and wasted life?" Susan wrapped her arms around her daughter and whispered in her ear.

"I'm sorry," was all she could muster, whispering it softly again and again.

Deanna nodded and kissed her mother on her cheek. "Sh, sh, sh, you don't have to say anything. It's over now. It will all be okay from now on." She patted her back just like Susan used to do to her when she was a little girl.

Releasing herself from Deanna's embrace, Susan met Reverend Jim's eyes. She mouthed a silent thank you. He nodded his head in approval and squeezed Susan's elbow. Susan braced herself not to shrink from his touch.

The warden broke up the little reunion by tapping her coffee mug on the desk. They all turned to her and waited.

"Ms. Jennings will be released on Thursday, November 1, 1984, into the care of Reverend Olson at 11A.M. You will be granted permission to live in your old home, providing you find lawful employment as soon as possible." She looked toward Deanna and smiled. "Please bring your mother some appropriate street clothes. She will go through an exit process with Doctor Waldron between now and then." She turned her focus to Susan, her smile broadening. "Ms. Jennings, congratulations. Let's not have any reason to see you back in here ever again."

Susan nodded her head again, mouthed a silent "Thank you" in the warden's direction and stumbled out of the room, escorted by the guards. She glanced over her shoulder before the door closed and saw her daughter wiping tears from her eyes and waving her off. Even the warden was caught wiping her cheek with a tissue.

Chapter Forty

Four weeks . . . I will really be going home in four weeks. I'll be home for Thanksgiving and Christmas . . . Home, now that is a strange word. It's Deanna's home now. And my home, the one I grew up in with so many memories, good and bad.

Susan rushed to the nursery quad to tell Pauly the good news. Pauly still had three months left of her twenty-four month sentence, but, she was relatively happy. Eighteen month old Desmond had stolen her heart and everyone else's in the yard. His dark shiny hair matched his mother's to a T, so unlike the fluorescent blue spikes Susan remembered from when Pauly first arrived on the "Farm".

At the first sight of Susan, Desmond toddled over with arms outstretched, willing to be picked up.

Susan accommodated the little guy and scooped him up into her arms. "Ugh," she said with a groan. "What are you feeding this kid? He weighs a ton."

"I know." Pauly replied with a laugh. "He's almost outgrown his crib. I think I'm going to have to train him into a youth bed when I get out."

Susan settled down into a chair, and Desmond wiggled off her lap, busying himself with a pile of large cardboard building blocks. Instead of stacking them, he just crawled up and over them, like a steam roller heading through town. Susan watched him play for a moment, and then couldn't hold back her enthusiasm anymore.

Her eyes sparkled with excitement. "I got it, Pauly. I got my parole. They are letting me out. Can you believe it?"

Pauly reached over and gave a quick squeeze to Susan's shoulders. "Of course I believe it. You're a good woman, Susan. Look what you have done for me. You helped me get my GED so I can find a job when I'm out. You're great with Desmond. He loves you to pieces. You never deserved to be in here in the first place. It was an accident. Who spoke for you? I thought your ex-husband wasn't coming around anymore."

"He's not. I had to do something crazy to get out. I called Brother Jim."

Pauly eyes widened into large brown pools. "What? The man that raped you?"

"I didn't have anyone else. Deanna isn't old enough, Mom is in a nursing home now and Thomas refused to help. I pretended I loved him. I told him we would be a family. He's my sponsor. But once I am out, I'm going to expose him. I had to get out, to protect Deanna."

"Wow. That has to be hard. Does he know about Deanna? That she is his daughter?"

"Yes, I had to tell him to convince him I wanted us to be a family. It was a horrible lie, but I'd do it again if it saves Deanna."

A lump formed in Susan's throat. She fought back the urge to cry. "I need to thank you, Pauly. It's because of you I am getting out. Deanna came to support me. And it wouldn't have happened if you hadn't sent Deanna my journal. Deanna told me it came from you. Once she found out the truth, about what happened to me . . . you know, what made me drink, she was able to forgive me."

Pauly looked sheepishly at Susan, partly avoiding direct eye contact. "I didn't know if I was doing the right thing. It was private, after all. I thought maybe you'd be mad at me for sending it to her."

"Well, I was taken back at first. I never thought through who would might read it. It was just for me to heal, but I know it was for the best. It was the only way she would ever forgive me. You did the right thing sending it to her."

Pauly breathed a big sigh of relief, and Desmond crawled up and nuzzled his head into her neck. She patted his back absentmindedly and rocked him to sleep.

"I have to ask. How did you get my journal to Deanna? The last time I saw it, one of the corrections officers was heading out of my cell with it tucked under her arm like a newspaper."

"Georgia. She can do anything, especially with a little help from Doc. I found it in the trash dumpster. I was working in the kitchen and when I threw the bag into the compacter, I saw the gold edges of it sticking out from under a pile of garbage. I had almost hit the compact button before I saw it. I had to get a broom to try to fish it out." Pauly chuckled. "I was about ready to climb in before I finally got it. I knew it was yours right away. I'd seen you writing in it when we shared a cell. And nobody else around here has anything like that."

Pauly leaned forward, careful not to wake her sleeping bundle and stood up. One fat little leg dangled from her arms as she gently set the boy down in the crib. He made a squeak, turned on to his side and slid two fingers into his mouth. She stood silent a moment, staring down at her sleeping son and smiled to herself.

Turning back to Susan, "I tucked it inside my jumpsuit when I went back to the quad. My heart was beating so fast, I knew I'd be in big trouble if I was caught taking anything, even something like that, out of the kitchen. I hope you don't mind, but I read the whole thing. Oh my God, Susan!" She whispered so as not to wake the baby. "How did you ever survive? I think I would have killed myself, or maybe just him."

Susan shrugged her shoulders, embarrassed and ashamed at what was now public knowledge. "I thought it was my fault. He kept telling me that, over and over again."

She was silent for a few minutes, caught in her old memories. "It's taken me a long time, but now I know it wasn't my fault. It was his." A slight smile crossed her face. She could finally place the blame where it belonged.

"Anyway", Pauly changed the subject. "I knew Deanna should read it. So I went to Doc and told her what I found. I knew I was taking a chance she may take it from me. But I explained I thought you should have it. She gave me Deanna's address and said if we got caught, she would swear we never had that conversation. Georgia smuggled it out." Laughing, "That girl can get anything in or out of here. She has all the connections."

Susan stood up and wrapped her arms around her friend's shoulders. "Thank you Pauly. Thank you." With that, she kissed the tips of her fingers and pressed them lightly against the sleeping baby's cheek, and closed the door quietly behind her.

***

Twice a week for the next four weeks, Susan met with Doc for her re-entry counseling. The chairman called it an exit process, but for Doc, it was more about entering the world than exiting the "Farm."

"I'm terrified," Susan confessed. "How will I support myself? I can't expect Brother Jim to take care of me."

"We have connections on the outside." Doc assured her. "I can help you find something. There are programs to help ex-cons get employment. You are great with words. Perhaps we can get you into the journalism field, maybe a proof-reader for a local newspaper. Let me see what I can find out for you."

Susan looked up at her long-time friend and counselor. She tapped her pencil on the desk, her foot shaking where it dangled over her crossed leg. "Do you really think I could do that? Would they even give me a chance?"

Doc reached across the deck, resting her hand over Susan's, calming the nervous gesture. "Well, let's see. But there's another possibility as well. It may take some time to make any money at it, but a worthwhile pursuit. Something you are already doing."

Susan looked up at Doc, eyebrows furrowed inquisitively. "What? What am I doing?"

"Your stories, your children's stories. They are wonderful. You could have them published. Become an author, you are already a writer."

Susan shook her head. "Those were just for fun. They were just a way to work through my emotions, my failures as a mother." *Is that really true? Or did I secretly dream someday I'd publish them?*

Susan leaned forward, staring into Doc's grey eyes. "Do you really think they are good enough to publish and to actually make a living at?" Susan's heart started to pound with the realization maybe she did have a talent, something to sustain her on the outside.

"I'm not a publisher, I'm the prison shrink, remember?" Doc laughed, her eyes crinkled at the corners. "But they seemed really good to me. Do your homework. Check it out. Find out what is involved with getting them published. Why not? Why can't you be a successful children's author?" She shook her head and answered her own question. "There is no reason, none whatsoever."

Chapter Forty One

Deanna changed clothes three times. The blue jeans and turtleneck looked too casual. The green jersey dress didn't feel right either and so she settled on a cream cashmere sweater and black slacks. She brushed her hair out soft instead of pulling it back like she had become accustomed. It hung smoothly to her shoulders, fly away strands finally tamed by a new conditioner. She didn't put on any mascara, afraid it would end up with black streaks running down her face. Loose powder and a little eye shadow and lip gloss was enough.

Reverend Olson's black Chrysler minivan pulled into Thomas' driveway at exactly 7 A.M. It was a three hour drive to Marysville. Deanna sucked in her breath. *Okay, I can do this. For Mom, I can do this.* Deanna could tell he was nervous too. They didn't have much to say in the car. He asked about Thomas and Janice. It was polite talk, not anything important.

"How is your grandmother? Is she going to be able to meet Susan at the house?"

"Yes, she is going to stay with us overnight. Then we need to get her back to the home. I am afraid this might be too much excitement for her. I really don't want her to have another setback. She has been really amazing. Ever since the parole hearing, she has been completely lucid. My dad is picking her up in a little while and bringing her to the house.

"I guess having something to look forward to gives her reason to try. The Lord works in mysterious ways."

Deana chuckled over the irony of the whole situation. *If he only knew how strange it really is.*

They reached the prison gates and gave their identifications to the guard. He made a phone call and gave them visitor passes. They headed toward the warden's office. Inside, they waited in the sparse waiting room. Looking around, Deanna eyes took in the room. Everything looked so shabby. The Berber carpet was nearly threadbare. The walls that were once white had faded to a dirty yellow. They sat in straight back chairs and stared at cheap prints in plastic frames on the opposite wall. Deanna had run through this room on the way to the hearing, but never looked at it until now.

At exactly 11 A.M., the door opened and there stood Susan. Deanna thought she looked beautiful. Her hair shone, the reddish highlights still shining through a few streaks of gray. The navy blue chenille wrap-around sweater and soft blue silk blouse Deanna had picked out looked lovely on her. The cream slacks hung on her being a size too big. Deanna had to make a guess on sizes.

Susan stood awkwardly, holding a paper bag with her meager belongings, looking into Deanna's eyes, looking for a cue. As soon as Deanna made one step forward, Susan met her and wrapped her arms around her daughter. She almost collapsed with relief and joy. They laughed and cried at the same time. Reverend Olson hesitated for just a minute, and then joined into the group hug. She caught the scent of peppermint. Susan stiffened for just a minute from the embrace, and then succumbed to the joy of her freedom. Everyone started talking at once. Susan thanked them over and over again for coming to the hearing.

A stiff uniformed guard stood in the doorway holding a piece of paper in her hand. She gave them a few minutes, and then she cleared her throat to get their attention. They untangled themselves enough to look her direction, but Susan held fast to her daughter's arm.

"These are your exit papers. You must follow the directives exactly. You have been briefed, but this is to remind you. You are to report to your parole officer every week. If you miss one time, you are subject to being returned here."

She looked at Deanna. "Have you made arrangements for her to stay with you?"

"Yes ma'am. We have a room waiting for her." Deanna gave Susan a squeeze on the arm.

"Very well, then you are free to go. One of the guards will escort you out." She looked at Susan and smiled. "Good Luck Susan."

Susan couldn't believe she was free. The crisp blue November sky didn't have a single cloud. In the distance, away from the grey concrete walls and barbed wire, most of the trees were aglow in red and orange leaves fluttering in the cool breeze. The light exploded in Susan's eyes as she squinted into the sunshine, sucking in her breath, overloaded with the sights, sounds and smells of freedom. She could smell the approaching cold front, and drew a deep breath like a cool summer drink. For a moment is felt too much to take in. Deanna held firmly to her hand, giving her a moment to gain her bearings. Susan glanced back at the stark grey building that had been her home for two years. She imagined she could see Pauly and Georgia waving goodbye. She waved back, knowing they did not see her.

Reverend Olson opened the passenger door of his minivan for Susan. Deanna got in the backseat. Everyone put on their seatbelts. The last time Susan had been in a car was the county van that had transported her and two guards to the cemetery for Daniel's funeral. *Say something, stupid. How are you going to survive if you can't even carry a simple conversation with your daughter?*

She watched the barbed wire fence fade away from view as they drove down the long drive into the street, Susan was overwhelmed. She felt reborn. She was also terrified.

What if I can't cut it? What if I can't get evidence against Jim? What if we are jumping out of the frying pan into the fire? Can I really pull this off?

Deanna broke the silence. "We have a room all ready for you at Gram's house? Did you know? Dad helped me move my things back over there. I only took a few things to his and Janice's house." It felt strange talking to her mother about her father and her step-mother.

Susan nodded her head. "I know," she said as she finally found her voice. "It will be wonderful to be back in the house. How is your grandmother?"

"Oh, much better, she knows who I am now and everything." She didn't want to give away the surprise that waited for her at the house.

Everyone relaxed and the conversation flowed much easier for the rest of the drive. Deanna told Susan about her plans for college and this wonderful new boy she had met at school. As they approached the house, the scenery was both familiar and foreign to Susan. The homes that surrounded the property looked the same. A new housing development had sprouted from the old corn fields and only a small part of Nils' massive flower garden remained, cared for by a long standing neighbor.

The house that Thomas and Susan had lived in next door was gone. There was a new two-story colonial in its place. The old house didn't look much different. Large comfortable wicker furniture was stacked in the corner for the winter. The long front windows were paired with dark green shutters, and the new front door had an elegant etched glass insert.

Several cars were parked in the driveway. Susan's heart began to pound. She didn't want a lot of strangers here, possibly people from the church. Jim took Susan's small bag from the back. She thought it was both sad and embarrassing that the little bit of possessions she had to call her own fit into a paper bag.

Deanna took her mother's hand, and they walked up the steps onto the big front porch. The door burst open and her cousins, George and Joe came rushing out, grabbing Susan up in their arms. They passed her around like a football, her feet barely touching the floor.

"Susan," George bellowed with a deep booming voice she remembered so well. "Our little munchkin cousin is home safe."

Susan couldn't help but break out into laughter. "Munchkin? Are you serious?" She hugged his neck tight, feeling the stubble of his beard against her cheek."

"Toss her here." Joe punched his brother affectionately in the arm. "Quit hogging' her." George passed her off to Joe without her feet ever touching the floor. It was like she was twelve years old again and had just returned from a long vacation, not a convicted felon, home from two years in prison. Everyone laughed and cried and hugged. Joe finally set her down in the living room. She took a deep breath and sighed.

"I'm sorry Sue." George hung his head in shame. "I should have visited you, in there. I just couldn't. I . . . I just couldn't."

Susan swatted his arm affectionately. "Forgiven! That's all behind us now. I don't even want to think of that place anymore."

I am home. She looked around. It hasn't changed much at all. Sitting in Nils' old brown leather chair by the fireplace, Esther waited patiently as she watched her daughter.

Susan turned toward the fireplace and saw her sitting there. "Mamma!" Kneeling in front of her, Susan kissed her cheek and laid her head in her mother's lap. Esther stroked her hair. *"Du är hemma nu älskling.* You are home now baby. It is going to be okay, you are home."

Chapter Forty Two

The transition was strained for both mother and daughter. George and Joe settled Esther back at the nursing home, before boarding airplanes for California. Susan and Deanna stood in the kitchen suddenly aware of the silence in the house.

"Want some tea?" Susan reached for the tea kettle, glancing over her shoulder at her daughter. She looked around for the familiar ceramic bowl which had held tea bags since she was a little girl.

Deanna was not a big tea drinker. She would have preferred a diet Coke or coffee, but she nodded her head in agreement. "Sure. It was nice to see Uncle George and Uncle Joe. They sure seemed happy to see you."

Susan smiled at the memory of them lifting her off her feet and spinning her around on the front porch. "They're great guys and were loads of fun when we were kids. They're not really your uncles, you know. They are my cousins so they would be your second cousins."

"I know. But it just seemed like the best way to address them. They are too old for me to call them by their first names."

Susan handed Deanna a steaming cup and passed the sugar bowl in her direction. "So, here we are, just the two of us. Are you as nervous as I am?" She offered a nervous smile in her daughter's direction.

Deanna let out a big breath. "Oh, it is so good to hear you say that. I thought it was just me. I know we have some getting used to here. Please be patient with me if I say something wrong. I have been angry at you for so long; I am still trying to put my feelings in reverse."

Susan came around the table and gave Deanna quick hug. "Sweety, you take as much time as you need. I was totally at fault. So it's okay if you're still a little angry. But I will promise you this; you will never see me take another drink as long as I live. Nothing can happen that would make me make that mistake again."

Deanna looked up at her mother and smiled. "Thanks Mom. I believe you."

"What we need to do now is come up with a plan. Brother Jim, I mean, Reverend Olson, is going to be expecting a certain behavior from us, especially me. I led him on to get him to agree to sponsor me. He thinks I want us to be a family.

"Does he know I am his daughter?" Deanna didn't look up from the steaming cup in front of her.

"Yes, I told him, but he acted like he already knew. I don't know how."

Deanna remembered the conversation with Thomas about the suicide attempt. He had said he told him. But did he actually remember anything in that state? "Mom, I think Dad told him a long time ago."

"What? No, I don't think so honey."

"Dad and I talked. He said he went to the parsonage the day Jim tried to commit suicide. He said he told Jim that he was the father of the baby, of me." She looked toward her mother for some sort of reaction; she didn't know what.

"Are you sure? He was there? And he didn't stop him from taking those pills?"

"Dad said he just went over there to talk, but when he saw the note and the empty bottle of pills, well, he wanted him to die . . . because of what he did to you. So he didn't stop him."

Susan looked pensively out the window. So he knew. And Thomas was going to let him die. Does that make him the hero or the villain?

"Well, that is water under the bridge now isn't it? Until we can expose him, we'll have to play along with him. No, let me rephrase that, I will have to play along. I want you to stay away from him as much as possible."

Deanna opened her mouth to reply when Susan interrupted. "He hasn't touched you, has he? If he's hurt you . . . ."

"No, not really. He's just been a little too touchy-feely. I actually was falling for him. Can you believe that? I thought he was so handsome and I didn't even care how old he was. But now, yuck, now that I know he is really my father—and what he did to you."

Susan hated having to talk about this with her daughter. "Thomas is your father, Deanna, even if not biologically. That other man can never be called your father. So let's figure out how we can get him his due. If he abused me, and he began advances on you, I am sure there are other girls he has abused. We need to find out who they are and get them to testify against him. The statute of limitations is only for twenty years so my time is running out, but if we can find someone else . . . ."

Deanna stirred her tea, staring thoughtfully into the amber swirl. "I agree. There must be others. What about the other cities he was in? Where did he go when they transferred him?"

"I don't know but that can't be too hard to find out. The church will know, but he'll probably even tell us himself he doesn't suspect anything."

A knock on the door caused both of them to jump. Susan got up and looked through the peep hole. "It's him?" She whispered to Deanna.

Squaring her shoulders, she opened the door with a broad smile on her face. "Brother Jim! How nice to see you. Come on in."

Jim stomped his feet, removing the light flakes of snow that covered his boots. "Don't you think it's time to just call me Jim? Brrr, it's starting to get cold out there. It looks like we might have a nor-easters blowing in."

Susan held out her arms and accepted his scarf and coat as he slipped out of them. "We were just having tea. Would you like some?"

He followed her into the kitchen where Deanna tried to hide her discomfort with his presence. "Deanna, how are you doing?"

"Good, I'm good. We were— we were just catching up. Girl talk, you know."

"Can't say I am too familiar with girl talk, but I know you have some catching up. I think we all do." A broad smile crossed his lips; the dimple in his cheek peeked in and out. He moved close to Susan and brushed an imaginary hair from her cheek.

Susan resisted the urge to recoil and instead took a step back and reached up and tugged on a lock of hair. "Sure," she said with a forced smile, "it's been a long time."

Deanna couldn't stand it any longer, watching her mother squirm under the lustful eyes of the pastor. "Maybe we could do this some other time, Reverend Olson? Mom and I really need some alone time, you know, just mother–daughter stuff."

Jim backed away from Susan, "Deanna, you don't need to call me Reverend anymore. Let's just leave it at Jim for now, okay? I get the hint. I'll leave you two alone. But let's get together, right Susan?"

"Right . . . soon."

After the door shut quietly behind him, Susan expelled a huge breathe. "Wow, he still makes my skin crawl. This is going to be harder than I thought. If he touches me, I think I'm going to clobber him." They wandered into the cozy living room and chose spots on either end of the chenille sofa.

"Well, he creeped me out too, just watching him move in on you. Now that you are out, do you really need to go through with this? Maybe it is time to go to the police, file charges against him. Maybe even get a restraining order."

"Maybe, but he is my sponsor. How would that look?"

"It looks like it was your only choice. With Gram sick and Dad so whipped by Janice, he was your only choice."

Susan frowned at her daughter. "Don't speak like that about your father. I understand why he had to distance himself from all this. Heck, if I could distance myself, I sure would."

Deanna swung her good leg over the arm of the sofa. "Well, you still had no choice. I think we should go to the police. Would it help if I told how he has been with me?"

"Deanna, it is very important that you only tell the truth. Even if it felt inappropriate, you can't accuse him unless it actually was. So, was it?" Susan felt her heart pumping. Please don't let him have touched her.

"Well, I don't like it." Deanna thought for a moment and decided to tell her mother the truth. "I did, though. I did like it— at first, before I knew. I liked how he always found a reason to touch me, stroking my hair or my chin, and when he bandaged my leg, he rested his hand on my knee a long time. I even thought I was in love with him. Yuck."

Chapter Forty Three

Susan fidgeted in the straight backed chair, pulling long strands nervously from the roots. *Why should they believe me? I am an ex-con.*

"The Sergeant will see you now." A middle-aged woman with a thick middle and tightly permed white curls spoke from behind the counter of the police station. She nodded with her head and eyes in the direction of the old wooden door at the far end of the hall. Susan and Deanna headed down the narrow hallway when they were blocked by two uniformed officers that quickly emerged from an open door on the right with a rumbled old man, handcuffed behind his back. The stale smell of liquor and cigarettes filled the hallway. The officers were practically carrying the man by the arms down the hall and disappeared down another hallway to the left. Susan knew where they were headed. She had been there herself. *First to the booking room, and then on to the holding cell.* She froze in place, paralyzed by memories of arraignment, the trial, the van ride to the prison.

Deanna sensed Susan's fear. "It's okay Mom. We are just going to talk to the sergeant. You can do this."

Susan lifted her chin, and squared her shoulders. *I've got to do this.* "You're right, let's go."

Deanna rapped lightly on the glass in the center of the door. She could hear a voice behind the door. It sounded like a man's voice on the phone. She hesitated just a second, then rapped lightly again.

"Come in, come in" A booming voice came from behind the door. As they entered the room, a big burly arm, bare to his rolled up sleeve exposing a dark tattoo with a Navy insignia waved them in and motioned to the two faded red pleather chairs in front of his desk.

Susan and Deanna sat down and glanced at each other for confidence. The room reeked of a strong man's cologne. Every corner of the room was filled with stacks of manila folders, some in cardboard boxes, others spilling out of open file cabinets, still more stacked high on the grey linoleum floor. Sergeant Kowalski's massive oak desk mirrored the rest of the room. Files teetered precariously in huge stacks on either side and across the top, almost obscuring the man from where they sat in the low chairs. Kowalski barked orders into the phone, "Put the new kid on that. He can get the statements from the neighbors. Yes, yes, that kid,

Mooney, or Monday, whatever his name is." He hung up the phone without saying goodbye. He just slammed the receiver into the cradle.

"Sorry about that. There are too many punks in these neighborhoods now and all I got is snot-nosed rookies to help me out. Now, what can I help you with?" He peeked at the woman and the young girl over the stack of files.

Susan sat up straighter and moved to the edge of her seat so she could see the officer over the stack of files. "Sir, we are here to file charges against the minister of our church."

Sergeant Kowalski's eyebrows raised and disappeared into the deep wrinkles of his forehead. "Your minister? Now that's one I haven't had before. What did he do? Get sticky fingers in the offering plate?" A smirk crossed his lips.

Susan swallowed hard. "No, he raped me. And we are pretty sure he has raped other girls as well." She felt her cheeks flame with embarrassment and the heat creep down her neck.

The sergeant leaned back in his chair and almost disappeared behind the stacks of files again. He ran his big hand through thin grey hair combed straight back from his high forehead. "Rape, that's a serious charge. Exactly when did this happen?"

Inwardly Susan groaned. "From 1962 to 1965. He raped me repeatedly for three years."

"That was almost twenty years ago. Why didn't you call the police then? Why wait until now?"

"I was only fifteen. He was the pastor of our church. I couldn't face my parents." Susan hung her head, ashamed that even twenty years later he could still make her feel that way.

"Okay, but for three years? Are you sure you weren't maybe in love with him, perhaps this was a little love affair gone bad, and now he has said or done something to make you want to get even with him?"

Susan bristled at the accusation. "It was not an affair! It was rape, from the first time until the last. I was a minor. He was twenty four years old."

"But not too old for a young girl to be attracted to him though, am I right Mrs. . . .Mrs. What did you say your name was?"

Susan had lost her patience with this pompous ass. He was one of those good ole' boys that took the sides of men everywhere in rape cases. "Jennings, my name is Susan Jennings. And I want to press charges. Can I do it now or not?"

Sergeant Kowalski ignored Susan and looked at Deanna. "And what's your story sister? Did he rape you too?" He laughed like the idea was too absurd to give any credence to.

"Not yet, but he was working his way up to it. He touched me inappropriately."

"Well little girl, there is no law against touching unless he put his hands someplace indecent without your consent. Did he do that?"

Deanna could feel her face burning. "Yes, well no. It was only my leg, but above my knee."

"Why don't you tell me the circumstance? Just exactly what did he do? Oh, by the way, are you a minor?"

"I'm eighteen. But I was only sixteen then. He came to the center, the rehab center where I lived after the . . . the accident. He was helping me wrap my stump. I lost my leg below the knee."

Kowalski stood behind his desk and peered over the desk at Deanna's jeans. Her clothes and ankle boots covered her leg. Except for a slight limp, no one could tell she was walking on prosthesis. She squirmed under his scrutiny.

"Wait, wait! Jennings? Automobile accident . . . . Now I remember. Aren't you the woman that got sent to prison for killing her kid, and another guy while driving drunk?" He narrowed his eyes and stared at Susan as she hung her head. "I remember that. And another kid lost her leg. That must be you." He looked toward Deanna, then back to Susan. "When did you get out?"

"Last week," Susan answered. "On early parole. Now I've got to get that SOB put in jail. He ruined my life, he ruined my daughter's life and I know there are others out there too."

Susan could tell Sergeant Kowalski had already mentally dismissed their case before she went any further.

"I suppose you blame the minister for making you a drunk, making you drive drunk, making you kill your kid and maim your daughter. Well, I don't see it that way Mrs. Jennings. I call it personal responsibility. Nobody made you take a drink, or drive that car, or kept you from reporting the rape, if it really happened that way. You can't go through life blaming other people for your own failures."

Susan jumped to her feet. She leaned over the pile of folders, some of which brushed against her breasts and spilled onto the floor. "I am quite aware of my own personal responsibility, Sergeant Kowalski. And I can see you are not going to be any help whatsoever. But regardless of what you think of me, I will find the other girls he has abused, and I will not rest until he takes his personal responsibility!"

She turned on her heals heading out the door. "Let's go Deanna. This man can't help us at all."

Deanna followed her mother out the door, pausing only momentarily to glare back at the man, already dialing the phone, totally dismissive of his present company.

Susan and Deanna were both deep in thought as they made their way through traffic back to the house. Deanna flipped the radio on and fumbled with the dials until she found a pop radio station playing the pounding disco music that was the latest rage.

The pounding base of the beat caused Susan's temples to throb. "Can you turn that down please?" She didn't mean it to come across so cross, but when she saw Deanna cringe, she knew the words were too sharp. "Sorry baby, that sergeant really got me riled up. I didn't mean to snap at you."

Deanna reached over and turned the radio down to barely a whisper. "I know Mom, he was a real ass. He blamed you for everything." It was just like, like I did. She didn't say her last words out loud. "So, what do we do now? If the sergeant isn't going to file charges for you, how are we going to get Reverend, I mean Jim, arrested?"

Deanna pulled her grandfather's old white sedan into the garage and put it in park.

Susan noticed the building was beginning to lean, like an old barn that has seen its better days. "Well, we just have to find those other girls by ourselves. Recent ones, that will agree to press charges. We need to find out what other churches he was at before he was transferred back here. And maybe there is even someone right here in this church. You've been going to church with your Gram since you were a little girl. You must know everyone in the church. Ask around. See what you can find out. Girl talk— you know how to do it."

"I'll try Mom. But I haven't got very chummy with any of the girls since I got back, from the rehab center. Most of them look at me like I am some kind of freak. So I just went with Gram to services and left as soon as I could. But I'll do whatever it takes. Maybe if I join a bible study group. They have some for teenagers, even though most are younger than me. I'll do whatever I need to do."

They walked arm-in-arm down the crooked path from the detached, slanted garage to the old frame house. The sun briefly warmed the red bricks on the walk that contrasted with the fine dusting of white over small green blades.

"We'll figure it out. You work on the local girls and I'll see if I can find out where he was before his transfer. Now, change of subject. Thanksgiving is in two weeks. Do you think Gram will be well enough to spend the day with us?"

Chapter Forty Four

Two weeks passed quickly and the aroma of nutmeg and pumpkin filled the house the night before Thanksgiving. Susan and Deanna worked side by side in the big country kitchen, baking pumpkin pies, sautéing onion and celery for the bread stuffing. Esther was having a good week and the nursing staff were all for sending as many patients as possible home for the holidays. Susan watched the clock. Deanna had to pick her grandmother up by 3 P.M., forty minutes from then.

Susan stuck her hands under the faucet, washing off the flour from the pie dough. "The pies will be done in about twenty minutes. I've set the timer. We need to let the onion and celery cool. And the apples still need sliced the apples and the bread browned."

"I know Mom, I know. I've helped Gram many times with holiday dinners. I'll go get Gram. You can finish up while I'm gone. She is going to be so surprised when she sees what else we have made for her." Deanna winked at her mother and scooted out of the kitchen.

***

Another cold front drifted through the valley as Susan lit the candles and put the finishing touches on the table settings in the dining room. Dark walnut from the antique table peeked through the old hand-made lace tablecloth from Sweden. The soft, sable-colored cloth napkins matched Esther's fine *Fasan Benporslin* china with little brown birds on creamy white plates. Cut crystal goblets cast iridescent rainbow colors onto the walls from the soft candle light. Place settings filled the space in front of three chairs at the end of the large rectangular table. Susan knew this would be a special day for each of the three generations of women as they regaled in the first holiday they had celebrated together in two years.

***

Susan carried the bird on the gleaming silver platter and placed it in the center of the table. Mounds of mashed potatoes, candied sweet potatoes and casseroles of green beans and corn presented a colorful array of bounty.

Esther smiled sweetly at her daughter and grand-daughter. "This is all so lovely. It will take you a week to eat all the left overs."

Deanna laughed and patted her grandmother on the arm. "No it won't Gram. We are sending it all back to the home with you. But wait, we almost forgot." She got up and ran into the kitchen.

Susan shrugged her shoulders at her mother, pretending she didn't know what the surprise was all about. Deanna backed through the door with her arms raised in the air, a platter over her head. "This is for you Gram." She set the platter down in front of her grandmother.

Esther lifted the lid on the platter and gasped in surprise at the Yule log. *Sylta*, a traditional Swedish dish of jellied meat loaf, served cold, made of pork shoulder and veal. Her eyes filled with tears. "Did you make this?" She dabbed at her eyes, looking through happy tears at her granddaughter."

Deanna nodded her head. The blond curls framed her face and cascaded onto her shoulders.

"I cooked it down with vinegar and onion and herbs just like you showed me. Then I separated it from the bone, added gelatin, rolled and sewed it together. I let it cool in the fridge for five hours. I hope it is cold enough to slice nicely at the table. And I remembered the secret ingredient too." She beamed at her grandmother.

"Don't forget the pinch of garlic!" Esther finished the recipe for her. She clapped her hands in delight. "We have so much to be thankful for this Thanksgiving Day. Let's share our traditional family prayer. They joined hands and bowed their heads. *"Gode Gud, välsigna denna mat som vi är på väg att äta . . . I Jesu namn, Amen.* Dear God, Bless this food which we are about to eat . . . in Jesus name, Amen."

As they prayed, each knew what the others were thinking— about not only the gratefulness of being together, but also about the people they missed that could have been sitting in the empty chairs, Nils, Daniel and Ray.

Thanksgiving swept into Christmas and New Years and before they knew it, it was mid- January. Esther's health was declining rapidly and Susan and Deanna took turns with daily trips to the home to assist with feeding and dressing. Esther sometimes spent the entire visit babbling in Swedish, which neither knew enough of to converse. They only caught a few words like 'Nils' and 'flicka,' which they knew meant girl and a few others they had heard through their childhood.

Deanna had just returned from her last visit. "It's sad, Mom. I wish I knew what she was saying. But she doesn't look distressed. I think she is with Gramps in her imaginary world."

"I know, Deanna. But if she can be with him in her mind, I am not going to argue with that. It is where she is the happiest. Have you heard anything from the girls in the Bible study about Jim?"

"Well, not much. I made a comment on how good-looking I thought Jim was, even though he is older and Jennifer Johnson got all flustered and turned red. There is something to that, but she hasn't opened up to me yet. I'll keep working on her. How are you doing with other cities?"

"I came right out and asked him where he lived after he left here. He didn't have any reason to suspect anything. He said he first went to Cincinnati, then to Toledo. I looked up both of the congregational churches in those cities at the library. I'm going to pull the newspapers from those cities at the library and see if I can find any public scandals. Then it is time to go pay some visits to the churches and see what we can find."

"I'll go Mom. You can't drive. We can play detective."

Susan didn't like the idea of Deanna going. "We might discover some pretty unpleasant stuff here. Are you sure you want to hear this?"

"Hearing can't be as bad as what you went through, and what those other girls went through. Besides, the road trip will give us more time to get to know each other again. Did you find out what other cities he was in?"

"Jim said he was in Cincinnati from '66 to '73. Let's start there."

Chapter Forty Five

Snow covered the roads as Deanna pulled on to the highway. She slowly made her way; first north on Rt. 76, then west and southwest on Rt. 71 south to Cincinnati. The heat on her grandfather's old Chevy Impala either blasted her with stifling gusts of hot air, or alternatively did not work at all. She gripped the steering wheel tightly as she wove through the hilly countryside, which gradually leveled out into the flat farm land of central Ohio. Deanna glanced at Susan as they passed the exit to Marysville. She was glad her mother was asleep. Slowly the topography changed again, back to hills and swales as they approached Cincinnati and the river that snaked around the south boundary of the state all the way north-east to close to their home town of North Lima. Deanna mused that, in another time, they could have arrived by steamboat, along the muddy Ohio River.

The stops and starts of the vehicle as it left the highway for the more congested city streets awoke Susan. She stretched and looked around. "Are we in Cincinnati already? I'm sorry I fell asleep. I thought I was just closing my eyes for a minute."

"No problem, I was lost in my own thought. What's the name of the motel you booked for us?"

"It's the Finnegan Motel. It's on West Jefferson. She scanned the map that sat between them on the seat. It looks like it is only a few blocks from the exit. Take a right turn at the next street ahead."

The Finnegan Motel was nothing to brag about. Inside, the building looked old and run down, even worse than from the street view. A balding man in a white undershirt, chewing on something bulging from his check looked up at them from the newspaper he was leaning on at the faded laminate countertop. "Help you?"

"Yes, yes. I have a reservation. My name is Susan Jennings." She fished through her purse for her ID and a credit card.

He shrugged his shoulders and slid the card through the credit card machine. It came back with a message to call the bank. "Just a sec." He turned his back on her and picked up the phone.

"Yep, yep. J-E-N-N-I-N-G-S. Okay, nuf said."

"Bank says this card ain't been used for two years. They said something about reactivating it. But you're good. Room is down to the right, third door. Number three." He handed her a rusty looking key on a large plastic ring with Finnegan's and a shamrock printed on the side.

Deanna was used to things being old. Everything in her grandmother's house was old. Room number three of the Finnegan Motel was beyond old. A cheap mural of a rocky mountain side, possibly someplace like Ireland or Scotland was wall-papered across the entire back wall behind the bed. The opposite wall was completely covered in floor-to-ceiling mirrors. The green and yellow shag carpet was worn in a line around the bed, covered in a kelly-green quilted comforter.

Deanna peeked in the bathroom. At least it was clean, tiny but clean. She smiled at Susan. "Well, at least, the bathroom is clean."

"It's fine. I've been in worse. Let's get some lunch and then head over to the church and look up Reverend Palmgren. That's right. I called him and told him we were visiting some relatives in Cincy and wanted to attend church there this Sunday. He was the associate pastor when Jim was there. It is a big congregation. He is senior pastor there now."

After a quick lunch at a diner three blocks away, Deanna pulled the map out and looked for directions to the Cincinnati Swedish Congressional Church. It was only five blocks in other direction, passed the Finnegan Motel.

Reverend Palmgren greeted Deanna and Susan in the vestibule of the main sanctuary. "It is such a pleasure to meet you both."

Deanna smiled at him and gave Susan a sideways glance. It was hard not to burst into laughter. His hair was snow white and his full beard and round belly made him look like Santa Claus.

"You're thinking I look like old Saint Nick, aren't you?" He caught Deanna staring. "It happens all the time. Not a bad sort of fella to be like now, is it?" He tipped his chin in the air and bellowed, "Ho, Ho, Ho."

She gave up trying to hold back the giggles.

Susan stepped right to the point. "Can I be truthful with you Reverend Palmgren? We do want to attend your services, but we have another reason for being here. I'd like to talk to you for a while if I may."

The minister's white brows knitted together in confusion. "Of course, my dear. That is what we are here for. We are always here to listen to our flock, even when they come from faraway places like North Lindsay, is that it?"

"Lima, it's North Lima, a little suburb of Youngstown." Deanna corrected him.

"Let's go in my study and we can talk." He gently escorted Deanna by the elbow, just like her Gramps used to do, to the building next to the church. Susan followed behind. "Hilma, this is Deanna and Susan Jennings. They came all the way from North Lima to chat with me. This is my secretary, Hilma Estafson. She has been here at the church for forty years."

"It's nice to meet you Mrs. Estafson." Deanna and Susan said in unison. Susan filed that information away in her head. Perhaps she had information about Jim that even the good reverend didn't know.

Hilma patted her little white bun on the top of her head. "Thanks, and the same to you. Please, call me Hilma."

Reverend Palmgren led the two women into the large study to the left of the reception area. Inside rows of bookshelves, all neatly lined up according to height lined the back wall. A row of small pots of ivy collected on the window sill facing east. Beside a beautiful antique mahogany desk gleaming from lemon furniture polish that filled the air, there were two comfortable deep-cushion chairs in maroon velvet and a well-worn brown leather sofa. It was an inviting room, one where someone could unburden their problems and nourish their soul.

The reverend sank into one of the velvet chairs and motioned for them to sit down. Susan and Deanna took both ends of the sofa. "Hilma, can you bring us some tea please?"

Deanna smiled to herself. He reminded her of her grandparents, with their same gentle airs and comforting rituals of tea.

Hilma brought a tray with an old ceramic tea pot sandwiched between three delicate cups and saucers. A small plate of round shortbread cookies complimented the set. She quietly slipped out the door, leaving the door slightly ajar.

The minister picked up the dainty cup with his huge left hand. "Never could get used to those big mugs people use these days. I still love a cup and saucer. So, how can I help you today?"

Deanna sipped at her tea. It was chamomile with lemon. She set the cup down.

Susan spoke first. "I want to talk to you about the pastor of our church. I think he used to serve here a long time ago. Reverend Olson, Reverend Jim Olson." She watched the old man for a hint of recognition.

"Olson you say. Hmmm . . ." He stroked his beard with his right hand. A few shortbread crumbs that had caught in the white fuzz dropped onto the thick wool rug. "What year did you say that was?"

Susan hadn't said yet but she answered. "I think somewhere around 1966 or '67. I am not exactly sure of the dates."

He looked at Deanna. "That must be before you were even born? May I ask the reason for this inquiry?"

Deanna looked at Susan. The stump on her leg suddenly started to throb. "Umm, I was born that year. August of 1966. I think he might be my father."

A look of surprise caused his little beady eyes to suddenly open wide, showing large white circles around bright blue pupils. He looked at Susan. "I see. Is this true?"

Susan nodded her head and dropped it to her chest. She felt the same guilt and shame as when she was a teenager at Brother Jim's mercy.

Deanna fidgeted in her chair. She took a deep breath. "My mother is the one that told me. The thing is . . . she was raped." She let out a deep breath of air.

"Oh my!" He looked toward Susan. "And you think he fathered this child?"

Deanna jumped from her chair, ready to protect her mother. "She doesn't think, Reverend Palmgren. She knows. That is why they transferred him here. It was to escape the scandal in our town. But now he is back, as our senior pastor."

Susan finally found her voice. "We believe he may have assaulted other young women over the course of years. We are here to find those girls. And get them to press charges against him." The emotion of the moment caught her off guard and she buried her face in her hands, fighting back the tears that pooled in her eyes.

The pastor did not speak for several minutes. He let her cry softly into her hands. Then he handed her a box of tissues from the bookshelf behind him. "Susan," he spoke softly. "Even if he did do that awful thing, it was a long time ago. Wouldn't it be better to forgive him his transgressions and leave the punishment to the Lord?"

"No, No. It would not be better. Because of him I became an alcoholic. Because of him I caused a car accident which killed my little boy and left

Deanna a cripple. Because of him I just spend two year in prison. "

Deanna nodded in agreement. She lifted her pant leg and rapped her knuckles on the metal prosthesis she was wearing under her jeans. "So what we want from you is the truth. Were there girls in this church whom he molested too? We need to know. And we need to find them."

"I have no recollection of any misconduct in this church since I've been here. And I've been here since 1963. I remember young Reverend Olson. He came to us very upset. I understood he had tried to commit suicide. He found solace here among our brethren. And I know of no one he ever harmed. I'm sorry but I can't help you. I hope you both find some peace about this. Hatred and revenge will only destroy you. It serves no purpose in our lives."

Deanna stood and looked down at the old man. She was not sure if he was telling the truth but she knew he would not give her the answers she needed. "We are staying at the Finnegan Motel on West Jefferson if you think of anything that can help us. Come on, Mom, I think we are done here." She turned to walk out the door. Susan followed her out the door on wobbly legs.

Mrs. Estafson did not look up from her desk as they hurried by.

Chapter Forty Six

Deanna got behind the wheel and headed back to the motel. She reached over and squeezed Susan's shoulder. "I'm sorry Mom. We knew the odds were a thousand to one he would say yes."

"It is just so frustrating when nobody believes me. Let's poke around a few more days. Something might come up."

They decided sleeping in the questionable bed was not a good option, so they picked up two light weight blankets at a nearby store. They slept together between them on top of the faded emerald coverlet.

The next morning, Deanna sat with her good leg slung over a chair in her room as she hunted the Cincinnati map for the library. The old black phone resonated from the night stand. "Hello?" Who could be calling them here?

Muddled words from the manager with snuff stuffed in his cheeks said there was a call for her from the Swedish Congressional Church. Maybe Reverend Palmgren had some news after all.

"Hello? Is this Deanna or Susan Jennings? This is Hilma Estafson, from the church yesterday?" She sounded like she was whispering. "I couldn't help but hear what you said to the pastor yesterday. It's about Reverend Olson. I have some information you may want to know. But I can't talk here. I take my lunch around noon. I'll be at the Big Apple Pancake house on Larkin Ave. I gotta go."

The phone went dead in Deanna's hands. She hadn't said a single word except "Hello".

Susan and Deanna were waiting for Hilma at the Big Apple Pancake house fifteen minutes before noon. They took a booth as far into the corner and away from the crowds as possible. Hilma waved to them from the parking lot window before she entered the building. She pointed in their direction when the hostess greeted her at the door.

"I'm sorry. I tossed and turned all night trying to decide whether to call you today. I didn't mean to eavesdrop on your conversation, but the pastor always tells me to keep the door ajar when he is in there with someone of the female persuasion." She offered an apologetic smile as she maneuvered her ample body into the booth.

Susan smiled at the woman. "Thank you Mrs. Estafson. I'm glad you heard the conversation. Do you know something?"

Hilma leaned forward and rested her bosoms on the table. She dropped her voice to barely above a whisper. "Call me Hilma, please. There was this girl. She came into the office one day crying hysterically. Reverend Gustafson was the senior pastor then. Gus, that's what we called him, shut the door all the way so I couldn't hear all of it. But as the girl was leaving she said she was going to press charges and she mentioned Brother Olson. It was all very hush-hush. I never saw anything in the paper so she must not have gone through with filing the charges with the police. But next thing I knew Brother Jim Olson was being transferred."

Deanna thought for a moment before she answered. "Do you know the girl's name? Does she still live here in town? When was this?"

"Hmm, let's see." Hilma swirled the pancake syrup around on her plate but did not take a bite. "I had just come back from a leave of absence. Gall bladder. Boy that thing hurt like the dickens. I didn't think I was ever going to feel good again. Back then, they did full blown operations for gall bladder. Cut me stem to stern. It was 1973."

"The girl, Hilma. Do you remember her name?"

"Roberta Hopkins, but we all called her Bobbi. She was the cutest little thing. She was about fifteen at the time. With strawberry blonde hair and the greenest eyes you ever saw. She was young for her age." She looked at Susan. "You know, not very developed yet. Hard to believe anyone would harm an innocent little child." Hilma dug into her pancakes, attacking them like she was punishing someone.

Susan prodded her forward. "Good Hilma. Now, do you know if she still lives here?"

"No, my dear. And she never came back to our church." She leaned over and whispered again. "I think she converted to Catholicism. Tsk, Tsk Tsk. She shook her head. But I guess you couldn't blame her. Gus paid her no mind. I don't think Brother Palmgren knew anything about it. He was a young man then. We were a large church back then; Gus was senior pastor, Brother Palmgren was the associate pastor and Brother Olson was the youth pastor."

Getting direct answers from Hilma proved to be harder than they had expected. She easily got off track and rambled on and on about insignificant details.

"Is she married now? Have a new name?" Deanna was getting anxious. Come on Hilma, spit it out.

"No, no. She never married. She moved to Lafayette. I heard from one of the parishioners that she works at the library there."

Hilma looked at her watch. "I really gotta run. The pastor wants his tea everyday right after lunch. I hope I was of some help." She tossed some bills on the table and waddled out the door.

Susan and Deanna sat there finishing their meal discussing the game plan. Susan was ready to get on the road. "If we get going right away, we could make the two hour drive to Lafayette. What do you say, Deanna?"

Deanna reached for the check before her mother could grab it off the table. "What are you going to say to her? You can't exactly walk up to the lady and say, 'Hey I think my pastor may have raped you. Still want to press charges?"

"I'm not sure. I'll have to approach this with some tact." Tact was something Susan had very little practice at.

Chapter Forty Seven

Deanna and Susan sat in the Madison County public library in Lafayette, Ohio staring at the women behind the counter and rolling carts of books down the aisles, systematically filing them away by the Dewey Decimal system. Deanna did the math in her head. If Bobbi Hopkins was fifteen in 1973, that would make her twenty seven now. The lady rolling past her with the cart had to be sixty if she was a day. The one helping the young mother with the twin boys in the children's section was closer to forty. Not many people in their twenties chose librarian as their career choices. Maybe she wasn't working today. Maybe she doesn't even work here anymore. The possibilities were endless.

Coming out from the back room with an armload of books was a young woman with dark blonde hair. As she passed the window and the light caught in her hair, red highlights created a gentle mix of colors, striated with hues of a maple tree in autumn. She passed Deanna and Susan, glanced their way, offering a shy smile. She was rail thin, and hunched over the books in her arms, as though she was protecting them against an unseen enemy. She wore long black leggings over a bulky cream sweater that settled just above her knees.

"Mom" Deanna whispered. "That's got to be her. I know it is. Now if I can just get her to talk to us." Deanna feigned interest in a book on the history of the Ohio River. Susan pondered how to begin a conversation with her. When the girl crossed in front of the desk again, Deanna took the opportunity.

"Excuse me," she spoke in her soft library voice. Are there archives of old local newspapers somewhere?"

The young lady set her books on the table and leaned over to answer her question. "It depends how far back. The really old ones are on micro-phish. What year were you looking for?"

Deanna took a breath and crossed her fingers below the table. "1972 or 73. I am looking for anything about a scandal at the Swedish Congressional church in Cincinnati. "

The girl face turned white and her knees almost buckled beneath her. She grabbed on to the table to hold herself upright. "Wha . . .wha . . . what do you mean?"

Susan wanted to soften the blow to this girl who obviously knew something. "Do you know something about that? Please sit and talk to us for a minute."

Because her legs were too wobbly to walk away, the girl sat down in the chair next to Deanna. Her hands were trembling. "Yes, I lived in Cincinnati most of my life. Why are you doing this?"

"I'm sorry. We should have introduced ourselves. My name is Susan Jennings and this is my daughter, Deanna. And you are?"

"Roberta Hopkins. Bobbi for short."

"It's nice to meet you Bobbi. We have reason to believe that a minister from the Congressional Church may have harmed some young girls back then. You see, he raped me when I was fifteen. I was too afraid to do anything then, but now I am ready to press charges before my statute of limitations expires. That is next year. They transferred him to Cincy to cover up the scandal in our home town. We figured if he did that to me, he probably did it again when he moved."

Bobbi picked at a piece of lint on her sweater. She did not look into Susan's eyes. "What was this man's name?"

"Olson, Brother Jim Olson. He was the youth pastor at our church at the time, and Hilma Estafson from the church said he was youth pastor there as well. Did you know him?" Please say yes, Bobbi. Please.

"I knew him. He is a bad man."

"Did he hurt you, Bobbi?"

Roberta slowly nodded her head. Her eyes glassed over and she wiped a tear that escaped down her cheek. "No one believed me. Not even my mother. I told her what he did to me. She called me awful names and said I shouldn't say things like that about a man of God. I went to the senior pastor. I told him I wanted to file charges against him. Gus, I mean, Reverend Gustafson didn't believe me either. Brother Jim was right. He told me no one would believe me. Next thing I knew he was gone. I don't know where they sent him. But I never went back to church. My mother never forgave me for making accusations against the minister. It was awful at home. I finally moved out. Then I moved here."

Deanna placed her hands gently on Bobbi's. "It is not too late. You can still press charges. We have to stop him before he hurts even more young girls. Will you help us Bobbi? Help us put him away for a long time."

Bobbi slowly shook her head. "I just want to forget about it. I wanted to grow up, get married, and have a family. But those dreams are gone now. No matter what happens to him, my life is ruined." She hesitated for a minute, and stood up to leave. "I'm sorry I can't help you."

"But . . . but Bobbi." Deanna pleaded after her. Susan reached across and patted Deanna arm. She understood how Bobbi felt. Bobbi hurried into the back room and closed the door.

Chapter Forty Eight

Back at the house, Susan paced the living room floor, if Sergeant Kowalski wouldn't listen; she had to find someone else who agreed to press charges. She needed an attorney to help her.

The doorbell rang and interrupted her thoughts. Standing in the doorway was Jim Olson.

Susan put on her best smile and opened the door. "Jim, how good to see you. Come on in. How are you?"

Jim shrugged out of his wool top coat and placed a kiss on her cheek. "Wonderful Susan, I thought I'd stop in and see how my favorite girls are doing."

For just a second she drew back, and then altered her stance to be amenable. She felt uneasy being alone with him in the house. "Can I get you something? Tea or coffee?" She gave herself precious space between them as she headed toward the kitchen.

He followed her into the kitchen. "I am good. Tell me Susan, how is your mother? I haven't had a chance to get out to the home in a few weeks. Last time, I didn't think she knew who I was."

This was safe ground. Susan relaxed just a little. She shook her head. "Not good, sometimes she doesn't know us either. And she speaks almost entirely in Swedish now. I don't know enough to converse with her. She seems to be in a fantasy world with my father. At least she is happy most of the time."

Jim crossed the room in three steps and placed his hands on Susan's shoulders, pulling her forward until she was against his chest. "It is hard to watch your loved ones slipping away. I am here for you, Susan. I can be your comfort and support." He slid his hands from her shoulders down her back into a tight embrace.

Her mind flashed back twenty years. *His arms are pressed tight around my waist as he lifts me off the floor and carries me to the bedroom, my schoolbooks forgotten on the kitchen table. The room is dark and he doesn't turn on a light. Dark curtains pulled tight block the daylight. His hands are on me, undressing me, hurriedly, not gentle but tugging at my sleeve that gets caught on my arm. Run, scream, fight . . . all these thoughts run through my head, but I don't move. I let him lie me on the bed. I feel the heat from his body, even before I can feel it. The smell of peppermint on his breath next to my ear makes me nauseous but I don't move. I don't make a sound.*

Panic rose in her chest. She pushed away from him, forcing his arms to release her. "Jim, don't! I am fine. Really, I don't need this." She quickly stepped behind the counter, offering a barrier between them. She placed a mug of coffee in front of him on the counter. "I appreciate your concern, and you sponsoring me, but I need to go slow. You understand, don't you?"

Jim backed away from her, shoving his hands in the pockets of his trousers. "Of course I understand. So, where's Deanna?"

"She's just out running for some errands for me. She'll be back soon."

The tension in the room was palatable. Jim headed for the door, his coffee untouched. "Well, I've got to run Susan. As I said, I just wanted to check in on you, see if you needed anything."

Susan handed him his coat at the door. As she closed the door behind him, she collapsed against the frame. *I don't know if I can pull this off. Every time he gets near me I want to scream. He's got to be able to feel the tension in the room.*

Deanna walked in just minutes after Jim left. "Was that Jim's car I saw on the street? Was he here?" She looked at her mother.

Susan was shaking, her arms wrapped tightly around herself.

"Mom, are you okay? What did he do?"

"Nothing really . . . he just hugged me." She tried to shake it off. "We really need to press those charges. I don't think I can keep up this act very much longer. I wish Bobbi had been more cooperative."

Deanna dropped into the chair at the big kitchen table. "I don't think she is going to be any help, Mom. But she did admit to being molested by Jim. Maybe we can go back to her later, if we find a few more girls. You know, strength in numbers."

"There has to be others. He was in Cincinnati for seven years. Did you get the feeling she knew of others?"

"She was way too caught up in her own trauma. But we could still search the newspapers on micro-phish. Do you want me to go back tomorrow and look through them? It sounds like the church kept covering for him, so I doubt we will find anything in the papers."

"You are right. See if Bobbi has a published number in the phone book. We may need to get back in touch with her and try again."

Deanna and Susan spent the next few weeks trying to get information from anyone who knew Jim before his transfer. Everyone had nothing but raving reviews about him. Susan was convinced that he only focused on one girl at a time. Like with her, he liked the control. And he was very careful to choose girls that were already insecure, before they had confidence in their own bodies or their own beliefs. So if she was the only one in North Lima, and Bobbi was the only one in Cincinnati, there had to be at least one in Toledo.

Deanna was sure that since she had rejected his advances, there was someone new at the church he was stalking. She continued to make comments to Jennifer Johnson before and after Wednesday night Bible studies. "He came to visit me in the rehab center. One time he helped me wrap my bandage and I thought I would just die when he touched me leg. I don't care if he is old enough to be my father; I think he is hot, don't you?"

Jennifer's face flushed a bright pink and she nodded. "Can I tell you a secret?" She leaned forward so only the two of them could here.

Deanna leaned in.

"He kissed me once. Well, kind of. He hugged me. I worked in the nursery one Sunday and I was cleaning up all the toys after the parents had picked up the kids. He came in to thank me for volunteering to take care of the kids. I don't mind. I love being with little kids. Then he gave me this big hug and kissed me on the cheek."

"Wow, has he ever done anything like that before." Deanna did not want to see this girl abused, but if she was, she needed to know the truth.

"Well, he's real touch-feely with me. He always finds a reason to stroke my face or brush up against me. I know it is crazy, but I think he is flirting with me. I really think he likes me."

Deanna sucked in her breath. *Touchy-feely – those were the same words I used to describe him to*

Mom. "Well, he is certainly good looking. But don't let him cross the line with you."

"Oh no," said Jennifer. "He is a man of God. He wouldn't do anything wrong. If he wants more than kisses from me, he's got to marry me . . . like that is going to happen." She laughed and skipped into the church, feeling a little prettier for the attention of a good looking older man.

Chapter Forty Nine

The roads were clearer when Susan and Deanna made the trip to Toledo. In spite of the frigid February cold from Lake Erie, there was no snow or ice in the forecast for the next few days. They easily followed the signs to the tiny little church on the map.

The building was picturesque to the point of being unbelievable. The church was small a four-square clapboard, painted white with a tall slender steeple complete with a single brass bell in the belfry. The building stood apart from any other structure for several blocks in either direction. To the left, a gravel parking lot had room for thirty cars at the most. To the right, a small cemetery of ancient stones tenderly cared for with a well-manicured lawn and small American flags graced many of the stones.

Deanna parked in the gravel lot with one other car. They stepped from the car and stretched, glad to be out of the confines of the car. The crisp winter air smelled fresh and the sun glistened off the long narrow windows. The double doors to the church opened and a woman waved a greeting from the wide steps.

"Isn't it a blessed day? I just love sunny winter days, don't you?" Wearing gray flannel slacks under a navy pea coat, Reverend Agnes Ackerman stretched out two delicate hands toward both of theirs.

"How do you do? My name is Deanna Jennings. This is my mother, Susan Jennings. Yes, it is a lovely day, and this is a beautiful little church. Right out of a Norman Rockwell painting."

Reverend Ackerman laughed. "Yes, yes, we were so fortunate to get this chapel after the Lutherans moved to a larger building. It was built in 1889, and except for adding the electricity and plumbing, it is exactly as it always has been. Our little flock is quite content here. What brings you to our humble house of God? I haven't seen you around here before. If you are looking for a mid-week service, I am afraid we don't have them anymore, just Sunday morning services."

Susan pressed her hand in the reverend's. "We are kind of on a research mission. May we take a little bit of your time?"

"Certainly, come on in. My office is behind the altar at the front of the church. Come, come, and let me show you the way."

Deanna and Susan followed the minister through the double doors. Light from the tall narrow stained-glass windows cast a warm glow on the dark mahogany pews. A huge single wooden cross was suspended from the ceiling high above the altar. Wires so thin, the cross appeared to float in the air. A rich red carpet runner ran down the single center aisle over wide plank flooring, up three steps to the choir loft and ended at the baptismal pool. A pipe organ with brass pipes in varying thickness and height filled the back wall. Deanna wanted to just sit in the first pew and take in the beauty of the room.

"Come this way." The reverend interrupted her thoughts and they followed her around behind the organ to a small room in the back. Sparsely furnished, though neat and organized, a large roll-top oak desk took up most of the room. With just enough room for two straight back chairs and a single filing cabinet, Reverend Ackerman had to step behind the chair to make room to shut the door.

Susan stood waiting for an invitation to sit down. The minister turned and saw her standing there and shooed her with her arms. "Here, let me take your coats, then sit, please." She perched herself on the edge of the desk.

Deanna slipped out of her leather bomber jacket and sat in the chair away from the desk. "Thank you. I am sure you are busy so we will try not to take up too much of your time."

"I was just working on next Sunday's sermon when I heard your car on the gravel. It's usually pretty quiet here during the week. I was going to talk about the patience of Job. People today are always in such a big hurry. I think it would be a good lesson to slow down a bit, don't you think?"

Deanna hoped they did not have to slow down too much more in their quest for answers. Time was running out for Susan and so far; they didn't have much to go on.

Susan read Deanna's mind and took the only other remaining seat in the small room. "I'm afraid we are in the wrong position to learn patience. We are some of those very people you are talking about who are always in a hurry." She offered a meek smile toward the woman. "What we are really doing here for is to find out about a former minister whom used to serve here."

"I see. I have been here two years last June. I took the place of a man who was transferred to the Youngstown area. We are only a small congregation and only have one clergy here at a time. So I may not be of any help to you. Do you have a name for this minister, or dates? I could check the records if it was far back in history."

"That is probably not necessary. The man we were looking for information on would have left here just before you came. His name is Jim Olson. Reverend Jim Olson."

Reverend Ackerman frowned at the mention of his name. "Oh dear. I do know that name. I thought he left the church. I didn't know he was transferred again. Please don't tell me he has done something horrible since he arrived there."

Deanna spoke next. "Not yet, but that is what we, my mother and I, are trying to stop. I think we better start at the beginning." She looked at Susan who nodded her head to let Deanna continue. "You see, he raped my mother, a long time ago. And I am result of that rape. He is my birth father. He has destroyed my mother's life, and inadvertently messed mine up pretty bad too. My mother wants to press charges against him, but her statute of limitations is running out. We feel pretty sure he has molested other girls since he has been transferred around several times. Now he is back at our church again." Deanna looked up at the minister who was sitting quietly listening with her hands over her mouth in dismay.

"Bless you sweet thing." She leaned over and patted Susan sympathetically. "What a horrible story. May I ask why you waited this long to press charges against him? I would think you would have gone right to the police as soon as it happened."

Susan words stuck in her throat. It never got any easier to say it out loud. "My parents are, well were, Dad is gone and my mother is in a nursing home, were very religious and everything in our family evolved around the church. I was only fifteen, the first time. It continued until I got pregnant with Deanna at eighteen. I was embarrassed and afraid. Jim told me nobody would believe me. He did a really good job of brainwashing me into believing it. So after he got transferred away to another town, I tried to put the whole thing behind me. I married the young boy I had been dating, and he raised Deanna like his own daughter. Until the accident."

"Accident?" Reverend Ackerman waited quietly for Susan to continue.

"Yes, you see, I thought I was handling all that shame, but actually, I only covered it up by drinking. By the time I was eighteen, I was a full blown alcoholic. And I kept drinking until one afternoon, two years ago, I was driving us to the mall and . . ." She stopped. This was so painful.

"Please go on, Susan. It's okay. I'm listening." The minister reached over and took Susan's hand in hers for support.

"My son and Deanna were in the backseat. My mother was up front with me. I hit another car. It was bad. Deanna spent three months in a coma and lost her leg."

Deanna pulled up her pant leg to show the minister her prosthetic. "Gram hurt her arm real bad, and Daniel and the man in the other car were killed." She stopped and took a deep breath. "It was an accident. Mom didn't mean to do it. But the police charged her with drunk driving and vehicular homicide. So they send her away to prison."

Reverend Ackerman retrieved two bottles of water from a small cooler under her desk. She handed one to each of them. "Daniel was your little brother?"

Deanna nodded, took a sip of the cool water and watched Susan as she spoke to the minister. "I was very angry at her for a long time. I wouldn't take her calls or read her letters for almost two years. Then her friend from the prison sent me Mom's journal. That was the first I knew about the rapes, about my real father. I couldn't hate her anymore. Mom's right. We have to stop him. He even got a little too friendly with me and probably would have gone farther if I hadn't found out the truth." She took her mother's hand. "Now Mom is out on parole and we need to find other girls whom he also molested. It is the only way the police will believe her."

Reverend Ackerman pondered how much to tell them. She knew Jim Olson had left the church because of accusations of molestation. But she hadn't been there to witness it, so she did not know how much of it was true. "There is a young girl from our church who accused him of the things you are talking about." It was hard for her to even say the word "rape" or "molested". I can give you her parents' names. She is only sixteen so it is best if you speak to her parents instead of her. I don't know why they didn't go to the police. Her name is Sara Glasser. She moved to Williamsburg, Virginia shortly after, well, the incident. I believe their address is on Henry St. Her mother is a historian at the museum." She handed Deanna a piece of paper with the name, address and phone number on it. "The Glasser's are wonderful people. I hope they can help you. That child is totally withdrawn. She rarely speaks anymore and had no friends that I can tell here in the church. I hope things are better for her in Williamsburg. Good luck to you Susan."

Susan and Deanna thanked the minister. Susan stuffed the paper into the pocket of her jacket. "Thank you so much, Reverend Ackerman. You have been a huge help."

Back at the motel where they rented a room for a few nights, they discussed the options. "Mom, we may have something here. Reverend Ackerman said Jim was the pastor there before her and she knew about Sara Glasser. We need to go talk to her, or her parents. It would be a parole violation for you to leave the state, but I can go."

Susan was glad there was someone else to substantiate her story but disturbed that another young girl had to endure the same trauma she had. "Let's call the mother first. See if she is willing to talk. No point in your going all the way to Williamsburg if she won't even talk to us."

Mom is right. What if this Sara is finally getting over it? Is this fair to bring it all back up again? But, I have to do it – for Mom – for the other Sara's out there.

The phone rang four times. Deanna was about to hang up when Mrs. Glasser finally answered. "Glasser residence"

Deanna stumbled for just a moment. "Ahh, Mrs. Glasser. You don't know me, but I am from

Ohio and I need to ask for your help. My name is Deanna Jennings."

Mrs. Glasser was short, quick to assess this as a telemarketer. "I am sorry, we don't need any of whatever you are trying to sell, and as much as I appreciate you are trying to work your way through college, or whatever you are doing, I just don't have the time or money to help you out. Have a good day." She hung up the phone.

Deanna sat with the phone in her hand. *She hung up on me. Call her back. You can't give up that easy.*

This time the receiver picked up on the first ring. Deanna was quick to get a few words in before the line when dead again. "I am not selling anything Mrs. Glaser. I need to talk to you about your daughter and Reverend Jim Olson." She held her breath, expecting the dull tone of a disconnected call.

"What did you say? Who are you again?" Mrs. Glasser was stunned by the mention of her daughter and Reverend Olson.

"My name is Deanna Jennings. I am here to ask your help in putting Jim Olson behind bars for what he did to your daughter, and others just like her."

"How do you know about my daughter? Did he do something to you too?

"I'd like to explain everything to you. But it is a lot over the phone. May I come and speak with you in person? Reverend Ackerman at the

Congressional church in Toledo gave me your address."

Mrs. Glasser hesitated for a moment.

"Mrs. Glasser, are you still there?"

"Yes, I am here. No, I don't want to upset Sara. She has been through too much. We are finally moving on."

"Is Sara, Mrs. Glasser? I know this kind of trauma can get buried for many years. We really need your help to stop him from ever hurting anyone like Sara again. Please reconsider."

"I tell you what. I'll listen, but I am not bringing Sara into this. When do you plan on being in town?"

"Thank you Mrs. Glasser, I can be there tomorrow. Where do you want to meet?"

"I'll meet you on the steps of the Capitol building in historic Williamsburg. It's at the end of the Duke of Gloucester St. Do you know where that is?" Her voice had changed to the high pitch of people in a state of fear.

"I'll find it. What time? I am nineteen, have blonde hair and I'm wearing a brown bomber jacket. I'll be there whenever you say."

"2:30 — I'll see you there at 2:30" The line went dead.

Chapter Fifty

The destination was Williamsburg, Virginia. Once settled into her seat, Deanna reviewed the notes her mother had given to her. She hoped this would have a better conclusion than in Cincinnati.

As the plane taxied into Richmond, Deanna took in the rich natural surroundings. The weather was considerably warmer and lots of green pine trees circled the tarmacs as they taxied to the gate. *I have a good feeling about this. The "good" Reverend Olson is about to go down.* Things moved smoothly from the gentle landing to a car waiting at the rental depot.

Deanna pulled out a map and plotted her path to the Capitol building. She was glad to get to see the historic district and hoped to get a glimpse at the campus of William and Mary. By 2:00, Deanna was standing at the triangle where The Duke of Gloucester Street converged with

Richmond and Jamestown Roads staring at the Christopher Wren Building of William and Mary.

If I ever get a chance to go to college, this is it. Old red brick roads, ivy growing up the sides of the buildings, they say this is the next to the oldest college in America. This place is literally calling me. I have to come back here someday.

Deanna turned and faced the Duke of Gloucester Street. Straight ahead, at the far end of the street, the historic Capitol building stood majestically as the center of the town. It's orange and grey bricks formed a checkerboard pattern around lead glass windows and a white the steeple created a sharp contract to the green foliage surrounding it. She made her way down the brick-layered street, stumbling a little from her prosthetic that had trouble gaging the different height of each brick. As she approached the brick wall and gate of the Capitol, a petite woman with a long green wool coat that reached just below the tops of brown knee-high boots caught her eye. She looked nervous and her eyes were glassy as though she had been crying.

"Are you Deanna?" She offered a gloved hand to Deanna.

"Yes, I am. Thank you for seeing me Mrs. Glasser. Is there someplace we can talk?"

Mrs. Glasser pointed to a small tea house two doors down the road. "There, it will be almost deserted this time of day, especially in February." She headed out in the direction of the tea house with Deanna struggling to keep up the pace.

Warm blasts from a large open fireplace engulfed Deanna when she entered. Fashioned in the eighteenth century theme of the city, a plump waitress in period attire greeted them and showed them to a small wooden table with two chairs by the hearth.

"I am sorry if I appeared rude on the phone." Mrs. Glasser began. "We have been through so much. Sara is just beginning to open up again. She barely spoke a word after . . . after what he did to her. What could you possibly know about that?"

Deanna went through the entire story again, beginning with her conception, the accident, and the revelation in the journal. "You see, I didn't really know about Sara until we followed his trail to Toledo. But my mother and I were pretty sure if we could find other churches where Jim served, we would find more signs of abuse. It's been almost twenty years and it appears he is still obsessed with young girls. Who knows how many more girls he abused? We have to stop him. The local police in our town didn't believe my mother. It has been so long. We figured that if we could find others willing to press charges, they would have to arrest him. He'll get his day in court, and hopefully we can put him away for a long time."

"Sara's story is not that different than your mother's. Reverend Olson first molested her when she was fourteen. But she never told me. He totally destroyed her self-worth. She was convinced it was all her fault. One day I walked in on her in the bathroom. She had a knife. She was trying to slice her wrists. Thank God I found her when I did. We admitted her to a psychiatric hospital. It was there we finally found out what had happened. My husband wanted to kill him. I think he would have if I hadn't convinced him that his daughter needed him at home, not sitting in a prison somewhere." She realized how that sounded to Deanna. "Oh, I'm sorry. That was insensitive of me."

Deanna smiled though the words cut in to her. "That is exactly why we have to stop him. Sara is the second victim besides my mother we have found. Why didn't you press charges against him? He always seemed to get away with it."

"We called the diocese of the church. They said they were going to excommunicate him. I just couldn't put Sara through all that pain again by putting her on the stand to testify. I had to look out after my daughter. So we moved here, tried to start to new life."

Deanna sighed. "How is Sara doing? Everyone says they just want to forget about it. But they don't forget, like my mother, they just hide it behind something . . . something like the bottle. And he goes on hurting more girls. Can't you see? We can't let this go on any longer." She gripped the arm of the tired little woman. "It has to stop, now."

A tear slid down the mother's cheek. She nodded her head. "I'll testify, but I have to talk this over with my husband. I still don't know if we can press charges if it would mean Sara would have to face him in court. She isn't strong enough. I am afraid it would send her right back to the hospital. What do you want me to do?"

Deanna gave her a sympathetic smile. "I don't know exactly, Mrs. Glasser. But if you would make a statement, I'll take it to our attorney. I am sure he will call you and explain what to expect. We can try to keep Sara out of it, but I don't know enough about the law to say for sure. My mother will be so grateful to you for doing this. I can't thank you enough."

That night on the phone, Deanna relayed the news to her mother. "I spoke with Mrs. Glasser. She said she would testify but she still wasn't sure about pressing charges if it meant having to involve Sara. Mom, Sara tried to commit suicide because of him. She was in a mental institution."

"That poor girl... What did you tell Mrs. Glasser?"

"I told her our attorney would get in touch with her. I asked her to write a statement. I did not really know what I was supposed to do from here. We never got this far before."

"Good, that is good. So are you coming home soon?"

"Yes, but Mom. When this is all over, I think I found where I need to be. I love this place. I walked around the campus of William and Mary. If there is a way, I am going to come back here someday and go to college. I mean it Mom."

Susan smiled through the phone. "I am happy for you sweetheart. And if that is what you want, we will get you there. That is a fine school. But first, we are going to put that bastard away for a long time. Oops, sorry about that."

Deanna laughed. "It's okay Mom, he is a bastard. See you day after tomorrow."

Chapter Fifty One

They finally had the evidence they needed. Deanna and Susan were ready. After speaking with her attorney, Braxton Graham, she was ready to approach Sergeant Kowalski again.

Graham accompanied Susan to the police station. Kowalski kept them waiting for thirty minutes past their appointment time. He nodded his head in the direction of the attorney. "Graham."

"Good afternoon Sergeant." Graham began with a broad smile. "I believe you have already met Susan Jennings? She is prepared to press charges against Reverend Jim Olson now."

Kowalski started to protest. "Come on, Braxton, you and I both know this is a romance gone sour years ago. Ms. Jennings has a bone to pick with the good preacher, fine, but I don't have time to bother with it."

"It is her constitutional right to press charges. She still has until February 14, 1985 for the statute of limitations to run out. I have in my possession a sworn affidavit from the mother of another victim by the "good preacher". So stop stalling, take her statement and go out there and arrest that son-of-a-bitch."

Kowalski shrugged his shoulders and reached for a folder that was several down in the heap on his desk. The files above it fell and scattered papers to the floor. "We will have to complete an investigation." He looked toward Susan with disdain. "We'll need to take your statement. Are you prepared to do that now?"

Susan looked at her attorney. He nodded. Susan raised her chin, alluding to a bravery she didn't really feel. "Yes, I am ready."

Susan skin crawled as she explained the entire sordid story of her youth. Kowalski continued to make innuendoes suggesting she had encouraged the advances; that she had in fact, been having an affair with the young pastor for those three years. By the time the statement was committed to paper and Susan had exposed her most hidden secrets to the officer, Susan's body and mind, were emotionally and physically drained.

Kowalski grudgingly completed the statement and showed Susan where to sign.

All Susan wanted to do was go home and scrub her body with strong soap; to scrub away the filth of the memories that now lay exposed and raw on her skin. "What next?" It was all she could muster on the way out the door with Attorney Graham supporting her with his strong arm.

"Olson will be arrested. He'll go through arraignment within twenty four hours. The police with conduct a preliminary investigation, and if they feel there is just cause, they will present the case to the Grand Jury. The Grand Jury will conduct its own interviews and reach a determination. The grand jury has a different burden of proof than a trial jury. This is good. They can hear second-hand testimony of Mrs. Glasser or the other ministers who knew of the offenses. Rape is a first degree felony in the state of Ohio. Once the grand jury indicts him, which they will, then he will stand trial. We are on a short window so I am going to pull every string I can to get the grand jury convened before the end of the year.

The police investigation proved reason for the Grand Jury. Nine members of the public convened in the grand jury room on December 28, 1984. Each took an oath swearing to keep secret all proceedings of the grand jury unless required in a court of justice to make disclosure.

The prosecuting attorney, Alexander Bronson was the first to question the first witness, Susan Jennings. He recalled he had been the one to send her to prison two years earlier for vehicular homicide. He offered her a curt smile, "Ms. Jennings. Good to see you again."

"Mr. Bronson."

For what seemed like the hundredth time, Susan repeated her story to the Prosecuting Attorney and the jury. When Bronson was done, the jurors had an opportunity to interview her. One frail little man with a shocking thick head of white hair questioned her reasoning for waiting so long to press charges.

"When I was a teenager, I was too afraid. Jim told me nobody would believe me. It was his word against mine. He kept telling me I was possessed with the devil. I was the evil person, not him. It was all so confusing. Then I got pregnant and he was sent away. When Thomas, that's my husband, well ex-husband now, agreed to marry me, I just wanted to have a normal life, with a normal family. I thought I could put it all behind me. But I was wrong. I hid my shame behind a bottle. I am not proud to say I am an alcoholic, but it was my only method of coping. And because of Jim, and my drinking, I killed two people and maimed two others. When I found out he was now pursuing my daughter, I knew I could not let him go on doing this to more young girls. I knew I finally had the strength to try to stop him."

A tall slender woman dressed in a black sari spoke next. "Are you sure your daughter is a product of the rape?"

"Yes, the blood tests for Deanna and Jim proved paternity. Besides, I had never been with another man besides Jim."

"Didn't you have a boyfriend? What about the one that you married?"

"Yes, Thomas. But I never let him get intimate with me. I was afraid the sex would be like with Jim, harsh and cruel. Thomas was shocked when I told him I was pregnant with Jim's baby. He was wonderful to marry me and keep my secret."

Deanna spoke to the grand jury about Jim's advances toward her. Even though his actions had not resulted in any sexual misconduct, it certainly exhibited inappropriate behavior for a minister to show to a minor child.

Mrs. Glasser testified to the trauma of Sara. The jury did not subpoena Sara but explained to Mrs. Glasser that if this resulted in an indictment, the court would most likely need Sara's testimony to convict Jim of any charges against her.

Reverends Palmgren, "Gus" Gustafson and Ackerman all were subpoenaed to testify. Susan was not privy to the conversations that took place behind the closed doors, but the grim expressions on each face gave her the satisfaction they had told the truth about what they knew.

To Susan surprise, Roberta Hopkins arrived as Susan was leaving the chambers.

"Bobbi, you came!" Susan wrapped her arms around her in a warm embrace. "Why did you change your mind?"

"After you left, I couldn't get you out of my head. You were right. I was never going to move on if I knew he was still out there hurting other girls. I came back and pressed charges. And they have subpoenaed me to testify for the grand jury." She looked over her shoulder. "Is he in there?"

"No, he is not there. Not even his attorney. It is just you and the jurors. Closed session, they call it. But I think we still have to face him in criminal court, after the grand jury indicts him."

"Roberta Hopkins" The bailiff announced in the hallway.

Susan gave her another quick squeeze. "You're up. Don't be nervous. Just tell them what happened. I am so proud of you. You're the best."

On January 5, 1985, the grand jury indicted Reverend James Olson on three counts of rape and multiple counts of corruption of a minor, endangering the welfare of a child, indecent assault and unlawful contact with a minor.

Susan and Deanna walked down the courthouse steps arm in arm; the sun streaming warm rays onto their faces. The trial will begin soon and they would have to relive the horror one more time. But on this day, they walked victorious. Brother Jim had been indicted by the grand jury, and that was no accident.

The End

Author's Note

Thank you for taking the time to read my debut novel. If you enjoyed it, please log on to my website http://wwwJoanneTailele.com and leave a comment on the Guest Page. Hard copy editions will be available in the fall of 2013. Also take the time to read the synopsis of my other upcoming books on my website. You may connect with me online with my blog, Writing Under Fire http://JoanneTailele.wordpress.com or Facebook at https://www.facebook.com/JoanneTaileleAuthor

Disclaimer

This novel is entirely fictional and any similarity to persons or events is strictly coincidental. Some information is purposely distorted to add to the story. The Swedish Congressional Church in the story is purely fictional and in no way is to be construed as derogatory to any particular church or denomination. Marysville Correctional Facility for Women does have a maternity/ child care quadrant; however the dates in this novel are fiction. Information was further incorporated by public domain websites, i.e.: http://www.sol-reform.com/Pages/sub/SOL/Ohio.html Note: Criminal Statute of Limitations - Twenty-Year Statute of Limitations for Criminal Prosecution of

Child Sexual Abuse : Criminal prosecutions of child sexual abusers must be commenced within 20 years of the occurrence. The statute of limitations will be tolled until the victim turns 18 or when responsible adult (not including family members) who has a legal duty to report abuse is aware of such abuse. Ohio Rev. Code Ann. §§ 2901.13(I)(1), 2151.421 (2009); State v. Elsass, 105 Ohio App.3d 277, 663 N.E.2d 1019 (Ohio Ct. App. 1995); State v. Turner, 91 Ohio App.3d 153, 631 N.E.2d 1117 (Ohio Ct. App. 1993).

Grand Jury Service, A Citizen's Guide Ohio Judicial Conference

The United States Army Center of Military History. . Villard, Erik The 1968 Tet Offensive Battles of Quay Tri City

Acknowledgments

Special thanks to all the people who have struggled with me through the process of writing this novel. In order by their involvement, I would like to thank the NANOWRIMO 2010 online writer's forum that gave me the encouragement to write the initial draft in thirty days. Special thanks go to The Writer's Village University online writer's group whom worked with me line by line with feedback for over a year. Those special people include Leona, Maruxa, Silby, and Ruby. Very special thanks to my local friends who have been my focus readers and for their time and patience in reading and re-reading my chapters. They are Brenda Bloom, Cindy Kunk, Robert Messier and Karen Biery. A very special thanks to Marie Johnson who assisted me with her expertise in the legal field with the trial and grand jury scenes. Special thanks to the Marco Island Writers and the encouragement and feedback received in various chapters. Thank you to my son, Andrew Cooper for his insight as a paramedic in the ambulance scenes. Thanks to my daughter, Candeus Cooper McDowall for her suggestions for shaping the life of Deanna as a teenager in the 1980's. Thank you to my other two daughters, Terri Gene Cooper and Amy Cooper Richards for always believing in me. Please accept my apologies to anyone I may have failed to mention. It has taken a city of help to put this together. Last, but certainly not least, thanks to my husband, Garry (Tai) Tailele for his never-ending patience and faith in me through this entire project.

23045119R00193

Made in the USA
Charleston, SC
08 October 2013